JANICE WHITEAKER

No Coming Back, book 2 in the Cross Creek series.
Copyright 2023 by Janice Whiteaker.
www.janicewhiteaker.com

All rights reserved. No part of this publication may be reproduced, stored in a retrieval system, or transmitted in any form or by any means electronic, mechanical, photocopying, recording, or otherwise without the prior written permission of the publisher and copyright owner except for the use of brief quotations in a book review.

First printing, 2023

ONE

TROY

TROY SCOOPED UP the last of the snow from Muriel's sidewalk, tossing it onto the top of the pile he'd been stacking up all winter.

He wedged the metal edge of his plastic shovel into the base of the mound of compacting snow taking up most of Muriel's tiny front yard, leaving it standing upright as he whipped off his baseball cap and swiped an arm across his sweating brow.

"I told you that you didn't have to drive all the way out here tonight." Muriel frowned out at him from the chair she always sat in while he worked, refusing to let him do it alone. "It's not like I was going anywhere."

Troy dropped his hat back into place before pulling the shovel free and carrying it to the bed of his truck. "You forget that I've met you before, Miss Muriel. Don't make me remind you of the time I thought it was safe to leave this shovel here."

When he turned back toward the porch Muriel was glaring at him. "I'm old but I'm not incompetent." Her chin lifted the tiniest bit. "And I did a fine job of shoveling my own sidewalk, thank you very much."

"You did a fine job of making yourself sore as hell for a

week." Troy walked back up the sidewalk he and a few of the other ranch hands poured in the fall, pulling off his gloves as he stomped up the steps they built over the summer. "So I don't think you'll be surprised when I say I don't trust you as far as I can throw you."

Muriel gave him a sly smile. The same one that always came a second before she tried to make him blush. "I bet you could throw me pretty far with all those muscles you've got."

The woman was a shameless flirt.

She'd also somehow become his best friend, and he was still on the fence about whether that was something to be embarrassed about.

Or proud as hell of.

"And I can bet that's one thing you'll never know." Troy sat down in the chair beside her, picking up the travel mug of coffee she always brewed up when she knew he was headed over.

Muriel let out a little sigh, her breath fogging in the cold January air. "It's probably for the best. Chances are good I'd end up with a broken hip anyway."

Troy chuckled as he tipped back the scalding hot liquid and swallowed down a mouthful, letting a few seconds pass before laying out an offer he'd made countless times over the past few months. "You need me to do any work inside?" He gave Muriel his best smile, hoping this might be the night he finally charmed his way into her house. "Things are slow at the ranch and I've got a bunch of free time on my hands."

It was only a half-truth. The ranch was as busy as always. It was his own free time that was lacking in opportunities.

After spending less than a year in Moss Creek, he'd already managed to go through most of the eligible ladies in town.

And unfortunately, not a single one seemed to have any interest in keeping him around long-term, leaving him with lonely evenings and an empty bed. Taking on the repairs he knew were hiding behind that front door would help him fill one of those.

Muriel waved him off. "I'm sure you have better things to do than waste your time hanging out with an old woman." Her eyes narrowed behind her glasses. "Speaking of, weren't you supposed to be on a date tonight?"

Troy sighed, stretching his legs out across the narrow porch where he and Muriel spent the majority of their time together. "Turns out that lucky lady's best friend's sister's cousin is someone I've spent time with."

Or something along those lines.

That was how he managed to end up on the *do-not-date list* he was sure existed. It wasn't that he'd actually gone out with every unattached woman in Moss Creek. All it took was a few for him to find out how small towns worked.

And how quickly the dating pool in them could shrink.

"Her loss." Muriel reached out to pat his hand. "Don't worry. The right girl for you is out there somewhere." She gave him a wink. "And you'll be glad you aren't caught up being my handyman when she finds you."

He doubted that would be the case. Not just that this perfect woman Muriel envisioned would find him, but that he would ever regret spending time with the older woman who reminded him of the grandmother he was beginning to struggle to remember.

If only the rest of his childhood was as easy to forget.

"The right girl for me would be happy to help me take care of whatever you need taken care of." It was another of the reasons he was sitting on Muriel's porch on a Friday night instead of being attached to one of his former flames.

Not a single one of the women he'd gone out with seemed to understand his relationship with Muriel.

They all thought it was cute at first. Loved that he took care of a little old lady.

Right up until it started interfering with the time he had to spend with them.

Then they expected him to leave Muriel hanging. Let her fend for herself.

And that wasn't anything he would ever be willing to do.

Because in the six months he'd known her, not a single one of Muriel's kids or grandkids had ever come to see her.

Her family let her down just as bad as his did.

Maybe worse since she actually knew all of her family.

"I would never regret being your handyman." Troy stood up from his chair. "You're stuck with me, Miss Muriel. Whether you like it or not." He glanced toward the closed front door and couldn't stop himself from giving it one more shot. "You sure there isn't anything I can do for you inside?"

He'd tried everything to get in that damn house, stopping just short of faking heatstroke when they were putting on the new roof in the lingering summer heat.

And every time she shot him down was making him more and more sure that whatever was in there was worse than he could imagine.

Muriel eased up from her chair, moving a little slower in the cold weather than she did when it was warm. "I am just fine." She patted him on the arm as she passed. "You go out and find something fun to do."

That was another big part of his problem these days.

Fun was turning out to be more elusive than it used to be.

He could go hang out at The Creekery with the rest of the ranch hands from Cross Creek. Play pool and drink beer until he convinced himself it was a great way to spend an evening.

It used to be.

But lately something had changed.

Shooting the shit and stumbling home didn't hold the same appeal it used to.

Troy stomped back down the steps, knowing full well Muriel wouldn't go inside until she knew he couldn't peek in around her. "You'll call me if you need something?"

Muriel gave him a wink. "I'll call you even if I don't need anything."

Troy grinned. "You better."

It was how he was pretty sure Muriel was his best friend. They talked on the phone just about every day. She was the first person he wanted to call when something good happened.

Or when something bad happened.

Or when he was bored and about to lose his mind staring at the same four walls.

He could claim it was because he wanted to make sure she was okay. Make sure Muriel hadn't fallen or any of the other litany of things that could happen to an older woman living alone.

But that wasn't the truth.

He just genuinely liked talking to her. Liked hearing her stories about what Billings used to be like and the dreams she had before she got married and traded them in for packing lunches and helping with homework.

It was the kind of history he would never know about his own life, and somehow learning about hers helped ease the ache of that missing piece.

By the time Troy was loaded into his truck and backing out of Muriel's driveway, she was closing herself into the house and flipping off the porch light, going in to spend her evening alone.

Just like him.

And tonight that was bothering him more than normal.

Bothering him enough that instead of turning for Moss Creek, he headed in the opposite direction, aiming his truck for downtown Billings. Hopefully he could find somewhere to sit and sulk without having to worry about everyone and their brother knowing about it before lunchtime tomorrow.

Troy reached the edge of downtown, passing one of the nicer hotels, slowing his truck when the sign glowing on the building next door caught his eye.

Booze and Bad Decisions

It seemed fitting, so he pulled into the lot next to it and parked, boots crunching over the cold-hardened bit of snow clinging to the sidewalk as he made his way to the door.

The name of the bar was heavy, but the mood inside was light and upbeat. A live band played eighties rock from a stage set up in one corner, belting out tunes the crowd packing the place seemed to be enjoying the hell out of.

It was good for them, but bad for him because there wasn't an empty seat in sight, and the thought of drinking beer standing alone in a corner was one step too depressing for him to consider.

He was about to leave when a man sitting at the bar got up and pulled on his coat before heading for the door, leaving one stool open in the middle of the lineup.

Troy dodged a few bodies as he crossed to the back wall where the bar was situated, moving quick to snag the vacated seat. He dropped into it, shucking his coat while he scanned the space around him.

A man a few years older than he was sat on his left, leaning close to the woman in the next seat down. She was laughing at whatever he'd said, one hand curved high on the inside of his thigh as her head fell against his shoulder. The man picked up her free hand and lifted it to his mouth, grinning as he brushed his lips across her skin, their matching wedding bands catching in the overhead lighting.

Maybe there was something even more depressing than

standing alone in a corner, because sitting next to a happily married couple certainly wasn't going to improve his disposition.

For the second time since walking in, Troy was about to leave.

But then he turned, catching sight of the woman sitting on his right.

She was the prettiest thing he'd seen in a long damn time, with straight blonde hair and wide brown eyes. The oatmeal-colored sweater-like dress she wore clung to lush curves a man could sink his fingers into and lose half his mind exploring.

But it wasn't just the way she looked that caught his attention.

There was a line of five fancy cocktails sitting in front of her, practically untouched. She frowned down at them, her full lips pressing flat as she twirled one strand of hair around her fingers.

He'd been in a lot of bars and met a lot of women, but never one who looked ready to throttle the alcohol she was served.

It made him wonder what in the hell those drinks had done to wrong her.

"Are you starting a collection?"

The woman's big brown eyes slowly came his way, resting on his face as her brows pinched together. "What?"

Troy tipped his head at what appeared to be an array of fruity, sweet concoctions that would have him puking by the third round. "Your drinks. Looks like you're collecting them instead of drinking them."

"Oh." The woman sighed, her shoulders dropping a little. "Yeah." Her focus went back to the line of options. "It turns out I just really don't like alcohol."

"Is this new information?" He settled back in his seat to wait for the bartender to notice he had a new arrival.

She sighed again, this one dragging out longer than the last. "Not really. I was hoping maybe the right motivation would change things, but they still all taste like ass." She pointed at the sweating glasses. "You want one?"

He couldn't help but chuckle. "You're not doing a very good job of sellin' them."

Her lower lip pushed out the tiniest bit, pulling his attention to the plumpness of the pout. "I guess I'm not much of a saleswoman."

Troy's focus stalled out on her mouth as he fought to think of anything besides sucking that sweet pout between his teeth. "I'm pretty sure that's not true."

He'd been beside her for less than a minute and chances were good she could sell him the clothes off his own back.

Probably because he was lonely as hell and all it took to make his dick hard was a single pout, which didn't bode well for his evening since this woman's pout didn't seem to be leaving anytime soon.

"It is true." She turned back to her drinks, grabbing the straw from one and stirring the melting pink slush around. "I'm a shitty saleswoman who can't drink alcohol and hates flowers."

The last bit sent his brain stumbling. "You hate flowers?"

Her dark eyes came back to his face. "Don't look at me like that."

He leaned back a little, lifting his brows in feigned innocence. "Like what?"

"Like I'm crazy." She pulled the straw free of the drink and pointed it at him. "Lots of people don't like flowers."

The frozen concoction clinging to the plastic started to slide. Out of reflex he leaned forward, catching the tip in his mouth and sucking off the frosty sweetness.

The woman's dark eyes widened, fixing on where his lips were wrapped around the straw in her hand.

Troy released the straw, giving it a flick with his tongue as he pulled away.

She sucked in a breath, the sound shooting straight to his already interested dick.

It'd been a hell of a long time since he'd had someone to really flirt with. Someone to chase.

Someone to seduce.

It was a high nothing else ever seemed to match. There was something about finding the most beautiful woman in the room and knowing he could make her his.

And the woman watching him with parted lips was absolutely the most beautiful in the room.

Maybe in the whole damn state.

Troy eased back, giving her a little more breathing room.

It was time for her to come to him. Time for her to make it clear she was picking up what he was putting down.

And wanted it to continue.

Her eyes stayed on him as he settled back into his seat, moving over his face before dipping down the length of his body. "Do you live here in Billings?"

"No." Troy gave up trying to get the bartender to notice him and snagged one of her neglected drinks, taking a quick sip before continuing. "I live in a little town about forty-five minutes from here."

Her light brown brows lifted. "That seems like a long way to come for a drink."

"I was in town visiting a friend." He took another sip of what was more like a milkshake than an alcoholic beverage. "Decided to stop for a beer on my way home."

The woman leaned a little closer. "And now you're stuck drinking my leftovers."

"I'm not stuck doin' anything." Troy forced himself to stay still even though all he wanted to do was move her way, see if she smelled as good as she looked. "I'm doin' exactly what I want to do."

Her head tipped to one side, that sweet pout back on her lips. "That's what I'm supposed to be doing too."

"Supposed to be?" He slid the drink away, abandoning it just like she had. Only he was doing it because he wanted to make sure his mind stayed clear. "Why aren't you?"

Her shoulders slumped the tiniest bit. "That's a good question." The lips that were driving him absolutely crazy pressed together for just a second before the lower one caught between her teeth.

Then she leaned closer. "You haven't told me your name."

"Troy." He paused before offering up the rest, just like he always did, wondering for a split second about what his last name could have been if things were different. "Merrick."

She inched in a little more, sliding her hand out between them. "I'm Amelie."

He wrapped one hand around hers, unsurprised at the tightness of her handshake. "It's a pleasure to meet you, Miss Amelie."

TWO
AMELIE

THE CROSS-COUNTRY FLIGHT must have fried her brain.

Pushed her into the same realm of insanity her best friend Evelyn occupied. Because right now, Evelyn's suggestion to find a 'sexy country boy' to bang all her problems away was starting to sound like brilliance instead of the bad advice her friend usually dished out over a bottle of red.

In fact, the longer she looked at the man occupying the bar stool next to her, the better her friend's plan to wipe the slate clean sounded.

Troy was ridiculously good-looking, with the bluest eyes she'd ever seen and a jawline so sharp it might be able to cut glass.

But in her experience, men who looked like he did left a lot to be desired in the bedroom. And if she was going to do this, she was most definitely going to do it with someone capable.

Which meant she needed to ask a few more questions. Dig out a few more clues.

"What do you do for work, Troy?"

"I'm a ranch hand." His focus was completely on her. "What about you, Miss Amelie? What do you do?"

The smooth way Troy said her name sent a little shiver of something down her spine, like he rolled it right off the tip of his tongue.

Which led to her undersexed brain making a list of all the other things he might potentially roll off the tip of his tongue.

Amelie cleared her throat, forcing her eyes from his mouth. "I work—" The past tense form of the word almost slipped out, forcing her to stop and start again. "I work in an art gallery." She tried not to let the reminder of her failure sour the tiny bit of hope she was finally feeling. "In New York."

Troy's brows slowly lifted. "The city, or the state?"

"Both." It had been her goal for as long as she could remember—to move to New York and chase down what some people considered an unattainable dream.

But she did it.

Sort of.

Troy's mouth pressed into an appraising line. "A city girl." His eyes dropped down to her mouth, lingering for just a second before jumping back to hers. "What's a city girl like you doing in a place like this?"

"Just visiting some family." Visiting was a nice way to put it. Way better than what she was actually doing, which was showing up on their doorstep to beg for a place to stay.

Troy's expression shifted, and for a second she could almost swear there was a hint of disappointment in his eyes. "Are you in town long?"

That was a great question. One she didn't have an answer to.

But she absolutely did have an answer for Troy. "I fly out in the morning."

If she decided to take this man to her room, it would have to be a limited engagement. One meant to serve as a palate cleanser and nothing more.

An 'out with the old and in with the new' sort of scenario.

Troy clicked his tongue. "That's a shame. I was trying to figure out what I would have to do to convince you to have dinner with me tomorrow."

Amelie did her best not to look as put out as she felt.

It would figure she'd find a gorgeous, charming cowboy that smelled good and wanted more than just an evening of fun.

Unfortunately, that was the way her luck was going.

But the way her luck was going would also mean Troy would turn out to be a world class twat she would catch fucking a new employee in her bed, so sending him on his way bright and shiny tomorrow morning was definitely the way this would have to play out.

Amelie curved her lips into a frown, hating that it wasn't as difficult to accomplish as it should be. "My flight leaves in the morning."

She hesitated, almost losing her nerve.

But this was about taking her life back. The same life she once swore would always be hers.

So, before she could talk herself out of it, Amelie leaned in close, pushing her tits against Troy's arm and her lips against his ear. "But I'm free tonight."

Troy sat completely still, not reacting at all to the fact that her boobs were pressed tight to him. "It's a little late for dinner, Miss Amelie."

It had been a long time since she'd had to decide if a man was interested in her or not, and she wasn't that great at it to start with, so it took a little of the wind out of her sails when Troy didn't immediately jump on the opportunity she was attempting to present. "Oh. Well I guess if you're not hungry..."

Troy shifted in his seat, the move subtle, but enough to drag his arm across her nipples in a way that immediately had them pulling tight. "I didn't say I wasn't hungry, Miss Amelie. I just said it was late to be eating dinner."

That didn't clear anything up for her.

Even worse, now she was distracted by the tingle of arousal sliding across her skin.

"So, you do want to take me to dinner?" This whole interaction was going downhill fast, proving art sales weren't the only thing she was terrible at.

She was also clearly a terrible flirt.

Maybe it made more sense to just cut her losses, suck it up, and spend the night alone. She could get her symbolic fresh start a different way.

Maybe a haircut. Or a Brazilian wax.

Possibly a tattoo.

But not a single one of those sounded nearly as appealing as spending the night with the man leaning close enough that his lips could almost brush her skin.

"Is that what you want, Amelie? For me to take you to dinner?" Troy's voice was low and seductive now, very different from the laid-back drawl he had before.

There was something about it that made her stupid. Stupid enough to give being brazen one last go.

"I want you to take me, but not to dinner."

She pressed her lips together as soon as it was out, immediately regretting being so forward with someone she barely knew.

But wasn't that the point of this? To prove she could be anything she wanted to be?

To prove that was still even possible?

Troy's nostrils barely flared and his gaze darkened. "I'm happy to take you anywhere you want."

She sucked in a breath. He was definitely interested.

Definitely probably.

"You are?"

He tipped his head in a slight nod. "Yes, ma'am."

Any inclination she might have had to change course ended with that *yes, ma'am*. How two words could be so affecting was beyond her, but maybe it had something to do with the fact that it made it seem like Troy wanted to please her.

To give her everything she was hoping to find.

Her decision was made.

"You could take me to my hotel room." Amelie could barely move enough air to get the words out as the possibility of hyperventilation threatened to ruin what was probably a once in a lifetime opportunity.

Men who looked like Troy didn't just grow on trees, and they certainly didn't show up to save you from dive bars.

Troy slowly spun in his seat until he was fully facing her, the long line of his legs bracketing hers in. "I will take you to your room on one condition."

Now she definitely was going to hyperventilate. "What's the condition?"

Troy's blue eyes moved to the line of drinks she'd attempted to convince herself to enjoy. "You have to promise me there weren't more of these before I came in."

Amelie shook her head. "I'm not drunk."

She was many things. Disappointed. Depressed. Embarrassed.

But definitely not drunk.

Troy didn't seem quite ready to take her at her word as he studied her face. "I just want to be sure you're making this decision with a clear head."

"I'm definitely very clear-headed right now." Maybe the clearest her head had been in a year. "But thank you for wanting to make sure I know what I'm doing."

Troy's eyes left her face for the first time since he sat down, slowly raking down her body before coming back to hold her gaze. "I wish I could say that was the only reason I was asking." He leaned in until she could feel the warmth of his breath. "But I also want to make sure you'll remember every second of tonight."

Then his mouth claimed hers, sealing in her gasp of surprise with a kiss that had her clinging to his shirt for balance as the noise and chaos of the bar spun around them.

There was no pretense and no hesitation in the act. He kissed her like he'd been planning it for a lifetime, each slide of his tongue and nip of his teeth making it impossibly clear that she was in way over her head.

But maybe that was the best way to be.

Troy broke off the kiss, but his big body stayed close, one calloused hand curving around her face as his blue eyes leveled on hers. "Still clear-headed?"

No. "Yes."

The lips that just left hers lifted at the edges into a sinfully sexy smile. "Looks like I've got my work cut out for me then."

He stood, dug out his wallet and threw a few bills on the bar, then grabbed her hand and pulled her toward the door, not even bothering to put his coat back on.

Amelie glanced back at the line of cocktails she'd ordered and ignored. "You didn't have to pay for my drinks."

"I hope you're kidding." Troy pushed open the door and led her out into the frigid air.

"I'm the one who ordered them." She nearly bumped into him when he came to an abrupt stop.

He looked her up and down, mouth pressing into a frown. "Where's your coat?"

She ignored the instinct to wrap her arms over her middle to conserve heat, but it was impossible to suppress the shiver that pulled her skin and her nipples tight. "I left it in the hotel because I didn't want to deal with it."

She had enough to deal with. Wrangling a giant coat at a packed bar might be what pushed her over the edge.

Troy's gaze dropped, fixing on where her puckered nipples poked through the lace of her bra and stood tall under the thin weave of her cashmere sweater dress. "So what you're tellin' me is you're stubborn."

Amelie's head bobbed back in surprise. "No."

No one had ever called her stubborn in her life. If anything, she was too damn agreeable.

Agreeable enough to unknowingly train the woman who was to become not just her replacement at the art gallery her ex-boyfriend owned, but also her replacement in his bed.

Troy shook out his coat and wrapped it around her, pulling it together in the front and zipping her in. "Only people who are too stubborn to let the cold control them skip a winter coat in Montana."

She fought her arms into the sleeves. "I just didn't want to mess with it."

Troy snagged one of her hands the second it was free. "Keep talkin'. You're only proving my point." He looked around. "Where are we going?"

Amelie pointed to the hotel right next to the bar. "There."

She'd decided to rent a room for her first night in town so she could have a little time to clear her head before facing down her grandmother in the morning and having to answer the ten million questions that were definitely going to be coming her way.

Troy didn't hesitate at all, his hand staying tight around hers as they made their way over the shoveled sidewalks, salt crunching under the soles of their boots.

"I'm not stubborn." She should probably let it go. It didn't really matter what this man thought of her since she would never see him again after tomorrow morning.

"You're definitely stubborn." Troy said it like it was the obvious truth.

"If I was stubborn, and didn't want the cold to tell me what to do, I would have worn pumps instead of boots." It was a stretch. Pumps would've looked a little silly with a sweater dress, but the primary reason she chose the knee-high suede footwear was for the traction they provided.

They also happened to look cute. Which was a complete coincidence.

"If you weren't stubborn you wouldn't still be arguing with me about whether or not you are stubborn." Troy moved into the hotel and straight across the lobby, punching the button on the elevator before dragging her inside and closing the doors on anyone who might try to join them.

Then his tall frame crowded hers, backing her into the corner closest to the panel. "But don't worry. I like stubborn women."

"I'm not stubborn." Why this was the hill she decided to die on was anyone's guess.

It was almost as confusing as the fact that she was arguing with a gorgeous cowboy she picked up at a bar so she could bring him back to her room and see him naked.

Touch him naked.

Maybe do a little sucking.

"I need you to pick a floor for me, Miss Amelie."

Troy's voice dragged her attention to the panel beside them. She reached out to stab her finger on the fourth-floor button before wrapping both arms around his neck and leaning close to put her lips on his.

She didn't want to argue with him anymore. Didn't want to try to convince Troy of what she was or what she wasn't.

She just wanted him to bang the broken bits of her into dust so she could sweep it away and start fresh.

Hopefully he was up for the job.

Troy pressed closer, pinning her against the wall as his fingers forked into her hair and his mouth moved from her lips to her neck, leaving a trail of heat and goosebumps as he licked and nipped her skin.

By the time the doors opened she was panting and in desperate need of more.

She grabbed the front of his shirt and dragged him out, moving embarrassingly fast to the door of her room.

But the key was in her purse, which was pinned between her body and Troy's heavy coat, forcing her to fight her way free of the bulky fabric to get to what she wanted.

"This is why I didn't want to wear a coat." Amelie wrestled the bag loose before fumbling through the pocket and pulling out the plastic card, immediately swiping it across the scanner.

"You didn't want to wear a coat because you knew it would take you a few seconds longer to get into your hotel room?" He shook his head. "I don't buy it." Troy leaned in a little closer as she swiped the card again, slapping it against the reader when it refused to recognize it.

"You didn't wear a coat because you're stubborn." Troy's hand came to hers, deftly sliding the card free before resting it over the digital lock. The deadbolt immediately unlatched. "It's the same reason you damn near beat this thing to death instead of trying to flip the card over."

Amelie snatched the card from him, irritation making her snappy. "I'm not stubborn." She shoved her way into the room, taking a few steps before turning to face him, barely waiting for him to come inside before pointing one finger his way. "Now take off your clothes."

They needed to stop talking before this argument ruined

everything and she ended up wallowing alone and waking up the same depressed mess of self-loathing she'd been for the past two weeks, instead of an empowered go-getter ready to make the world her bitch.

Troy stared at her, his only movement the slight arching of one eyebrow. "I don't think so." He slowly came her way, each step making her heart beat a little faster. "This is a 'ladies first' kinda night."

He leaned into her ear as the tips of his fingers gathered the bottom of her dress, pulling the fabric higher and higher. "And my clothes aren't coming off until you come for my hands and my mouth."

THREE
AMELIE

AND?

His hands *and* his mouth?

Amelie stared at Troy in disbelief. "I'm not sure you're being realistic." It was a nice thought, but the chances that this man, cowboy or not, could get her off once, let alone twice, were slim to none. "Two times is a lot."

Troy skimmed her dress higher, dragging it past her ass and over her stomach. "No one said anything about two times, darlin'." His fingers slid over her skin as he bared it to the cool air of the hotel room. "I just said twice before my clothes come off."

She laughed.

There was no way to stop it.

"I think you're getting a little ahead of yourself there, cowboy." She paused as her dress covered her face, waiting until Troy was carefully laying it across the chair before continuing. "You haven't even managed it once, so maybe you should see how much effort that involves before you start making promises you won't be able to keep."

She didn't come here expecting to get off.

Troy was hot, sure, but hotness and climaxes weren't always connected.

Hell, sometimes the more attractive a guy was, the less likely he was to think he had to do more than show up and stick it in.

Troy's brows lifted. "Is that so?"

She stood tall as his eyes moved down her body, taking in the scraps of turquoise lace that covered her boobs and bottom. "It is."

Another of those slow, sexy smiles worked across his lips. "Definitely stubborn."

Amelie started to argue, but Troy suddenly stepped close, covering her mouth with his as he banded one arm around her back, pulling her against him.

She was so distracted by the feel of his body and his lips that she didn't immediately notice when Troy's free hand slid into the front of the tiny panties she'd carefully selected before going out.

Just in case an opportunity presented itself.

But the second his fingers brushed her clit, every cell in her body turned its attention to that point of contact, focusing only on it as he stroked her with an unerring touch.

One that had her legs shaking in under two minutes as she struggled to stay upright.

Troy's arm tightened around her back as he sucked the lobe of her ear between his teeth. "I promise not to let you fall, Amelie. All you have to do is give me what I want." The steady slide of his fingers sped up, working back and forth between her thighs and making an obscene wet sound that she would be embarrassed about later.

Or not, since she would never see this man again.

A fact that made it easier to let go. To do exactly what he said and give in to the tightness coiling inside her.

To set it free.

Troy held her tight, supporting all her weight as the first of the climaxes he promised ripped through her, leaving her panting and weak.

And a little shocked.

But there wasn't a hint of surprise on Troy's face as he walked her backwards across the floor, that wicked grin back as his wide palm cupped tight between her thighs, the firm pressure making the pulsing aftershocks still throbbing there even more noticeable.

Her legs hit the mattress and a second later she was going down, tumbling back onto the king-sized bed, feet dangling over the edge.

Troy stood over her, eyes intense as they slid down her body. "I can't help but notice you've got on some pretty sexy panties, Amelie." He reached out to hook one finger in the see-through lace cup of her bra, yanking it down to expose her breast. "And they match your bra."

She was caught but wasn't interested in admitting that maybe she left the hotel with a more specific plan than she let on. "Can't a girl want to look pretty?"

"Of course." He plucked at the nipple already pulling tight under the heat of his gaze. "But you lookin' pretty has nothing to do with the panties you're wearing." Troy leaned down, bracing his body over hers as the heat of his mouth closed around the aching tip.

His tongue flicked against her just like it had the straw she pointed at him earlier. And it felt as good as she'd imagined.

Maybe better.

It wasn't long before her hands were laced in his hair,

pulling tight as he tugged the other cup of her bra down and shifted his mouth to that breast.

Before long the throb between her legs was back, like her body wanted to pretend she hadn't already gotten off. Each pull of his mouth shot straight to her core, collecting in a new unmet need.

One that made her feel a little desperate.

"Troy." She grabbed for his pants, wrestling with the buckle of his belt. "I want you."

His mouth barely left her body as it worked lower. "That's good to hear." He caught her hands in his, pulling them loose as he dropped to his knees. "But you're gonna have to wait until I've had my fill of you."

Amelie leaned up, bracing on her elbows so she could put her eyes on the cowboy who was supposed to have had one, simple task.

All Troy had to do was come in here, complete the assignment she'd given him, and then go on his merry little way.

But he was starting to prove himself to be an overachiever. And that could prove to be a problem because this had to be a one-time thing.

Her focus needed to stay on rebuilding her life.

Not getting naked and dirty with a cowboy, no matter how capable he might be.

And Troy seemed pretty damn capable.

Amelie yelped a little as he caught her behind the knees, using the grip to pull her down the mattress until her ass was right at the edge.

She grabbed at the cover under her back, holding on just in case he kept dragging her toward the floor. "What are you doing?"

"If you don't know what I'm doin' then you're about to be a very happy woman." Troy hooked her legs over his shoulders and leaned in to put his mouth right on her, the heat of it easily passing through the tiny scrap of lace still covering her pussy.

The contact was sudden and a little unexpected.

Most men talked a good game about all the things they were going to do, but when it came time to put their money where their mouth was...

They usually used their dick instead.

Amelie stared in shock as Troy's mouth lifted, his blue eyes meeting hers as he hooked one finger in the crotch of her panties and pulled them to one side. The last thing she saw before going cross-eyed was the hint of a smirk on his wicked lips.

Troy's mouth was just as unrelenting as his fingers were, tongue dragging over her clit in steady strokes until her back was bowing off the bed.

Possibly from levitation.

But it wasn't until his lips closed around her clit, sucking the already sensitive bud, and the air from her lungs, that the possibility of a second orgasm became reality. Climax number two thundered through her as she tried to roll away from the intensity of the pleasure this cowboy dished out like Smarties at a candy convention.

Troy held her tight, refusing to let her break free until he'd wrung every bit out of her.

And then some.

Then he slowly stood, keeping her legs braced up the front of his body, ankles against his shoulders as he leaned into her, rocking his hips in a steady rhythm.

But the way Troy's body rubbed hers was like no teenage dry humping she'd ever been a part of. It was slow and purposeful, not driven by hormones and inexperience.

Because Troy clearly had plenty of experience.

And he was starting to make her look bad.

Like she was the kind of woman who just laid back and took without offering anything up in return.

Which she was not.

Amelie unhooked one of her ankles from Troy's shoulder then looped her leg around his back, pulling him forward until his face was close to hers.

Troy's head tipped to one side as he glanced at the leg that was now bent almost all the way back. "You're flexible."

For some reason she was flattered that he noticed. "My best friend in New York is a yoga instructor, so I get free classes."

Troy wrapped one arm around her back and dragged her up the mattress. "Send her my thanks."

The mention of Evelyn made her smile.

Her friend was going to be proud as hell when she filled her in on tonight's events. "I'll be sure to tell her all about you."

"That sounds promising." Troy straightened, balancing on his knees. "I guess I'll have to make sure you have plenty to say." He caught the sides of her panties and slid them down her legs before tossing them to the edge of the bed.

"You mean besides that you kept your clothes on for an insanely long time?"

She was teasing him.

Mostly.

Being naked wasn't a big deal. She'd done some modeling in art school, so seeing strangers nude and being seen nude by strangers wasn't usually something she got all worked up about.

But she was more than ready to see what a naked cowboy looked like.

Specifically this cowboy.

"Insanely long?" Troy ran his fingers up the length of her legs, the slightly rough drag of his touch sending a shiver of anticipation along her skin. "We haven't even been in this room an hour."

Amelie bit her lower lip as Troy's hands moved to the hem of his thermal shirt. "And you don't think that's an insanely long time to keep your clothes on when there's a willing woman in front of you?"

Troy shook his head as he shifted the shirt up his stomach. "Not when we've got all night."

Her eyes were burning from not blinking, but the sight of Troy's abs wasn't something a woman missed a second of. Amelie licked her lips as he worked the shirt higher, exposing a thin smattering of light brown hair across a chest that was even broader than she initially thought.

But then his words registered.

"All night?" It came out a little squeaky and a lot breathy.

If it were any other guy she might have taken the statement with a grain of salt.

But so far, Troy was turning out to be a man of his word.

He tossed his shirt on top of her panties before digging into the back pocket of his jeans and pulling out his wallet. A second later a condom hit the bed beside her.

Amelie looked from the single condom to Troy. "All night plus one condom doesn't really add up, cowboy."

He worked his jeans open, uncoremoniously shoving them down his hips. "If you think there's only one way to have fun then you're about to be pleasantly surprised."

She opened her mouth to argue, but the sight of Troy's cock as it dropped free of his pants muddled her words, turning them into an unintelligible combination of consonants and possibly a gasp.

The man was hung.

Because of course he was.

If this wasn't the absolute definition of irony, then someone needed to have a talk with Merriam-Webster because their book needed an update.

She'd even be willing to write it for them.

Irony: Meeting a sexy cowboy with an insane ability to cause orgasms and a perfect penis right after deciding men were the root of all your problems.

Troy grinned, kicking the rest of his clothes to the floor before crawling over her. "I might need you to repeat that." He nosed along her neck. "I didn't catch what you said."

His long body was warm where it pressed against hers, the thick line of his cock resting on her belly as his mouth caught hers in a kiss that only added to the fog of frustration threatening to cloud her judgment.

But she couldn't let that happen.

She'd allowed a man to derail her life once. It wasn't going to happen again.

No matter how good of a kisser he was.

No matter how blue his eyes were.

No matter how charming and sweet he seemed to be.

"I said, you should have warned me you were bringing a Louisville Slugger to bed." She slid her hand down to trace along the velvety skin of his cock. "I might have reconsidered inviting you up here."

Troy nipped at the lobe of her ear. "Not a baseball fan?"

She nearly choked on the laugh that tried to sneak out.

He was funny too. Great.

"I'm just saying that's the kind of thing you warn a woman about." Amelie jumped a little when the front clasp of her bra unsnapped, releasing the pressure it put on her chest. "For future reference."

Troy lifted up, his face hovering over hers, eyes serious. "You're the one in charge of this show, Amelie. We only do what you want to do, so if you don't want—"

Oh hell no.

This was going to happen.

"I didn't say I didn't want to do..." Her eyes drifted to the condom. "Everything."

She was tired of knowing the last man to touch her put his hands on someone else.

In their bed.

She was tired of feeling like she meant so little to someone she gave so much more than she should have.

And honestly, she was a little worried that she would die tomorrow and sex with Trevor would be the last she ever experienced.

"I'm just a little intimidated by Baby Troy."

Troy stared at her. "Did you just call my dick Baby Troy?"

"What do you want me to call it?"

"I didn't hate Louisville Slugger."

Goddammit.

She was about to laugh again.

Amelie took a slow breath, trying to regain control, but Troy's hand slid up the inside of her thigh, cutting the inhale short.

"You tell me what we're doing, Amelie." He teased along the seam of her pussy with a light touch that felt good enough to make her think she might not actually know her own body's limits. "The only way we're using that condom is if you say we are." His touch pressed deeper, sliding between her labia to skate across her clit. "Because I'm just as happy to see how many creative ways I can come up with to make you come before you get on that plane in the morning."

He looked like he meant it.

And the threat was enough to have her grabbing the condom and shoving it at him. "Put it on now."

Troy's eyes moved from hers to the condom, hanging a

second before he pulled his hand from her body and took the foil pack. "Yes, ma'am."

He made short work of tearing it open and rolling it on.

Amelie tried to spread her legs, assuming the standard position, but Troy caught one and stretched it flat against the mattress before straddling it, one knee resting on each side of her thigh. He braced one hand behind her other knee, holding her leg out to the side as he lined himself into place, notching the thick head of his cock against her core.

Then he stopped, waiting until she looked at him.

"You're sure?"

She nodded, the movement a little jerky as anticipation and another wave of arousal dumped adrenaline into her system. "Positive."

She'd been unsure of so much lately, but not this.

Not Troy.

Now *he* would be the last man who touched her.

The last man who kissed her.

The last man who fucked her.

And that would be a pretty nice memory. Definitely better than the one he was replacing.

She thought he would immediately shove into her, but once again Troy proved to be so different from what she'd grown to expect.

The slide of his body into hers was slow and careful, a series of short thrusts that eased her into the invasion.

And it was most definitely an invasion.

"How you doin, Stubborn?" His voice was low against her ear. "Too much?"

"I'm fine." She let out a rush of air as he pressed deep. "And I'm not stubborn."

"Whatever you say." Troy's next thrust came a little faster, but the positioning of her leg against the mattress kept him from pushing in too far, and it wasn't long before the stretch of him inside her felt a little less, *too much*—

And a little more, *just right*.

His pace was steady and solid, each thrust coming exactly how she expected and exactly when she expected, and the consistency was having one hell of an effect.

Troy's lips moved against her ear. "Better?"

She squeezed her eyes shut, trying to stay focused. "Stop talking."

"Not gonna happen." Troy slid the hand from her leg and spread it across her lower belly, thumb on her clit. "It's the only way I know you're having as much fun as I am."

"I'm having fu—"

Her words strangled off as Troy's palm pressed down in a small move that had huge repercussions.

Now his cock dragged across something inside her with every pass.

Something that felt so good it made her toes curl and her breath stall.

Now there was no need to focus.

Nothing would distract her from whatever he started.

"Don't stop." Amelie clawed at his skin, unable to control her movements or the embarrassingly feral sounds coming out of her as Troy sent her over the edge for the third time in a climax that was unlike anything she'd ever felt before.

She was barely coherent when his body tensed, a low groan rumbling through his chest as his orgasm chased hers, leaving them both breathing heavy.

And her a little off balance.

A little concerned she'd done more than make another bad decision.

She might have made the worst decision of her life.

Because this whole plan was to use Troy to help her reclaim her past.

Help her move on and stop beating herself up over things she couldn't change.

But Troy may have just ruined her.

And there might not be any coming back from him.

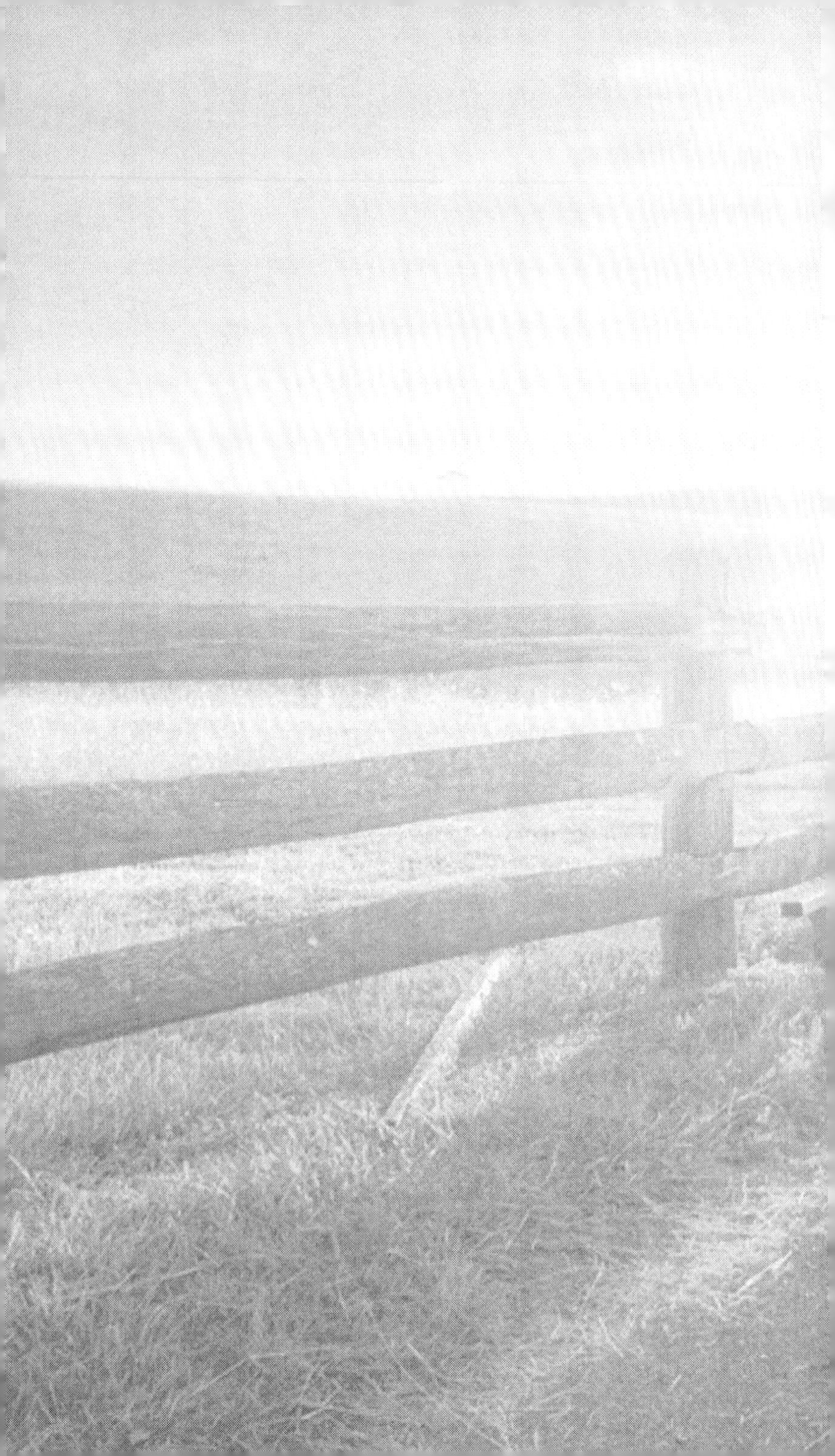

FOUR

TROY

TROY STARED OUT the kitchen window at the pile of snow that hit the ground overnight, stacking up on top of the sidewalks he'd just shoveled two days ago.

Normally the snow didn't bother him. It was just a fact of life in Montana. One he'd come to accept since choosing the state as his new home.

But this morning, everything was bothering him.

The cold.

The snow.

The fact that even his best efforts hadn't convinced Amelie from New York to reschedule her flight.

Or give him her phone number.

Or even just her last name.

What she did do, was unceremoniously send him on his way the next morning after a night of the most interesting sex he'd ever had.

Interesting in that they'd done so much more than fuck.

They'd argued.

Teased.

Enjoyed each other in ways that went far beyond physical satisfaction.

But obviously that was a one-sided sentiment since he was waking up alone.

Again

Troy dumped what was left of his coffee down the sink of the little farmhouse he'd been living in since the end of the summer, then rinsed out the cup before stomping his way through the kitchen and back up the stairs to the bedroom he'd yet to bring a woman into.

When Liza and Ben, the owners of Cross Creek Ranch, offered up the little cape cod, he'd jumped at the chance to move out of the bunkhouse and into a place of his own, thinking it wouldn't be long before he found someone to share it with.

He'd been wrong, and that didn't look to be changing anytime soon.

Because, as depressing as it was, it might be time to start facing the truth.

He was the guy women took home for the night, not the man they made space for in their lives.

Which was par for the course, but still stung like hell.

All he wanted to do was wallow. Spend the day holed up licking his wounds.

But Mother Nature had to come and screw up his plans by dumping out a pile of frozen bullshit that he knew damn well Muriel's stubborn ass would end up trying to clear away with a spatula and a hand broom.

So he got dressed and brushed his teeth before pulling on a knit cap and his heavy coat. Then he trudged out into the cold, starting up his truck to let it get warm while he shoveled the back deck and the path leading up to it.

The physical labor made him feel a little better. Got out some of the frustration he felt with himself.

He had to be doing something wrong. Something that made women run in the other direction as soon as the sun came up.

But then again, that was the story of his life. Right from the get-go people seemed to have a hell of an easy time walking away from him.

Leaving him behind.

He finished clearing the last of the snow and chucked his shovel into the truck bed just as his buddy Colt came down the drive.

Colt was another ranch hand at Cross Creek. He'd become one of Troy's closest friends as they commiserated over working on a ranch and living the single life.

But Colt had been more unavailable than normal lately, and it looked like the reason for that was sitting in the passenger's seat of his truck.

Troy ambled up to the side of his friend's pickup just as it came to a stop. The passenger's window rolled down to reveal a pretty redhead with a sweet smile. Colt leaned across the console, offering a nod in greeting. "Looks like we got more snow last night."

"Seems like." Troy thumbed over one shoulder in the direction of his running truck. "I'm on my way to go shovel Muriel's sidewalk so she doesn't get out and try to do it herself."

Colt grinned. He was part of the crew that helped pour Muriel's new sidewalk and replace her deteriorating roof the previous summer. "That sounds about right." He turned his attention to the redhead. "Muriel's a friend of ours. Your Aunt Gertrude would love her."

Colt refocused his attention on Troy. "This is Winter. Her aunt lives on the mountain. Her house is a few down from mine."

Troy gave Winter the best smile he could manage, hoping to mask the jealousy creeping in. "Nice to meet you."

Colt slung one hand over the steering wheel. "I promised I'd bring her out here to see the ranch and figured today was as good a day as any." He reached across the cab to trace his fingers along the inside of Winter's palm. "Is there anything you need me to take care of while we're here?"

Troy forced his gaze from where Colt stroked Winter's hand in a touch that was both casual and intimate. "Nothing besides the normal." He took a step back, needing a little space. "But you might want to check with Ben just to be sure."

Since their hay barn burned down in the fall, he'd taken on more responsibilities, hoping to ease the burden Ben and Liza were struggling to carry. They both needed time and space as they recovered from what was one hell of a rough summer. And Colt was usually right there with him, helping do what needed done.

But it looked like, at least for this morning, his buddy had a new sidekick.

Troy forced a smile back on his face. "You two have fun." He gave Winter a nod. "It was nice to meet you."

"Nice to meet you too." Winter's voice was as sweet as her smile. "Have a good day."

He turned away as they drove off, unwilling to let himself stew over a development he should be happy about.

Colt was a good guy. He was a hard worker who loved the hell out of his family. He deserved to find a nice girl to settle down with.

Unfortunately, rationalizing it didn't ease the sting.

Troy opened his truck door, knocking the snow from his boots on the frame before climbing in and heading out of town.

He hadn't called Muriel yesterday, but maybe he should

have because the closer he got to her house, the less miserable he felt.

His mood still wasn't great, but at least he would have someone to talk to for a bit. Someone who understood what it was like to be alone and all but abandoned by their family.

Hell, maybe he could even play the pity card and earn himself an all-access pass to the inside of Muriel's house. He was sure as hell going to be needing a distraction since all he wanted to think about was long blonde hair, big brown eyes, and a set of lips he would have happily booked a flight to experience again.

But the offer clearly wasn't on the table.

Since he hadn't given Muriel a heads-up that he was on his way, Troy decided to stop and grab them each a fancy coffee, choosing from the shop's seasonal menu just in case sugar and whipped cream was the answer to all of his problems.

But his hopes for commiseration with Muriel took a nosedive the second he turned onto her street.

A strange vehicle was parked in her driveway. It wasn't that the small SUV itself was strange, it was just that any car would be strange to see in Muriel's driveway. As far as he knew, no one came to check on her but him and a few of the people from Cross Creek.

Not her neighbors. Not her friends. Not her family.

It was one of the reasons they got along so well. He understood what it was like to be forgotten.

Abandoned.

Troy pulled up alongside the white crossover, parking his truck and grabbing the coffees before climbing out to get a better look.

The presence of the vehicle was odd on its own, but the fact that last night's snowfall was untouched, both on the SUV and the driveway around it, meant whoever it belonged to had been there since the night before.

And that meant Muriel must have let them in.

Troy stared up at the little house he'd been busting his ass for months to get a peek inside, never once making it past the threshold.

But it wasn't just him who couldn't get in. Ben had tried. Liza had tried. Colt had tried.

Muriel didn't let anyone in, so the fact that someone was in there with her was concerning as hell.

He cut across the yard, skipping the sidewalk to take the most direct route to her front porch, kicking himself that he hadn't called to check in on her yesterday.

If something happened to Muriel—

Troy banged on the door, not caring that it was still early. Not caring that he might scare the shit out of whoever was inside.

They'd just have to deal with it.

He shifted on his feet as he waited, each second that passed ramping up the bite of panic taking over.

Muriel had to be okay.

If something had happened she would have called him.

As long as she was able to call.

He raised his fist, ready to bang again, but his hand only met air as the door swung open.

A pair of familiar brown eyes stared back at him.

He blinked hard before taking another look.

But Amelie was still standing there, those lips he couldn't stop thinking about dropped open in shock.

"Troy." His name rushed out of her mouth, whispery and soft, just like it had more than a few times two nights ago.

He continued staring, unable to take his eyes off the woman he never expected to see again.

Somehow, she was even prettier than he remembered. Her long hair was tied up at the top of her head in a messy knot, and the sexy fitted dress she wore that night was replaced by a pair of thermal pajamas. There wasn't a trace of makeup on her scrubbed-clean face and a few creases were wrinkled into the skin of one cheek from where she'd been sleeping.

There was nothing better he could have hoped to find on the other side of Muriel's door.

Or worse.

Amelie glanced over one shoulder before stepping out onto the porch in her bare feet and closing the door behind her. "What in the hell are you doing here?"

"I could ask you the same thing." Troy forced his eyes to stay on her face as she shivered, crossing both arms over her chest to hide the tight peaks of her nipples. "I thought you were going back to New York."

Amelie pursed her lips, the move so similar to the pout that lured him in it was almost painful to witness. "I—"

Troy shook his head. "It's fine."

It was actually far from fine, but pride kept him from admitting it.

It was obvious when Amelie shoved him out the hotel room door that she wasn't interested in keeping in touch, but he'd wanted to believe distance played a part in that decision.

Except here she was. Still in town. Still close enough he could have taken her out to dinner. Could have seen her again.

Could have shown her he was more than just a good time.

Amelie's dark eyes dropped from his face to rest on the coffee cups in his hands. Her brows pinched together as she rubbed her arms and bounced from foot to foot. "I just—"

The door opened behind her and Muriel peeked out through the crack. Her eyes opened wide behind her glasses. "Troy. What are you doing here?"

She didn't seem any happier to see him than Amelie had been.

And that was like a knife to his already scuffed-up heart.

"It snowed." He nodded toward his truck. "I came over to shovel so you wouldn't have to worry about it."

Muriel's wide gaze moved from Troy to Amelie then back to Troy again. She edged out the door, pulling it closed behind her just as she had every other time he'd come over. "You didn't have to come all the way here." She focused on the cups in his hands. "But I'm not gonna complain since you brought coffee." She reached out to snag one before going to shuffle her way across the porch, pulling her coat tight around her shoulders as she took a sip from the cup.

Like she was just going to sit in that same chair and pretend this was a normal fucking day.

Amelie pointed her finger at Muriel before swinging it back to Troy. "I'm sorry, but how do you two know each other?"

Muriel wiggled deeper into the seat before taking another long sip of her coffee. She made an approving expression before turning to Amelie. "I told you about Troy. He's the boy who's been helping me around the house."

"The boy." Amelie's eyes slowly moved down his front. "Who's been helping you around the house."

She shivered again, but this time he wasn't convinced it was only the cold that caused it.

"Here." Troy held out the other cup of coffee. "This one is vanilla chestnut."

Amelie's stare was intense as it settled on the insulated cup. "That sounds really good."

Troy held it closer. "Take it."

"I don't want to take your coffee." She inched back a little.

"Stop being stubborn and take it." He might still be a little chapped over the fact that she lied about leaving town so she didn't have to see him again, but that didn't mean that he wanted her to freeze to death.

Amelie scoffed, squaring her shoulders and lifting her chin. "I'm not stubborn."

Muriel snorted.

Then started coughing. She patted her chest a few times before giving Troy and Amelie a smile. "Sorry. Wrong pipe." She squinted at them, looking from one to the other for a second. "Do you know each other?"

"No." Troy offered up the simplest answer. "I just assume you're going to wear off on anyone that hangs around you too long."

Muriel gave him a grin. "This one here has acted like me from the day she was born." Muriel's grin turned to a smile that was filled with a level of pride he'd never witnessed. "Amelie's my oldest granddaughter." She leaned forward, like Troy might need to hear her better. "She's an artist in New York City."

Troy turned to Amelie. "An artist?" He stepped back to lean against one of the supporting pillars of the porch. "What brings you to Billings?"

Asking more questions was a dirty move, but if he wanted to know why he couldn't keep a woman, then this was his opportunity.

And Amelie obviously didn't see a problem with lying to him, so he wasn't going to feel bad about putting her on the spot.

"Same thing that makes any woman fly across the country." Muriel took another sip of her coffee, making him wait a few agonizing seconds for the rest. "Because it was easier than digging a hole."

FIVE
AMELIE

MAYBE COMING TO her grandmother's wasn't as smart of a decision as she thought.

"I don't want to talk about this." Amelie turned and opened the door. "And I definitely don't want to do it out here. It's freezing."

She needed to get away. From the moment. From the situation.

From Troy and the horribly arousing things his presence was making her remember.

Initially, as she stared out at him standing there on the porch, she thought her exhausted brain conjured him up. A custom-made nightmare to add insult to injury.

But this man was most definitely real.

And if she couldn't figure out how to get him the hell out of here, she was screwed.

And not in a fun way.

In the way that would have her falling into the same trap that snared her mother and grandmother.

And almost managed to snag her.

Amelie made it a few feet into the house then turned to face Troy, ready to tell him he needed to go back home. That she would handle shoveling the snow and whatever else he helped her grandmother with.

But Troy walked right past her, his focus on the house as he moved from room to room like he was looking for something.

And she had a sinking feeling she knew what he was looking for.

Amelie watched as he went for the narrow flight of stairs leading to the second level.

Shit.

Each hit of his boots on the stair treads was like a note from the intro to Symphony No. 5.

Dun, dun, dun, duuuun.

Dun, dun, dun, duuuun.

She didn't know Troy well, but it didn't take a rocket scientist to figure out it was going to be a hell of a lot harder to get rid of him once he saw what was up there.

The door to the front bedroom clicked open.

She cringed as his footsteps moved back to the landing and to the second bedroom. That door opened, the telltale creaking of the hinges echoing through her sleep-starved brain.

"Amelie." Troy's deep voice echoed down the partially enclosed stairwell.

She stared at the stained ceiling above her head, holding her breath even though she already knew what was coming. "Yeah?"

"I'm gonna need you to come up here."

She slowly walked to the base of the stairs, refusing to look up as she lifted one foot.

"Go put some shoes on first." Troy's tone was sharper than she'd heard it before.

But to be fair, her experience with him was pretty narrow.

"It's fine." She ignored his request and moved up the steps, straightening her shoulders as she stared him down.

Troy stepped in her path, blocking the landing that led to the two bedrooms and bathroom that made up the second floor, arms crossed over his chest, a frown on his handsome face. "You're not coming up here without a pair of shoes on your feet." His frown edged toward a scowl. "There's insulation all over the place."

"I know." She swiped at her dirty hair, shoving back a few of the strands that had worked free of her bun while she tossed and turned on the sofa, trying to figure out how in the hell she was going to help her grandmother dig out of the literal mess she was in. "I got as much as I could cleaned up yesterday, but—"

Troy held up one hand between them, stopping her from getting any closer to the landing. "You were trying to clean this up?"

She glared up at him. "Of course I was trying to clean it up. Did you think I was just gonna leave it there?"

Troy's mouth flattened into a hard line, his expression serious. "Honestly, I don't know what I expected considering no one in your family seems to give two shits about your grandma."

The harshness in his words was shocking.

But what he said wasn't.

Guilt sent her crumbling to the stairs, butt dropping to the threadbare carpet covering the treads. Her head fell to her hands. "This is all my fault."

Troy immediately came down beside her, going to his knees a few steps down so they were face-to-face. "Did you know she was living like this?"

Amelie shook her head, blinking as her eyes started to water. "She always said everything was fine. I had no idea—" Her throat closed off, making it impossible to finish the explanation.

She should have come back sooner. Should have made the time to fly here and see for herself that everything was as fine as her grandmother claimed it was.

Because God knows no one else would do it.

Which was also her fault.

"Do you talk to her much?" There was something more than general curiosity in Troy's question, but she couldn't put her finger on what it was.

"I call her every other day." Amelie sucked in a breath, trying to stop the running of her nose. "I knew I was the only one who checked on her and I should have done more."

Troy sighed as he shifted to one side, settling onto the step just below her. "She's been telling me everything was fine for six months now, even though I was looking right at the fact that it probably wasn't."

Amelie peeked his way, taking in the strong line of his profile. "What do you mean you were looking at it?"

Troy tilted his face her way, his eyes lifting upward. "Who do you think replaced the roof on this house?"

Her jaw went slack, hanging open a second before she recovered enough to clamp her teeth back together. "You replaced the roof?"

"Not by myself." He leaned back, resting his elbows right beside her. "A few of us from the ranch where I work have been trying to get this place to where it won't fall down around her ears." He barely shook his head. "But I could never get her to let me come inside."

Amelie huffed out a little laugh. "If it makes you feel any better she wasn't too thrilled about letting me in either."

She showed up on her grandma's doorstep two mornings ago, feeling mostly prepared to figure out where her life should go from here. She expected Muriel would be thrilled to see her. Hoped it would be just like when she spent summers here as a teenager.

But right out of the gate she knew something was wrong.

"Why wouldn't she want anyone to help?" Troy scrubbed one hand down his face, the sight of his long, strong fingers threatening to distract her from the conversation. "I could have already had all this handled for her."

"She doesn't like people making a fuss over her. She'll swear everything's fine even if it's a complete dumpster fire." It was how her grandmother handled all the drama that tore their family apart.

She just moved forward. Pretended like it didn't bother her and like it was okay that her own sons cut her off over something trivial.

"So she's stubborn." Troy's blue eyes came to rest on her face. "It must be genetic."

Amelie huffed out a breath as she rubbed her burning eyes. "You're aggravating as hell, you know that?"

Troy's lips lifted in a wicked smile she was a little too familiar with. "I'm a lot of things, Miss Amelie." He slowly stood before turning and leaning close. "But you already know that."

Before her cheeks could even have the chance to flush with what might be embarrassment but was more likely arousal, Troy turned away and stomped back down the stairs. "Get dressed. We're going shopping."

"No." She shook her head. "Absolutely not."

This was spiraling out of control and she had to find a way to stop the spinning before she lost her mind. "I can't go shopping with you."

It had already been difficult enough to shove Troy out of her life, and that was before she knew he was the 'boy' who'd been taking care of her grandmother.

Troy slowly prowled back up the stairs, her heart beating faster with each step.

Why did he have to be so good-looking?

And why in the hell couldn't he be an asshole? The kind of man who was only worried about himself?

It would figure this would be the one time she wouldn't pull one of those into her orbit.

"I have been trying to get into this house for six months, Amelie." He rested his hands on either side of her, leaning down until their eyes lined up. "If you think I'm going to pretend I didn't see what's at the top of these stairs, then you're about to find out I'm just as stubborn as you are."

"I'm not stubborn." She couldn't stop the argument from jumping out.

She wasn't a fighter. Never had been.

That's why she didn't talk to anyone in her family. All they did was fight. Yelled and screamed until they bullied you into submission.

But it didn't feel like fighting with Troy. It felt like honesty, and it was easy to give since he was a stranger.

A stranger who'd seen her naked.

Touched every inch of her body.

Had his mouth—

"Then it looks like you found two things I'm not going to argue with you about." Troy lifted one hand, raising a finger. "I am fixing that mess," he added a second finger, "and you absolutely are stubborn." He straightened, crossing his arms. "So the question is, are you going to help, or not?"

Amelie stared up at him.

She should run right back downstairs, pack her bags, and go to the airport. Get as far from this man, and all the problems she knew he would bring to her life, as possible.

But there was nowhere else for her to go.

Her life in New York was over. Ended exactly the way her parents said it would—which she would never admit to them.

That's why going home to Colorado wasn't an option either.

"Fine." She pushed to her feet, bumping Troy back as she stood. "But there's got to be rules."

Troy's mouth curved. "A stubborn rule maker." His blue eyes sparkled. "I like it."

She pointed at the center of his face. "None of that." She wiggled her finger up and down his body. "And none of that either."

Troy's brows lifted. "I can't talk or," he glanced down at where her finger stalled out in the center of his chest, "breathe?"

Amelie glanced down at the bottom of the stairs, looking for any sign of her grandmother, then inched closer. "No more of what happened the other night."

Troy held her eyes. "Are you saying you regret what happened?"

"No." Sleeping with Troy was exactly what she'd intended to do, and she wasn't going to pretend differently. "But it was a one-time thing."

The curve of his lips lifted even more, working into that seductive as hell smirk that could light her panties on fire. "I counted way more than one time."

Amelie stabbed her pointing finger at his lips. "And no more smiling at me like that." She leaned to peek downstairs, lowering her voice even more. "If my grandmother finds out that we..." She struggled to finish.

And Troy seemed to enjoy the hell out of it.

He inched in a little closer. "What did we do, Amelie?" His deep voice was soft enough only she could hear. "Tell me."

She struggled to breathe and it had nothing to do with the heavy weight of dust and debris still hanging in the air. "You know what we did. You were there."

"Remind me." Troy was two steps below her which put his face almost level with hers, bringing him close enough that the familiar scent of his skin teased around the musty smell filtering down from upstairs. "Just in case I forgot."

In case he forgot?

Amelie leaned in until the tip of her nose almost touched his. "I guess if you already forgot then it won't be too big of a hardship for you to pretend like it never happened." She shouldn't be offended. It was one night. He'd probably had more one-night stands than he could count. She was just another notch on his belt.

But she wanted to at least be a memorable notch. Not one that was easily forgotten.

Especially since she was going to have a hard time forgetting Troy.

And not just because he was right in front of her now.

"If you forgot then that's your problem." Amelie elbowed past him, more upset than she had any right to be.

Troy caught her by the arm, snagging her before she could get away. "Don't get all huffy."

"I'm not huffy." Amelie wiggled her arm from his grip. "I'm just—"

She was tired. Physically and mentally. Overwhelmed by both the mess she left behind in New York and the one she found in Montana.

And she was frustrated.

Who in the hell had a one-night stand with the same man who'd been shoveling her grandmother's sidewalks?

And replacing her roof.

And bringing her fancy coffee.

"Fine. I'm huffy, but trust me, I have plenty of reasons to be." She looked Troy up and down, which was a mistake that only resulted in her brain offering up a mental picture of what he had hiding underneath his clothes. "I'm not sure if you noticed, but I have a lot on my plate right now."

And he only knew half of it.

Her whole plan for this trip to Montana was to regain a little of the girl she used to be. The one who believed she could accomplish anything she set her mind to. The one who believed everything she wanted was within her reach.

It was the whole reason she'd shoved Troy out of her life even though so many things about him made her want to spend just a little more time with him.

But she knew firsthand how quickly a man could derail a woman's plans, even when she was positive she would never let that happen.

"You can't clean that mess up on your own." Troy pointed to the second floor. "You shouldn't have been up there cleaning last night, because I can guarantee you didn't have a filtering mask on while you did it."

"What's a filtering mask?"

Troy's nostrils flared and he let out a deep, disappointed sounding sigh. "You are a lot of things, Amelie, but I am positive you aren't capable of fixing everything that's wrong up there."

"I can do anything I want to do." It was a sentiment she used to live by but lost somewhere along the way. Hopefully saying it out loud would be the first step to believing it again.

"Fine. Let me rephrase." Troy closed his eyes and took a

deep breath before starting again. "We don't have time for you to figure out how to clean up that mess upstairs all by yourself."

"You don't know that. I didn't give you a copy of my schedule." Technically, she had as much time as she wanted.

It wasn't like she had a job waiting for her. Or an apartment to move into.

Or any concrete plans to find either of those things.

"Your schedule isn't the issue." Troy tipped his head forward, leaning close. "Do you have any idea how much it costs to heat a house with no ceilings?"

She didn't, so she stayed quiet.

"Your grandmother doesn't have the finances to keep paying to run that furnace like she is."

Amelie pressed her lips together, willing herself to keep her mouth shut so she didn't spill any more of the secrets her grandmother was keeping.

Because Troy was right.

She couldn't clean this mess up all by herself.

And her grandmother couldn't keep running the furnace. That's why it was turned off. Mostly.

Troy's eyes narrowed, his head barely tipping to one side.

Then he took off up the stairs.

Amelie chased after him, hoping she could stop him before the dots fully connected.

Her bare foot was just about to hit the landing when she was suddenly lifted off the ground, feet dangling, as Troy hauled her up against his side with one arm.

He frowned down at her. "Do you know what it feels like to get fiberglass insulation in the bottoms of your feet?"

"There's no insulation out here. I cleaned it all up." She wiggled around, trying to get free.

Troy looped his other arm around her waist, hauling her a

little higher as he moved back down the stairs, finally setting her down about halfway. "Stubborn woman."

"I'm not stubborn."

"Good." Troy pressed one hand against her back, urging her to continue down the stairs. "Then you'll be happy to go get dressed so we can go shopping and start cleaning this mess up."

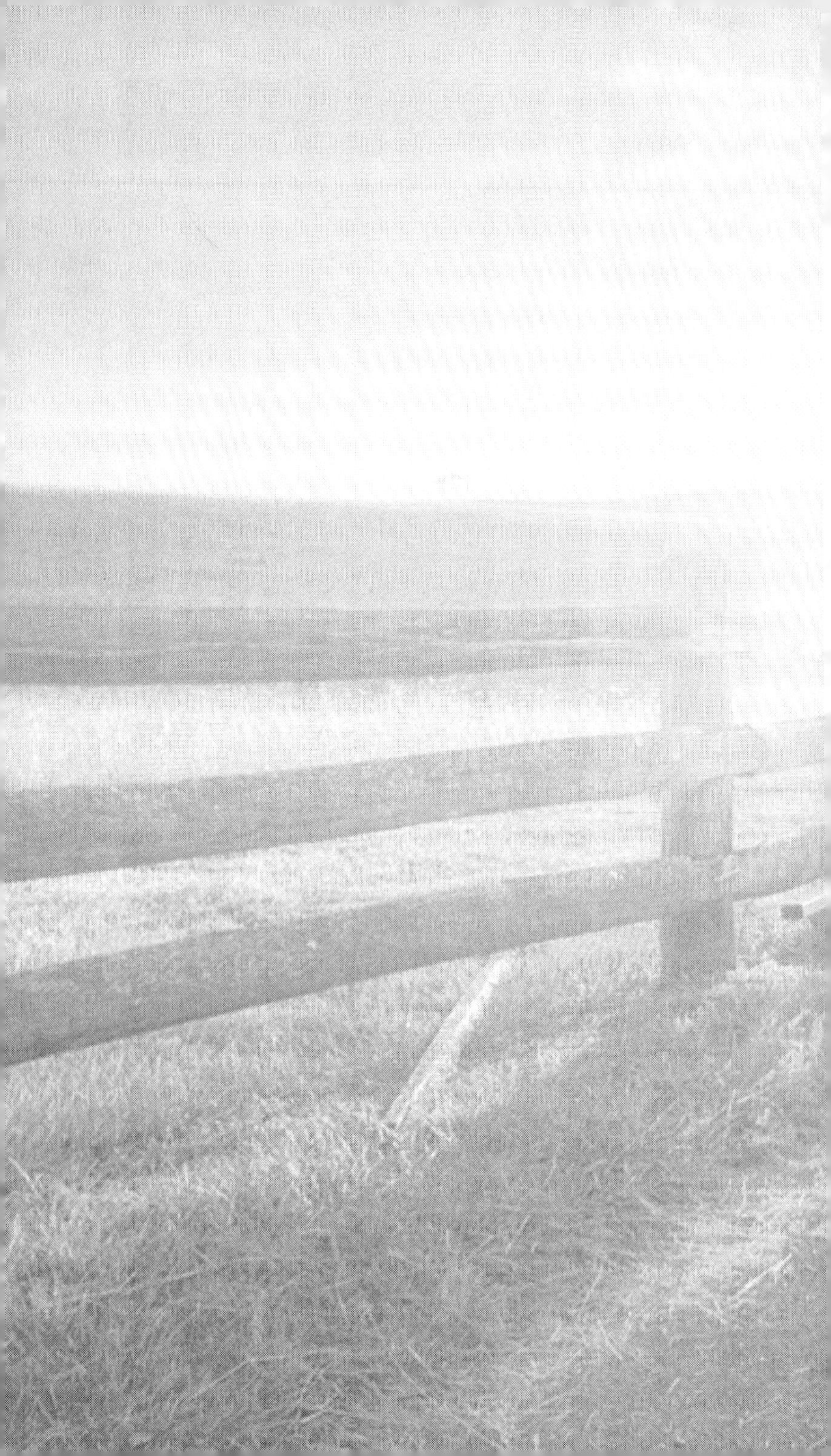

SIX

TROY

"IS THIS REALLY necessary?" Amelie stood at the top of the stairs as he strapped one of the respirator masks they picked up at the hardware store onto her face, being careful to make sure it was well-sealed but not digging into her skin.

"Yes." He finished and took a step back, looking her over. "Feel okay?"

She reached up to adjust the protective glasses balanced on her nose. "I feel like a bug."

He grinned in spite of the irritation he'd been fighting since finally getting the all-access pass to Muriel's house he'd been wanting for months. "You're a cute bug."

Amelie's brown eyes rolled toward the only bit of ceiling still in place on the second floor. "We said no flirting."

"*You* said no flirting."

Troy had listened patiently as she trailed him through the store, filling their cart with the basics of what they needed while Amelie dished out a whole list of rules he had no intention of following. "*My* rule is no bare feet on the second floor." He leaned closer to her. "And we both know how well you followed that rule."

Amelie's eyes widened behind the plastic glasses. "So, what? You aren't going to follow my rules if I don't follow yours?"

"That seems fair." Troy shot her a wink. "I'm glad you suggested it." He turned Amelie before she could argue back, directing her into the first of the two bedrooms they needed to clear out. "I'll be right in."

He quickly strapped on his own mask and eyewear before grabbing the roll of contractor bags and going in behind her.

It was obvious she'd tried to clean up at least a little of the mess, but Amelie just wasn't equipped to put much of a dent in it.

Since Muriel wouldn't let him inside, he hadn't realized how much underlying damage there was when he replaced the roof. The ceilings had still been in place when he pried off the old sheeting, but sometime after that they'd started to drop, collapsing down onto everything in their path and covering the whole place in crumbly drywall dust and moldy blown-in insulation.

Which Amelie had dug through with her bare hands and no face mask.

Troy set the roll of bags on the top of a dresser that was mostly cleared of dust and debris. He pulled one loose and shook it out before passing it to Amelie. "Hold this open."

"Why do I have to be the bag holder?" She immediately argued, but took the plastic, gripping it tight in her gloved hands.

"Because I can lift more weight than you." Troy snagged his snow shovel from the hallway and went to work scooping up the clumps piled up on the matted carpet.

"That's sexist." She leaned back as he dumped in the first shovelful.

"It's the truth." He scraped up another pile and added it to the bag. "We can arm wrestle later to prove it."

Amelie scowled at him. At least he assumed she did based on the slash of her eyebrows and the narrowing of her eyes. "You're an ass."

"Not an ass." He'd been called a lot of things in his life, but an asshole wasn't one of them. "I just seem to enjoy the hell out of pressing your buttons." He tried to end it there, but couldn't stop himself from leaning a little closer and offering a reminder. "All of them."

He should be at least a little put out that Amelie lied about leaving town, and maybe he was. But that little lie also fed into his need to prove he could win anyone over.

Because deep down he loved a chase. Always had. He loved proving he could make just about anyone like him.

And they always did. Even the women who didn't want to continue spending time with him liked him.

Which made the fact that they chose to move on even more frustrating.

Amelie rolled her eyes up toward the rafters and he could swear she said something that involved Jesus under her breath.

But it didn't quite sound like a prayer.

"Troy? Amelie?" Muriel's voice carried up the stairwell. "There's no reason for you two to spend all your time messing around with that."

Troy backed toward the stairs, leaning out the open doorway to shoot Muriel a glare she probably couldn't see through all the gear strapped to his face. "We talked about this."

Muriel was definitely embarrassed by him seeing the inside of her house. She'd avoided him like the plague after he came in, hunkering down on the porch until he and Amelie left for the store. When they got back she was nowhere to be found, but the door of her first-floor bedroom was closed. Eventually she found her way out and attempted to do damage control, which consisted of trying to convince them that the mess wasn't as big of a deal as they were making it out to be.

Which explained how Amelie had no clue Muriel's house was in the condition it was in. She might have been calling every other day to check in, but her grandmother most definitely kept her in the dark about the deterioration of her home.

So while he might be a little chapped over Amelie claiming she was leaving, he couldn't be upset that she didn't know what the inside of Muriel's house looked like.

Muriel crossed her arms at the bottom of the stairs, looking just as unhappy as she had when she came out of her bedroom to deny the disaster he'd discovered on the second floor. "I don't even go up there. There's no reason to make a fuss—"

"There's mold up here, Muriel. That means it's floating around your house and it could make you sick." Not to mention the fact that the place was bleeding any heat she managed to pump into it through the handful of space heaters she was using to keep the main floor warm.

Muriel huffed out a breath that bordered on becoming a raspberry. "A little mold isn't going to hurt me." She propped her hands on her hips. "Now come down here so we can have some lunch."

Amelie stepped out beside him. "We have to clean this up, Grandma." She matched Muriel's stance, fists on hips, as they stared each other down. "And the longer we stand here and argue about it, the longer it's going to take."

Muriel held her ground a few seconds longer, but eventually stomped away, mumbling to herself.

Troy leaned into Amelie's ear. "That's definitely where you got your stubbornness from."

Amelie snatched the garbage bag back up and hauled it into

the center of the room. "I'm not stubborn. I keep trying to tell you that, but you're obviously a shitty listener."

He lifted his brows at her from where he stood in the doorway. "I must not be too shitty of a listener, because I sure managed to hear exactly what you liked—"

Amelie reached up and grabbed the front of his mask, using it to pull him close. "We're not talking about that." She widened her eyes, demanding compliance. "Remember?"

Troy shrugged. "Fine." He was flexible. "Let's talk about something else then." He had so many questions for her, but one was really gnawing at him more than the others. "Where in the hell is the rest of your family?"

Amelie let out a little breath, like she was relieved at the topic change. "Colorado." She adjusted the top of the bag so it hung open and grabbed a section of drywall off the bed and dropped it inside. "My dad and his brother moved there not long after they graduated college."

Troy abandoned the shovel in favor of following Amelie's lead. He went for the bigger sections laying across the bed, stacking them into the bag as they talked. "Why don't they come visit her?"

"That's a long story, but the condensed version is because they're assholes." Amelie picked up a clump of insulation but didn't drop it in the bag. Instead, she just held it, eyes focused on the spot she'd cleared.

An aging stuffed animal, its fur stained by time and exposure to everything that dropped from the ceiling, rested across the pillows stacked against the headboard.

The toy had definitely seen better days, but its shabby look didn't seem to affect the sentimental value it clearly held for Amelie.

Troy carefully picked the small bear up and tried to gently

brush some of the dust and insulation from its fluffy fur. "It looks like this little guy has seen better days."

Amelie reached out to take it from his hands. "I brought him here when I was ten." Her eyes barely crinkled at the edges, making it seem like there was a smile hidden under her mask. "I used to come here every summer and spend a month with my grandparents."

"I bet those were special times for you." He had a few special times of his own, but the memories were fuzzy at best and only got hazier as the years passed.

"It was my favorite thing to do in the whole world." Amelie smoothed down a patch of matted fur. "I would've moved here if I could have, but my parents would never let me."

He didn't like hearing that maybe Amelie's childhood wasn't all sunshine and fairytales. Suffering as a kid was the kind of thing he hoped had only happened to him, but the older he got the more he realized his upbringing wasn't a rarity. It made him feel less alone, but didn't make him feel any better.

Amelie sighed. "But I guess that was par for the course with them." She shoved the toy into the garbage bag, stacking on a few more clumps of drywall before swiping one arm across her forehead. "I need to get something to drink."

She rushed from the room, leaving him standing in the space that was obviously difficult for her to face—not just because of the state it was currently in, but because of the memories that it held for her. Good and bad.

Troy reached for the bag she'd abandoned, digging down until he came to the toy. He pulled it out, shook off the new layer of filth it had collected, and went out to the landing to stuff it into the pocket of his coat.

It would take him hours to get all the insulation out of its pink fur, but that didn't really matter to him. What mattered to him was making sure he never saw that same look on Amelie's face again.

Because it hit a little too close to home.

By the time she came back upstairs, he'd filled the bag they started, along with two more, shoveling them full before tying them off and lining them down the wall.

"Wow." Amelie's dark eyes moved over the space. "You got a lot done while I was gone."

"I'm pretty decent at cleaning up messes." He tied off another bag and added it to the line. "To be fair, I do a decent job of making them too."

He studied her face, watching as she looked over the space, sadness pinching her expression.

He knew what it was like to be caught in the past. Fighting it more days than not.

Which was why he needed to ask her a question she probably wouldn't want to answer.

"Why did you tell me you were leaving?"

Amelie's lips pursed, twisting to one side. "Would it have mattered if I wasn't?"

"Yes." He wasn't sure how much clearer he could have been about his intentions. "Then we could have had that dinner I promised you."

Amelie's head tipped to one side. "I didn't think you were serious about that."

"Why would I have asked if I wasn't serious?"

Amelie stared at him for a minute, eyes wide. "I thought you were just trying to..."

She stopped short of offering him the insight he was looking for, but he wasn't going to let it go. "You thought I was trying to, what?"

Amelie's eyes drifted away from his and she shrugged. "I

don't know. I guess I assumed you were just trying to get into my pants."

The answer surprised him. "Did I seem like the kind of guy who just wanted to get in your pants?"

"Yes." The answer came too quickly for it to be a lie.

"Huh." Troy scratched at his scalp even though not a single bit of insulation had gotten anywhere near his head.

Sure, he liked to flirt as much as the next guy. Maybe a little more. But most of it was harmless. It was just his way of making sure everyone liked him. That they knew he was friendly and easy to talk to and unproblematic.

"Don't feel bad about it." Amelie pulled off her mask, revealing her whole face to him for the first time since they'd been back and started working. "I was just trying to sleep with you too."

The admission threw him for a little bit of a loop. "I didn't think that was the sort of thing women normally did."

It was part of the reason he went back to her room. He was hopeful that Amelie would want to see more of him afterward. That she would realize he was worth keeping around.

But that's not the way it played out, and he was starting to get a better picture of why.

Amelie scoffed, her mouth hanging open. "Sometimes women need itches scratched too, Troy." She stepped in front of him, tipping her head back to keep her frown directed at his face. "And not all of us are looking to be tied down."

Could the answer be that simple? Could he just have been unlucky enough to stumble along every woman in Moss Creek who wasn't looking for a serious relationship?

It seemed unlikely.

"So that's why you told me you were leaving? Because you don't want to be tied down?"

Amelie gave him a little nod. "Something like that."

Her explanation put him in a disappointing position.

He was hoping spending time together would help Amelie reconsider her initial decision to send him on his way.

They had chemistry. He felt it every time she looked at him. Every time she argued with him.

Every time she swore she wasn't the stubborn woman he knew she was.

He thought maybe they could find out if that chemistry would translate into something more. Something real.

But Amelie seemed hell-bent on keeping her distance.

And maybe that was just as well. The situation could get real tricky real fast and he wasn't going to risk what he had with Muriel for anything.

"Fair enough." Troy pushed his own mask up, resting it against the top of his head as he grabbed the first two trash bags, gripping one in each hand as he made his way out the door and down the stairs. He tossed them into his truck bed before coming back in, stomping off the snow from his boots and heading back upstairs.

He went into the bedroom to grab the next two bags as Amelie snagged his coat from the floor of the landing. "You should put this—"

The coat dangled from her hand and that small stuffed animal he saved from the garbage dropped to the floor.

Amelie peeled off her gloves as she slowly crouched to pick it up, staring at the toy as she straightened and turned Troy's way. Her eyes finally lifted to his and he immediately started trying to offer up an explanation.

"It just seemed important to you and I thought maybe I'd try to take it home and see if I could clean it up." He had very few good memories of his own childhood and he hated the thought of throwing one of Amelie's in the garbage.

"I'm not sure I can make it any better, but I figured I would at least try—"

Amelie jumped at him, arms latching around his neck as her soft body slammed into his, chest to chest, thigh the thigh—

Mouth to mouth.

SEVEN

AMELIE

THE BAD DECISIONS were racking up at this point.

Unfortunately, every bad decision she'd made where Troy was concerned seemed way more right than it should.

Including the one that resulted in his lips being on hers.

She wasn't usually an impulsive person, but after spending the entire day facing down the fact that Troy clearly cared about her grandmother and stepped up to take care of her when her own sons wouldn't, Amelie was feeling more than a little reactive.

Which was what led to the situation she was currently in.

And damned if she could make herself be upset about it.

There was already something familiar about the way he kissed.

The way he smelled.

The way he tasted.

And it was a little like a drug. One she couldn't seem to stop herself from taking a hit of.

But making bad decisions where a man was concerned was what got her in the predicament she was currently facing, so as much as she hated it, this had to stop.

Amelie pushed both palms against Troy's chest as she stepped back, pressing her lips together in the hopes that it might help her pretend she couldn't still feel his. "We need to stop."

Troy let her go easily, even though he was breathing a little harder than normal. "Yes, ma'am."

"Goddam—" She jumped at him again.

Him and his fucking, *yes, ma'am* bullshit.

She laced her fingers in his wavy blond hair, holding tight as Troy's arms pinned her body to his, every inch of his long frame hard where it pressed against her.

It was almost like he knew what the sound of those words did to her, which was frustrating since she'd only just realized what those words did to her.

Troy didn't hesitate the minute her mouth was back on his. He picked right back up where they left off, racing alongside her, like they were playing a much sexier version of red light, green light.

And he was frustratingly good at it.

He pressed her up against the cleanest patch of wall in the room, lips moving across her jaw and down her neck as he shucked his gloves. The width of his bare palms immediately slid over her body, one gripping the curve of her ass while the other found the peak of one nipple through the bulky fabric of her sweatshirt. It seemed like he'd been waiting all day for the opportunity to touch her. Another chance to have her under his hands.

No one had ever made her feel like that before. Like she was something they couldn't get enough of. It was intoxicating. Especially since she'd been having a similar struggle.

But she could have made it through, kept her hands to herself, if it wasn't for that damned stuffed animal.

The hand Troy had on her breast dipped lower to toy with

the waistband of her knit joggers. "Can I touch you?"

If she wasn't already wrapped around him, the fact that he was asking permission would have had her climbing him like a tree. "You're already touching me."

"Point taken." His teeth scraped along the lobe of her ear before releasing it. "Then I guess I'm asking if I can make you come."

Her knees went weak, nearly buckling as anticipation and excitement curled through her belly, creating a perfect storm that immediately shot south, threatening to steal any coherent thoughts that might be left in her brain.

She was supposed to be shoving this man away. Keeping a reasonable amount of distance between them so she didn't get distracted in her quest to create a life that was her own. But it's not like Troy was asking her out on a date. He wasn't trying to form some sort of future plan that would result in him getting everything he wanted and her being nothing more than his sidekick.

He was just offering a physical release.

And a physical connection wasn't really a problem. It was the mental and emotional type that caused issues.

"Yes, please."

A low sound rumbled through Troy's chest, making her toes curl inside her sneakers. "So polite."

His hand was already halfway into her pants, fingers immediately seeking out their target and zeroing in with astounding accuracy.

A physical connection would definitely be fine. Not a problem at all.

Amelie gripped tight to the soft fabric of his flannel shirt as Troy stroked against her like he'd done it a hundred times before, each pass of his strong fingers making her breath come faster and faster.

Troy's other hand suddenly released her ass and clamped over her mouth. "I'm real happy to know you're having a good time, but I'm not so sure we want the rest of the house to know."

She hadn't even realized she was making noise. All that was registering was the steady slide of Troy's touch between her legs.

Which never stopped and never slowed, even as his hand pressed to her lips and his eyes locked onto hers, watching as she fought each whimper that tried to escape his hold.

It wasn't long before her thighs started to shake and her vision started to narrow. Amelie squeezed her eyes closed, doing everything she could to keep her outward reaction to a minimum as the climax ripped through her.

"Good girl. Just like that." Troy's murmured praise only made it more difficult to control the sounds still managing to work free.

Because right now she wasn't being good.

She was being very, very bad.

And maybe that's why his words affected her so much.

Being told you're good for being bad was not something she was used to, and it felt nice. Like maybe she wasn't as awful of a person as some people wanted her to think she was.

She was still breathing heavy as Troy slipped his hand from her pants, carefully adjusting the waistband into place before tugging her sweatshirt back down.

If only he could right the clutter stacking up in her brain as easily.

Amelie swiped at the bits of hair pulled loose by the mask Troy insisted she wear, pushing them out of her face as she tried to regain her composure.

If she ever actually had any.

"I didn't mean to do that." She was already kicking herself, not just because of what happened, but also because of how much she wanted it to happen again.

"Are you going to call this a mistake?" Troy's voice was surprisingly flat. Like maybe she'd hurt his feelings.

But Troy was the kind of guy who went home with a girl from a bar, so assuming he had any sort of emotion wrapped up in this would be foolish. It was part of the reason she thought he was the perfect partner for her plan to wipe the slate clean. He wouldn't be invested, and therefore it would be easier for her not to get invested either.

But right now Troy wasn't looking at her like an uninvested man.

"Not a mistake." Amelie tried to smooth the situation over because, like it or not, having Troy around was starting to look like a necessary evil. "I would call it an accident."

She accidentally jumped at him.

Twice.

She accidentally let him give her an orgasm.

Or three.

It was a series of mishaps, really.

"I just felt a little—" she searched for a word that wouldn't make her seem emotional, "reactive. And it caused me to behave in a way that I didn't think through. It was a complete accident."

There was another update for Merriam Webster.

Accident: climbing up a cowboy before fully processing the ramifications.

She was going to have to start writing these down.

Troy's brows lifted. "An accident?"

Amelie nodded, glad that he was starting to understand what she was trying to say. "An accident."

Troy stepped close, crowding her until her back was once again pressed against the wall. "I've got bad news for you then, because I fully intended to do everything that just happened."

She stared up at him, a little panicked, and also a little turned on.

Again.

If that was even possible.

Troy inched in a little more. "And you should know that every time I touch you is on purpose. I meant to do it this time and I plan to do it again."

Amelie struggled to breathe as he leaned into her ear, voice low. "I'll see you bright and shiny tomorrow morning, Miss Amelie." He straightened, blue eyes intense as they held hers. "And I wouldn't plan on having any more workplace accidents." Troy smirked as he emphasized that last word, tapping her chin with one finger before turning and walking out the door, boots loud on the stairs as he left.

She was still pressed against the wall, staring across the room, when her grandmother's voice carried up the stairs. "Amelie? Is everything okay up there?"

"Yup. I'm fine." She was far from fine.

So much of what had happened to her over the past few weeks was far from fine, so maybe this was her new normal.

Being unfine.

Amelie pushed away from the wall, blowing out a breath as she glanced around for the stuffed animal that started it all. Of course, it was nowhere to be found. Not here anyway.

But she knew exactly where it was.

She also knew that it could not lead to another 'workplace accident', no matter how fluffy and clean it was returned to her.

She walked out of the room, making her way back down the steps to where her grandmother was getting situated in her armchair. Muriel looked Amelie up and down. "You must have been working hard. Your cheeks are all flushed."

Amelie wiped at one side of her face, the warmth of her skin proving her grandmother was right. "The mask Troy made me wear is hot."

It was a fib, but she didn't imagine her grandmother would want to hear the truth—that she accepted a sexual favor from the man who'd been shoveling her driveway and running her to doctors' appointments for the past six months.

That was one more reason she had to find a way to set some boundaries with Troy.

Her grandmother adored him. There was no way she would risk ruining the connection they obviously had. Or risking the assistance he seemed eager to provide since she needed all the help she could get right now.

Amelie looked over the living room, making a mental list of everything that had to be done. The carpet needed cleaning. The furniture was worn and in desperate need of replacing. The walls could use painting. Shelves were covered in dust and cobwebs clung to the ceiling. None of that was actually a big deal. Those were things she could easily accomplish on her own.

But there were other, more pressing issues that she simply wasn't skilled enough to tackle. Like the ceilings upstairs. The busted water heater. The furnace that only blew cold air. The electric outlets that no longer worked.

It was like every time she turned around she discovered another major problem her grandmother had simply learned to live with. It was overwhelming and exhausting.

But there would be no rest for the weary tonight. There was too much to get done.

Amelie collected her dirty clothes from the zippered compartment of her still-packed suitcase. "Did you bag up everything you wanted me to take to the laundromat?"

"Honey, you don't have to do that. I can wash whatever

needs to be washed." Her grandmother immediately started to argue, just like always, insisting she was fine and could handle everything herself.

It was the same reason she was clueless about the state of Muriel's home. Her grandmother was always downplaying everything that happened, from the knee replacement she had, to the case of the flu she got last year. You never really knew how bad things were until after it was over.

"I have to go for myself anyway, so I might as well bring everything I can. It won't take me any longer to do yours too since I can run all the loads at once." She'd already collected the pile of sheets her grandmother hadn't been able to wash in the sink, along with half the clothing from Muriel's closet, stuffing everything into the largest basket she could find.

But chances were good she'd missed something that desperately needed a run through the wash.

"There's no reason to go to all that trouble. Just set out what needs to be cleaned and I'll wash it in the sink tomorrow." Muriel said it like it was a simple task. One that didn't involve heating water on the stove or wringing out everything by hand.

"You're not washing all the laundry in the sink." Amelie grabbed the giant basket she'd stuffed to maximum capacity. "Not when there's a laundromat right down the street that can get everything washed and dried in under two hours." She hauled the basket of laundry toward the door, swinging it open without considering what might be on the other side.

Or in this case, *who* was on the other side.

Troy had one hand raised, ready to knock. His fist stayed where it was, hanging in the air as his eyes fell to the giant quantity of dirty laundry she was toting.

His frown was firm and instantaneous. "You've got to be kidding me."

Amelie shot him a glare, hoping it might distract him from

what he'd seen. "Why are you back?"

"I forgot the list I made upstairs." He glanced down at the laundry again before bringing his eyes up to hers. "Do I need to ask what you're doing?"

She shook her head. "Nope."

Troy let out a long sigh as he reached in to steal the basket, grabbing it away and carrying it out.

Amelie chased after him. "I can carry that. I'm not incapable of handling my own laundry."

"I don't doubt that." Troy opened the door of his pickup truck before angling the seat forward and wedging the laundry into the back. "But this isn't only your laundry, is it?" He shoved the seat upright and turned to face her.

Amelie sealed her lips together, intent on keeping at least a few of her grandmother's secrets from Troy.

Troy propped his hands on his hips, scowl deepening. "How long has her washing machine been down?"

Amelie lifted her chin, averting her eyes. "That's something you should probably discuss with my grandmother."

Troy gripped the edge of the open door, his eyes narrowing as he leaned closer. "Your grandmother doesn't tell me shit."

Why was he acting like this was her fault? She was just as much a victim of her grandmother's truth hiding as he was.

Maybe more.

Amelie crossed her arms and straightened her shoulders, facing him down. "Welcome to the club."

Muriel was great at fighting for the benefit of others. Making sure the people she loved were heard and seen. But she didn't enjoy having that focus turned back on her, which was frustrating as hell.

Troy's gaze stayed on Amelie a second longer before lifting to the house. "Is there anything else in there that needs to go with us?"

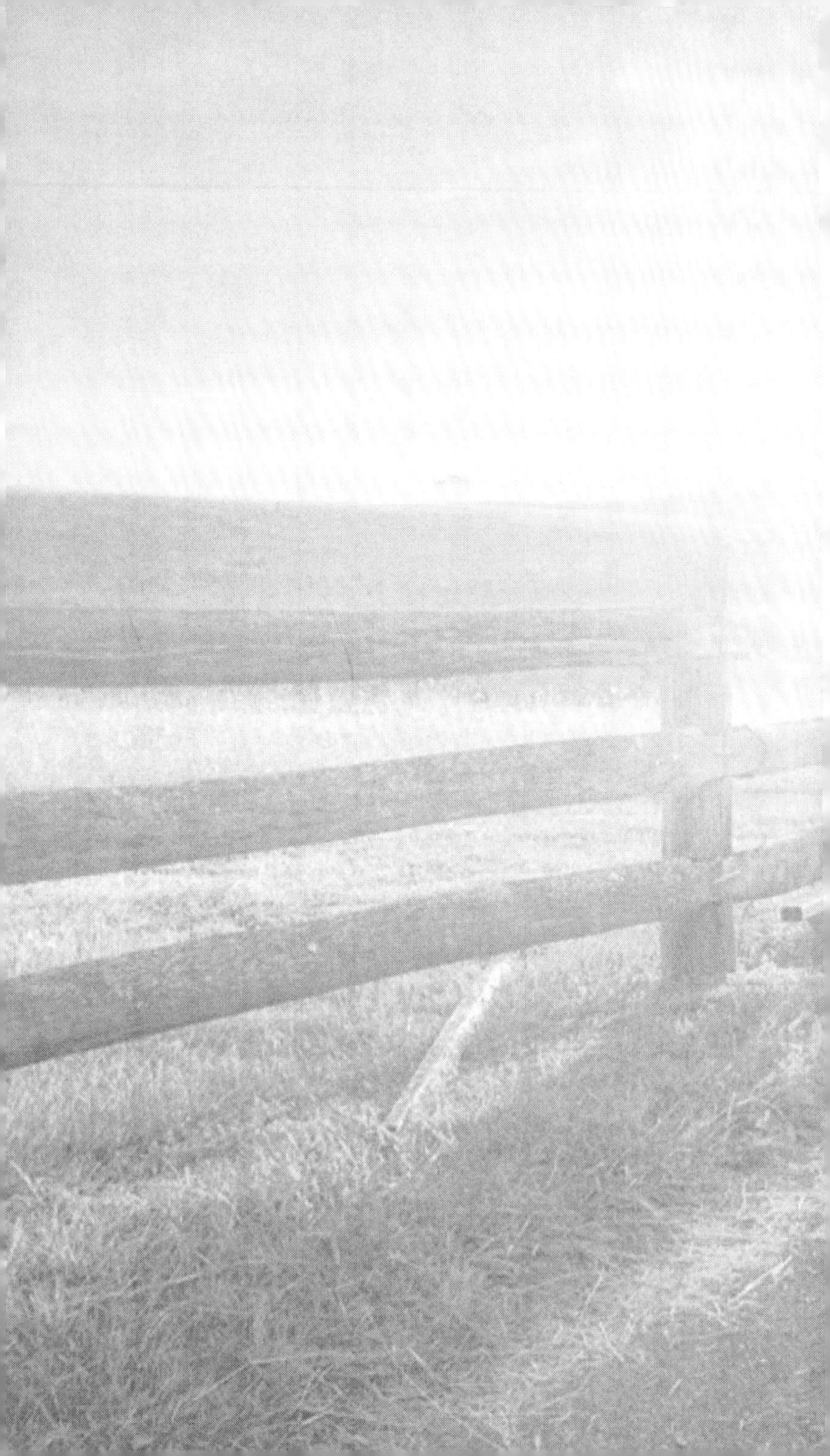

EIGHT

TROY

TROY STARED DOWN at the piles filling almost one entire wall's worth of counters at the laundromat. "That's a lot of dirty laundry, Amelie."

This wasn't just a day or two of accumulation. It wasn't even a week's worth.

This was the laundry of someone who'd been without a washer for quite some time.

Amelie rubbed at one eye as she worked to sort everything into stacks. "Can we not talk about this right now?"

She finished designating the items into groups and grabbed a pile of flower-printed sheets, carrying them to the first washer. She stuffed them in before adding detergent and dropping the lid into place, yawning long and loud as she loaded quarters in and set the cycle.

When she came back to grab the second load he was ready with a new set of questions. "Why are you so tired?"

Amelie gathered up the pile of towels she'd finally admitted also needed to come with them. "You've seen my grandmother's house. Why do you think I'm so tired?"

He had seen Muriel's house. Finally.

And it was just as bad as he imagined it to be.

But at least he expected it. Amelie probably walked in without a clue about the extent of the damage that was inside.

Part of him was a little worried that extent was more encompassing than he currently realized.

"So there's the ceiling upstairs." Troy held up one finger. "And the broken washing machine." He lifted a second finger. "She's heating the main floor with space heaters because it's too expensive to run the furnace." Troy added a third finger. "Is there anything else I need to know about?"

Amelie's eyes didn't come his way as she turned with the towels. "Nope."

He watched as she repeated her earlier process with the new load, piling them in and setting them up to wash.

She'd definitely inherited Muriel's stubbornness.

Chances were good he wouldn't get the whole truth out of either of them, which meant he was just going to have to figure out what all was wrong for himself.

Because there was no way he was letting Muriel continue to live like she had been.

Which brought up another set of questions.

"Are you going to tell her kids about all this?" He'd love to be a part of that.

He'd asked Muriel about her sons a dozen times, doing his best to seem casual and not like he was accusing them of abandonment.

He'd rather do that to their faces.

He understood not being able to afford the cost of visiting her, but the least they could do was have someone check in and make sure everything was the way she claimed. Her sons had to know Muriel would do anything to avoid someone making a fuss over her.

"There's no reason to tell them anything." Amelie shoved a

row of quarters into the machine and started the washer before turning to face him, her shoulders sagging a little. "They pretty much don't have anything to do with her."

He'd known Muriel for long enough to recognize that she could be a little bossy. Occasionally difficult. Sometimes a pain in the ass.

But nothing horrible enough that her own children should have turned their backs on her.

"Why would they do that?" He was struggling to come to terms with the fact that anyone would walk away from a mother who loved them.

Amelie hefted another load from the counter and went to work adding it to a third machine. "Because they suck."

Her movements got a little more aggressive as she stuffed the pile of dark colors into the drum. "My grandparents were simple people. They worked hard, but didn't have a ton of money." She dropped the lid into place and moved on to the next load. "My dad and his brother went away to college and both got really good jobs making a ton of money. They wanted my grandparents to move to Colorado, but they were happy here so they said no. I think that's where it all started."

"They were upset that your grandparents didn't move?" Troy grabbed a set of quarters from the counter and slid them into place while Amelie loaded the washer.

"They were upset that my grandparents didn't listen to them. They thought they were smarter and knew better and it pissed them off that my grandparents didn't just go along with whatever they said." She gave him a little smile as he shoved the quarters into the machine. "Thank you."

"I'm happy to help." He'd been trying to take care of Muriel for the better part of six months now and it felt good to finally be able to see what all he was dealing with. "Thank you for letting me help."

Amelie faced him, leaning one hip against the washing machine as she crossed both arms over her chest. "I didn't realize I had an option."

For a second he thought she was serious, but then the edges of her mouth barely twitched.

"So you were planning on hanging that sheetrock upstairs all by yourself?"

She stood a little taller, chin lifting. "I would have figured it out."

Obviously she'd never held a piece of drywall over her head for any length of time, but somehow he believed she would have made it happen.

Amelie might not see it, but she was absolutely stubborn as hell.

Stubborn enough that she would have come up with a way to take care of the mess upstairs on her own.

And probably suffered for it.

A lot like how Muriel could shovel her own sidewalks.

"But now you don't have to, which will save you a lot of time."

The smile teasing her lips bloomed, full and wide. "I guess I'll just call you Time-Saver Troy."

"That reminds me." He reached into his back pocket and pulled out his phone. "What's your number?"

Amelie glanced from his phone to his face.

So she didn't trust him to have her phone number, but she trusted him enough to sleep with him?

"You need to have someone close that you can call if there's an emergency." He didn't want to lay out the obvious, but clearly he had to. "Your grandma's fallen before and I don't want something like that to happen again and you to be stuck alone."

Amelie's smile flattened into a frown. She let out a long sigh. "Of course she has."

She hesitated a second longer before rattling off her number.

Troy tapped out a text message that was just his name and sent it. "Now you have mine in case you need me for anything."

Need probably wasn't the right word since Amelie would never admit—to him, herself, or anyone else— that she was the kind of woman who needed anyone.

Which was unfortunate.

It wouldn't be the worst thing for someone to finally need him.

She gave him a half-smile as her phone made a chiming sound. "Thanks."

Amelie collected and loaded the last of the laundry, their whole haul taking up six washers when it was all said and done.

Troy pointed to a set of chairs sitting in front of the windows lining the entrance. "We should go sit while we wait."

Amelie was looking more and more exhausted with every second that passed. It was clear she hadn't had enough rest in the past few days, and at least one of those nights was his fault.

He waited for her to sit before taking the seat across from her.

Coming up with something to talk about was tricky. He was in an odd position with her, one he wasn't quite sure how to navigate. Talking about what was between them felt too complicated to address, so he settled on picking back up where they left off.

"Tell me more about Muriel's sons." They seemed like the safest topic to discuss that wasn't boring or pointless.

And he didn't want to waste any of the time he spent with Amelie talking about boring or pointless things.

Because, even though her reaction to him might be confusing, his reaction to her was not.

Amelie sighed, sinking lower in her seat. "I don't even know where to begin with them." She relaxed back, letting her head rest against the window. "I haven't seen either of them in probably six years." She shrugged a little bit. "My grandmother isn't the only person they no longer talk to."

"Is that their choice, or yours?"

Amelie pursed her lips, eyes moving to one side as she considered the question. "Probably both at this point."

She stretched her legs out in front of her. "I don't know that I have any interest in letting them be a part of my life, even if they wanted back in it." She started to slide, the distribution of her weight in the chair inching her toward the floor and forcing her to sit up a little straighter. "I don't know that I want to allow people to be part of my life if they're just going to make it more difficult, you know?"

He did know. Unfortunately.

Only he was on the opposite end of the equation.

"Was it easy to cut them off?"

Amelie huffed out a little laugh as she tried again to get comfortable in her seat. "Definitely. They don't bring anything but drama and chaos."

When she started to slide against the vinyl seat again Troy reached down to pick up her ankles, levering them up and into his lap. "I guess it would be difficult to deal with someone like that."

It was hard not to put his own personal feelings and experiences on Amelie's situation.

Muriel's family abandoning her stuck in his craw right from the get-go, but Amelie choosing not to associate with her father was very different from his situation.

She had a reason to cut him off. A good one.

"What about you?" Amelie finally relaxed, looking significantly more comfortable now that she wasn't worried about falling out of her seat. "Please don't tell me you have a perfect family. I might cry."

"Cry?" He rested one hand across her shin, letting himself believe it was only to help keep her feet in place. "Why would that make you cry?"

"Lots of reasons." Her eyes moved over him.

Troy glanced down at where his fingers brushed across the gap of bare skin peeking out between the top of her sneaker and the hem of her pants. "My family definitely isn't perfect."

It was a topic he didn't like to discuss because it was painful and embarrassing and pointless.

But Amelie seemed to be in a similar situation. One that made him feel like she might understand where he was coming from.

"My mom had me when she was nineteen." He stroked against her skin, focusing on where he touched her as he continued explaining the half of his past he knew. "My grandmother took care of me when I was little because my mom wasn't interested in dealing with a kid." The few memories he had of his grandmother were good, but blurred with time and too painful to revisit. "She died when I was eight and then my mom had to deal with me."

Which was the extent of what she did.

She made sure he was fed and clothed, but that was about it.

Amelie's expression was serious. "What about your dad?"

Troy shrugged, hoping to look unaffected by what he was about to explain. "I don't know. I guess he figured a kid would get in the way of the life he wanted to live so he never had anything to do with me."

Amelie's brows pinched together. "Never?"

Troy shook his head. "He skipped town the second my mom told him she was pregnant and she never heard from him again."

Amelie was quiet for a second, but her eyes didn't leave his face. "Have you ever tried to find him?"

"Why would I? He didn't want to have anything to do with me then. I can't imagine he'll want anything to do with me now."

It was hard not to resent a man that wasn't willing to take accountability for his actions. And even though he'd give anything to have someone who wanted to be a permanent fixture in his life, reaching out in the hopes that his father might have had a change of heart wasn't anything that appealed to him.

Mostly because there was no room in his life for someone who didn't want him. He'd dealt with that long enough.

Amelie pressed her lips together, making him worry she was about to say something he didn't want to hear.

Something like, *maybe you should try, just in case*.

Or, *maybe he's not as bad as you think*.

That was what usually happened when he opened up to someone about the man who fathered him.

"I get it." Amelie blew out a long breath as she reached up to fiddle with the messy wad of hair at the top of her head. "I don't have any interest in trying to force a relationship with my dad either. I don't feel obligated to let him be a part of my life even though a lot of people think I should."

The fact that she understood lightened a little of the weight the conversation created in his chest. "Exactly."

"Do you talk to your mom much?" There was a hint of hope in Amelie's voice. Like she wanted to believe his mother was a bird who could change her feathers.

But she was not.

"No." Troy brought his free hand up to rest against her other shin, liking the way that added point of contact helped him feel a little less alone. "Sometimes she remembers to call me on my birthday, but that's about it."

Even then, it was usually pretty clear that she was calling to remind him of the day he ruined her life by being born. She never outright said it, but that was always the implication floating just beneath the surface of all their conversations.

Amelie was quiet for a very long time and the lull of the washing machines behind them started to steal his focus.

"I'm glad you found my grandma." Her serious expression softened, full mouth curving in a little smile. "She won't ever forget your birthday."

Troy smiled back. "She talked my boss into telling her when it was and made me a cake, with candles and everything."

Muriel served it up on her front porch, wearing a paper hat and singing at the top of her lungs.

It'd been one of the best birthdays he'd had in as long as he could remember.

"That doesn't surprise me." Amelie's eyes moved to the washers as one beeped. "Looks like it's time to start switching things over." She pulled her feet from his lap and stood, yawning again as she went back to their task. Troy helped her switch everything over, getting all the dryers going before they went back to their seats. This time Amelie drifted off almost immediately, her head tipping to one side as she dozed.

He relaxed while the dryers worked, her feet back on his lap, the quiet moment unfamiliar in an unexpected way.

He'd been to a laundromat plenty of times.

But always alone.

It never occurred to him how different something so mundane could be.

When the dryers started going off, Amelie roused from her nap and they went back to the counters to finish the task.

Together.

By the time they'd unloaded and folded all the towels and sheets and clothes, he was dreading having to go back home alone.

Even more than usual.

―――

THE LIGHTS WERE still on inside Muriel's house when he pulled into the driveway, parking beside Amelie's rental.

Amelie was slumped down in the seat next to him, sleeping soundly enough he hated to wake her up.

But it had to be done.

Troy reached across the console, gently sliding his fingers along the inside of her palm, the same way he'd jealously watched Colt touch Winter what felt like forever ago.

Amelie's eyes opened almost immediately, coming straight to him.

"Looks like your grandma waited up."

"She's a night owl." Amelie yawned as she climbed out of the truck, turning to flip her seat forward before trying to wrestle the bag of laundry from the back.

Troy rushed to her side, stepping in to work it loose. "Is that why you're so tired? Because she's keeping you up?"

"I mean..." Amelie peeked his way as they walked up the steps to the porch. "She's not the only one who's ruined a night's sleep for me this week."

Troy grinned as he followed Amelie into the house, carrying the bulk of what they washed. "If you're expecting an apology—"

His words died off at the sight of Muriel.

She was standing in front of the bathroom, a steaming pot of water balanced in her hands.

Troy dropped the bag of laundry. "You're kiddin' me." He turned his eyes to Amelie. "The water heater's out too?"

She pursed her lips, which was enough of an answer.

"So you've got mold, space heaters, a busted washer, and no hot water?" He was going to throttle both of them.

Just as soon as he got them somewhere warm and clean.

"Pack your shit." He met Amelie's eyes. "You're both comin' home with me."

NINE

AMELIE

"NO." AMELIE SHOOK her head. "Absolutely not."

There was no way she was going to Troy's house.

For a myriad of reasons.

Troy lifted his brows at her. "You're really going to argue with me about this?"

She could tell by the look on his face that he was about two seconds away from calling her stubborn again, and that might be enough to push her over the ledge she was already dangling from.

She was tired. She was dirty. She was frustrated.

All she wanted was to suffer through an ice-cold shower before crashing on the couch.

Amelie took a deep breath, digging around for what little patience might still be inside her. "I'm not arguing. I'm simply telling you that we are going to stay here tonight." She turned to look at her grandmother, knowing Muriel would provide the support and backup she needed.

"Well…" Muriel's lips pressed into a considering line. "Maybe it wouldn't be too bad to be somewhere we could take a hot bath without boiling ten pots of water."

Amelie's mouth dropped open as she stared at her grandmother. "Are you kidding me?"

Was this the same woman who refused to tell anyone there were issues with her house because she didn't want to be fussed over?

"Good." Troy walked over to Muriel and snagged away the pot of steaming water she still held. "It's settled then." He took the water into the small galley kitchen and poured it down the sink. "Get your stuff packed and we'll head out."

Muriel immediately hustled into her bedroom, like she couldn't wait to go along with Troy's terrible plan.

Troy came out of the kitchen and crossed his arms, expression stern. "You're spending an awful lot of time standing still for a woman that I know is about ready to fall over from exhaustion."

His eyes slid over the couch she'd slept on the night before, his jaw getting tighter as he took in the pillows and blankets strewn over the lumpy cushions. "You need to sleep in a bed tonight, Amelie. You can't work like you did today and then try to sleep on the couch."

Amelie stood as straight as she could manage. "I'm pretty sure I could sleep anywhere right now."

Troy wasn't wrong when he said she looked ready to fall over.

She was.

Ready enough that it was really hard to come up with the effort it would take to fight this.

And sleeping in a bed did sound good. Almost as good as a hot shower.

Plus, it would only be one night. Tomorrow, she would be better rested and ready to list all the reasons she and her grandmother were just fine staying here.

Amelie huffed out a sigh of resignation and went to the bathroom to collect the few items she'd lined across the counter, bringing them back and adding them to her still mostly intact suitcase before zipping it all up and rolling it toward the door. Troy grabbed it from her and carried it out to his truck, opening the door like he was going to wrestle it into the cramped backseat.

Amelie snatched the keys to her rental from the table beside the door and hit the unlock button. The small SUV beeped and the lights blinked, drawing Troy's attention to it.

She wrapped on her coat before joining him in the driveway, opening the back hatch and standing aside as Troy loaded her suitcase.

Once he slid the bag into place, he closed the hatch and turned to her, smirking. "That's a pretty cute little car."

Amelie shrugged. "It handles decently in the snow and has heated seats."

She didn't drive when she lived in New York and it was nice to get back behind the wheel. It was one of a few things she didn't realize she missed as much as she did.

"Heated seats don't sound too bad." Troy snagged the fob and looked it over. "No automatic starter though." He opened the driver's door and leaned in to start the engine, spending a few seconds adjusting the vents and heater before closing the door. "How about you go back inside while this warms up."

Amelie headed back for the house, assuming he was right behind her, but when she turned to make sure he closed the door, Troy was nowhere to be seen.

Nowhere in the house, anyway.

She went back out on the porch to discover him clearing the snow off her windshield. "What are you doing?"

He paused, looking from the car to her. "I feel like it's pretty obvious."

"I didn't mean literally." She stomped back down the steps. "I mean why are you doing it?"

Troy didn't stop this time and continued using the brush side of his scraper to knock away the snow clinging to the side windows. "I may not have been brought up the best, Amelie, but I do know that it's considered respectful for a man to clean off a woman's car."

Amelie pinched the bridge of her nose, squeezing her burning eyes closed as she fought the knee-jerk desire to simply argue back with him.

Troy told her things at the laundromat that she didn't think he normally shared, including how his mother treated him as a child, and the fact that Troy turned out to be the kind of man he was said a lot about how hard he worked to be better than he was set up to be.

"You don't have to do all of this." She didn't want to seem unappreciative—like she didn't recognize how far he went above and beyond—but Troy needed to know she wouldn't take advantage of that. That she didn't expect it.

"I know that." He swiped off the last of the windows before shaking the snow clinging to the brush free and sliding it behind the driver's seat of his truck. He turned back to face her, blue eyes resting on hers. "I don't do it because I have to. I do it because I want to."

The sound of the front door slamming pulled their eyes to the house.

"I'm ready." Her grandmother shuffled across the porch, hauling her own rolling suitcase. "Let's get this show on the road."

Troy rushed to help Muriel down the steps, keeping her on his arm as he guided her to the passenger's seat of his truck and loaded her in. Amelie took advantage of his distraction and picked up her grandmother's suitcase, adding it into the back of her small SUV. Before she was done, Troy was already back at her side, frowning.

"I was going to do that."

"So what, I should just sit in my heated seat while you do all the work?" She closed the hatch, matching his frown. "I don't think so."

They stared each other down as both vehicles idled in the driveway, seconds ticking past as the cold started to sink through the soft, but thin, pants she wore.

Finally Troy's lips lifted. "Stubborn."

Amelie scoffed before stabbing him in the chest with one finger. "You're the stubborn one." She swung her finger toward his truck. "Now get in your truck so we can go before I get hateful."

Troy's smirk widened, and she knew what he was going to say before he said it.

"Yes, ma'am."

Amelie pressed one hand to the center of his chest, pushing him out of her way. "Smartass."

Troy grinned at her through his window as he backed out of the driveway, waiting in the middle of the road until she was behind him before heading out of the neighborhood and away from Billings.

Just like he told her the night they met, his house was about forty-five minutes away, which meant it took an hour and a half out of his day each time he came to check on her grandmother.

And that wasn't counting however long he spent shoveling her driveway.

Or taking her to a doctor's appointment.

Or bringing her fancy coffee.

The man was really starting to get on her nerves.

By the time they pulled onto a narrow lane leading to a

small white farmhouse, Amelie was scowling deep enough to form a permanent crater between her eyebrows.

Troy pulled his truck into a spot at the back of the little house and got out to motion for her to take the place right next to him. She parked and climbed out into the cold, stomping her way to the back to unload their bags.

Troy took her grandmother straight inside, managing the task much faster than she expected.

"You really don't want me carrying your bags, do you?" He crowded in beside her and hauled her bigger bag out of the back.

"I don't want you doing a lot of things, but that hasn't stopped you."

Troy was suddenly very close. Close enough she should take a step back.

But her damn feet wouldn't cooperate.

"I seem to remember it differently." He leaned into her ear. "I remember you asking me *not* to stop." His fingers brushed a bit of loose hair back. "Begging me to do more."

Heat rushed through her veins.

Like she was kerosene and this man was a living, breathing match, capable of lighting her up with nothing more than a flick of his fingers.

"I don't want to talk about it." Her attempt to shut him down was weak at best, but she was running on fumes.

Which he would probably also set ablaze.

"That's fine. We don't have to talk about it." Troy's voice was low and deep as he inched closer, breath warm against her ear. "But you should know I think about it all the damn time."

When he backed away his expression was smug.

Like he knew exactly what he did to her and enjoyed the hell out of it.

"Jerk." Amelie grabbed Muriel's bag from the back and

NO COMING BACK

dropped its wheels to the ground, yanking up the handle so she could stride past Troy like she was perfectly fine.

And not concerned at all about melting into a puddle at his feet the next time he whipped out a well-timed *yes, ma'am*.

"It's toasty warm in here." Muriel held open the door as Amelie worked her way up the steps leading to the small deck that spanned the backside of the house.

She stopped just inside to stomp the snow off her shoes, letting it fall to the rug before kicking her sneakers off and lining them up next to a selection of boots sitting in a neat row.

As her grandmother promised, the house felt freakishly warm, but that was probably because she was used to a drafty space warmed by a few space heaters.

"You can hang your coat up in that closet if you want." Troy came in behind her, closing the door and flipping the deadbolt before taking off his boots and dropping them into place beside her sneakers. He rolled both suitcases into the small kitchen that sat at the back of the house and looked out over the deck. "Anyone hungry?"

Muriel went straight to the fridge, unabashedly opening the door and perusing the contents. "You're pretty well-stocked for a bachelor, Troy."

"Grabbing fast food isn't an option out here." He snagged a bottle of water from the bottom shelf and held it out to Amelie. "A man learns how to feed himself real quick unless he wants to starve."

Muriel made an approving sound before closing the door and walking along the L-shape of the counters. "Neat and tidy too."

Amelie wasn't interested in seeing any more of the ways Troy was head and shoulders above the rest of the men walking around the planet. It didn't matter.

"Can I take a quick shower?" She was itchy from digging

around the insulation and drywall that destroyed the second floor of her grandmother's house, and the whore's bath she took the night before hadn't done much to make her feel clean.

"Of course." Troy tipped his head at the stairs. "Bathroom's off the bedroom on the left."

Amelie grabbed her suitcase and hauled it up the narrow staircase, being careful not to bang it into the walls. Whether she wanted to think about it or not, it was clear Troy worked hard to take care of his home and she didn't want to rough it up.

The room at the top of the stairs was just as clean and well-kept as the rest of the house. A queen-sized bed sat in the center of the room with a dresser right across from it. A matching chest shared the wall that seemed to lead to the bathroom Troy mentioned. She headed straight for it, flipping on the light to find a tub/shower combo that looked like absolute heaven.

Amelie quickly grabbed her toiletries and a set of pajamas before jumping in to scrub away the ick clinging to her skin and hair. The water was hot and the spray was strong, and when she stepped out onto the thick plush of the bath mat she felt like a new person.

If only it was really that easy.

After slathering on a layer of lotion and pulling on her pajamas, she wrapped her hair in a towel turban and flung open the door.

To find Troy digging through the top drawer of the chest right next to her.

His eyes quickly skimmed down the front of her pale pink cotton top and pants. "Feel better?"

"Much." Amelie eyed him as he pulled out a pair of flannel pajama bottoms.

Then she looked over the rest of the room, taking in the masculine colors of the quilt and the line of items sitting on the dresser. "This is your room."

"I'll be out of your way in just a sec." Troy grabbed a t-shirt, wadding it up in his arm as he closed the drawer. "I just needed something to sleep in."

"I'm not sleeping in your room." She was apparently all about bad ideas lately, but that one would take the trend a little too far. "I'll sleep in the other room."

There was another door across the hall so she headed right for it, twisting the knob and flipping on the light.

But her bare feet stopped two steps into the empty space.

There was no bed. Nowhere to sleep but the floor.

"I've got your grandma all set up in the recliner downstairs since she can't make it up the stairs. She was already snoring when I came up here." Troy tipped his head toward the bed she now knew he slept in every night. "That means the bed is all yours."

Troy brought them to his house knowing he wasn't going to have anywhere to sleep.

Brought them to his house knowing it would make his night hell.

And then he was going to get up and insist on working his ass off tomorrow to help her clean up a mess that wasn't his problem or responsibility.

It was just as frustrating as everything else about him was.

The whole damn man was aggravating to the point that she was starting to lose her mind.

Had to be.

It was the only explanation for why she was suddenly wrapped around him, arms at his neck, front plastered to his, holding on for dear life as his mouth claimed hers in a kiss that only added to the list of issues Troy was causing in her life.

Their intertwined bodies banged into his room, bouncing the door against the wall as they grabbed at each other, yanking at clothing in an effort to wrestle everything from between them. It was a game Troy was better at, because she was shirtless almost immediately, gasping as his hands moved over her skin, fingertips rolling her nipples as she attempted to stay the course, her fingers fumbling with the buttons on his shirt as his tongue slid along hers.

It was a futile effort. But at least she was still in her right mind enough to realize it.

Amelie shoved at his chest, pushing him away as she fought to catch her breath.

Troy stood perfectly still, watching her with an intensity that made her shiver.

He was waiting.

Waiting for her to decide what happened between them.

Knowing he would walk right back down those stairs if that's what she asked made the decision so much easier than it should have been. She raised one hand and pointed to the opening they'd just come through. "Close the door." Her eyes moved down the length of his body. "Then take off your clothes."

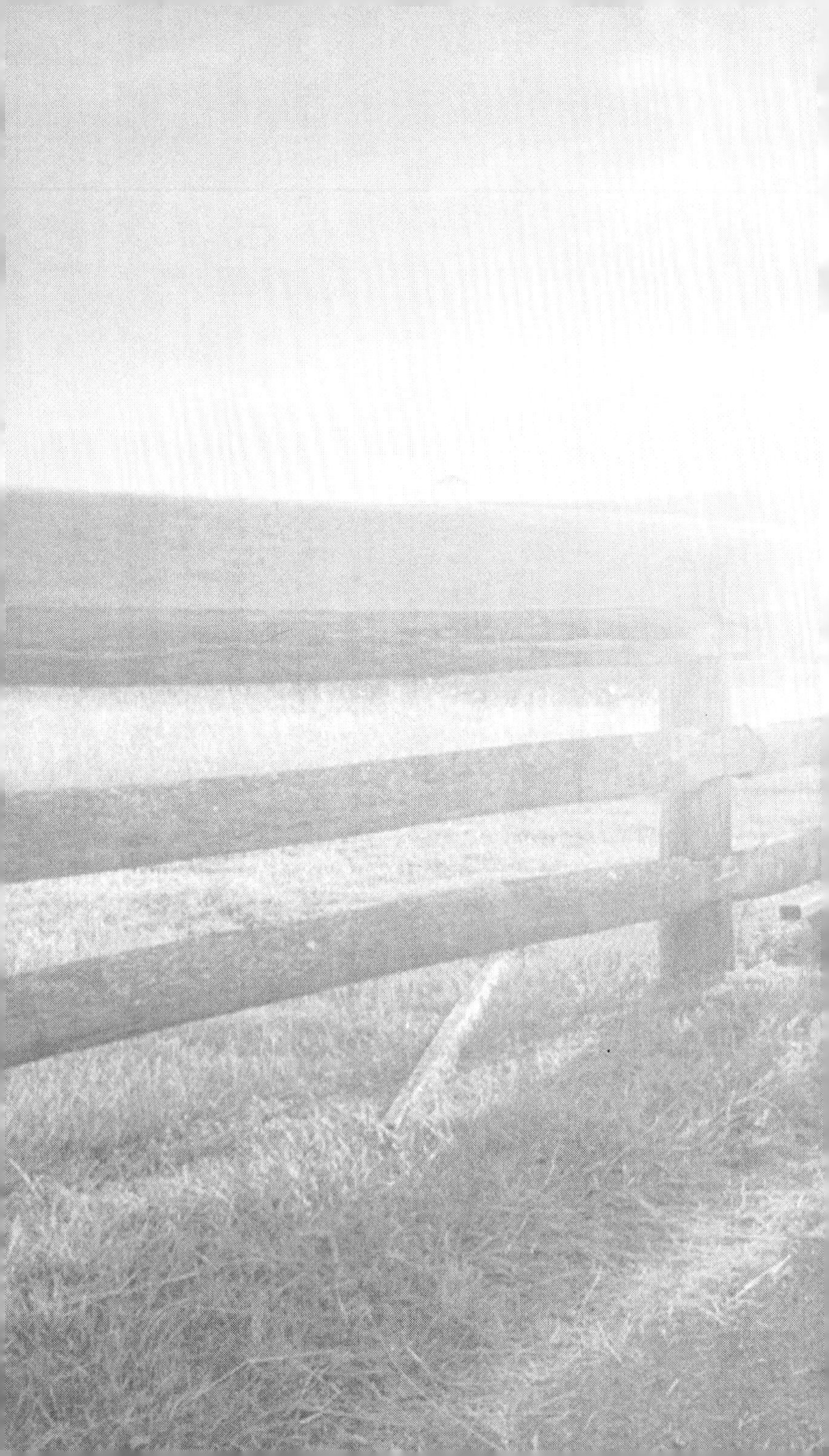

TEN

TROY

AMELIE LOOKED TOO damn good standing in his room, hair wet and wild, body bare from the waist up as she dished out orders he was happy to follow.

Troy silently closed the door, carefully letting the latch fall into place just in case Muriel was a light sleeper.

Then he pulled his shirt over his head, giving Amelie exactly what she asked for this time. He'd already proven what he could accomplish with his clothes on, and it didn't help his cause any.

Maybe giving her what she wanted would.

Amelie's dark eyes followed his every move, skimming along his skin as he stripped away his pants and everything under them. Then he stood tall, letting her look her fill. Letting her savor these last few seconds of control before he took it back.

Her eyes snagged on the solid line of his dick. "That thing is a damn monster."

He couldn't help but chuckle.

His cock wasn't really that abnormally big, but he'd let her think it was. Especially since she seemed so damn impressed by it.

"Good thing it doesn't bite." Troy prowled toward her, tired of being so far from where she stood.

He wanted to see her across his bed. Wanted to watch her hair move over his pillows.

Wanted to fuse the scent of her skin to his sheets.

Amelie watched as he closed in on her. "That's debatable."

He laughed again. "You didn't seem to mind."

She gasped as he grabbed her, but her body immediately softened against his, both hands sliding into his hair. "I was too full to complain."

He pulled her close, nosing along her neck. "Was that the problem? Because you didn't seem to have problems making other noises."

Amelie sucked in a breath when his fingers found one nipple, rolling it as he worked his mouth over her soft skin. "I didn't make noises."

"You did." He loved how willing she was to argue. The way she didn't hesitate to come back at him, even at times like this.

It made sex something besides just a physical release.

It turned it into a conversation of sorts. One that brought him closer to her than a simple intimate interaction could accomplish.

"And as much as I hate to say it, you'll have to keep that to a minimum tonight." Having her in his bed for the first time with Muriel downstairs wasn't ideal, but he would take Amelie any way he could get her.

"I don't make noise." She whimpered a little as he gave her nipple a sharp pinch, proving her own lie.

"What was that you said?" Troy traced his fingers lower, sliding them into the elastic waist of her pajama pants and under the cotton fabric of her panties.

Amelie bit down on her lower lip as he teased along her

seam, seeking out the spot that would test her commitment to staying silent.

It was tempting to see exactly how loud he could make her be, just to prove his point. But it would come back to bite him if Muriel realized what was going on between them.

And something was most definitely going on between them, whether Amelie wanted to admit it or not.

Her fingers dug into his biceps as he found what he was looking for and began to circle, keeping the motion slow enough that Amelie would get frustrated. Because when Amelie was irritated she wasn't as focused on all the reasons she'd come up with that this wasn't a good idea.

Amelie wiggled closer, hooking one foot around the back of his leg in a move that opened more of her up to his touch.

The gesture wasn't innocent. It was done completely on purpose. He knew what she wanted, but it wasn't quite time to give it to her.

Not yet.

Amelie sagged against him, her fingers tightening in his hair as she rolled her hips in time with the slow circle of his finger.

She dragged his mouth back to hers, lips taking what she wanted in a kiss that threatened to make him forget that he needed to be careful.

Needed to take his time.

Needed to keep her from noticing how close they were becoming.

Amelie broke the kiss, her breath coming in choppy bursts as she shoved down the stretchy fabric of her pajama bottoms. Then she grabbed him again and leaned back, the sudden shift of her weight throwing him off balance and tipping him down to the mattress with her.

The feel of her soft body under his stole his focus, redirecting it in the worst possible way.

The movements that were once careful and calculated became rushed and a little desperate as he fought to be closer to her.

To have her the way he did that first night.

To hear his name on her lips as she came undone around him.

It was all he'd thought about since she'd sent him on his way after a night that he'd been hoping might be the beginning of what he'd been chasing for a long damn time.

And now she was here.

In his house.

In his bed.

All he had to do was figure out how to keep her there.

Troy pinned her against him with one arm around her waist as he dragged her up the bed before yanking at the covers, wrestling them under their tangled bodies before pulling them back up, covering them with the heavy warmth of the quilt.

Amelie lifted her brows at him. "Cold?"

"Your hair's wet." Troy eased over her as he slid one hand into the tangle of her damp locks, dragging them away from her skin. "And you've spent the past two nights freezing your ass off in a house with no heat."

It was the last thing he wanted to think about right now, but it was impossible not to tell her what was on his mind.

"I don't want to talk about that." Amelie hooked her legs around his waist, the shift in position dragging his focus to where the wet heat of her pussy pressed against him. "I just want to forget about everything."

Is that all he was to her? A distraction?

He might have believed that yesterday.

Not now.

Amelie might not want to admit it, but there was definitely something between them. Something more than the attraction neither of them seemed interested in fighting.

"You have a lot of faith in me," Troy smiled as he rocked against her, sliding the length of his cock along the slick warmth of her slit, "if you think I can make you forget everything."

Amelie wiggled against him, trying to get a little more friction on her clit. "Shut up. You know you're good in bed."

"Careful. All these nice things you're sayin' might go to my head." He slid against her again, changing the angle to give her the contact she was seeking. "Make it bigger than it already is."

Amelie groaned and the sound was half-pleasure half-exasperation. "If it gets any bigger it won't fit inside me."

"We can't have that." Troy leaned to snag a condom from the bedside table. "It would be a tragedy I'd never recover from."

In a perfect world he would take his time with her again, spend hours sucking and licking every inch of her body the way he did their first night together. But it was late and Amelie had to be exhausted.

And chances were good she'd be in this very same place again tomorrow, curled up in his bed, ready and willing.

Amelie rolled her eyes at him as a smile worked onto her lips. "I'm sure you'd survive."

"How about we don't find out?" Troy worked the rubber into place before going up on one knee and rolling Amelie over to her stomach.

She yelped at the sudden shift in positions, but the wiggle of her ass as she lifted it his way made it obvious she wasn't against the change.

Troy slapped one curved cheek, eliciting a gasp that didn't sound like it was because he surprised her.

Amelie peeked at him over one shoulder, bottom lip caught between her teeth and cheeks flushed. "Careful, cowboy. I might hit back."

He leaned down to nose along her neck. "You can smack my ass whenever you want, Miss Amelie."

She wiggled her ass again in a dare he wasn't willing to back down from. This time she groaned when his hand connected with her soft flesh, the sound shooting straight to his aching dick.

"You might want to be the one who's careful." Troy rested his front to her back, pinning her to the bed with his weight as he worked his cock between the press of her thighs. "You'll end up too sore to sit down tomorrow if you keep it up."

She pushed back against him, curving her spine in a move that lined their bodies up perfectly, allowing him the angle he needed to press into the heat of her body.

He moved slowly, giving her time to acclimate before he set the pace he already knew she liked. This position was perfect for making sure he didn't shove too deep. Amelie seemed to think he was walking around with an abnormal amount of dick, so he was going to have to work her up to realizing she could easily handle everything he had to offer.

Luckily he had all the time in the world. Especially now that he had her where he wanted her.

Troy worked one hand under her belly, sliding his fingers down to slick around the spot where his body penetrated hers so he could feel her stretched around him.

He leaned into her ear, nipping at the shell as his fingers moved over her slick skin to find her clit. "How's that feel?"

"Why do you always want to talk?" Amelie's voice was strained as she grabbed at his sheets, fisting them tight.

"Because I like talkin' to you." Troy circled the hard nub as he rocked in and out of her, hips bouncing against the fullness of her ass with each thrust. "I like knowing you're enjoying what I'm doing to you."

"It's distracting." Amelie whimpered as his fingers started moving a little faster.

"You're going to have to get over it." He ran his lips down to her shoulder, sucking at the skin there. "And learn how to multitask."

He didn't just want to fuck. That was never what he'd really been after.

He wanted a kind of closeness that a merely physical connection couldn't provide.

"You're so damn frustrating." Amelie's face pressed into the pillow as one hand came back to grab at his thigh, fingers digging in as her body started to shake.

Her climax was sudden and unexpected.

And proof that she was very capable of giving him the sexual experience he wanted.

Troy rolled to his side, bringing her with him. The hand between her legs curved tight to her mound as his body spooned around hers. Each thrust of his hips pulled his balls tighter as he fought the need to come. He didn't want to give this moment up just yet.

Because there was no telling what would happen when it was over.

But there was only so much he could do when every sound she made threatened to send him over the edge. And when Amelie arched her back, allowing him to sink deeper than he had before, it was over. There was no more savoring. No more stalling.

It took everything he had to not lose control and drive into her until his skin slapped against hers, claiming her the way he wanted as he emptied into the condom between them. But it had to be done.

Amelie was unsure about him in a lot of ways and he needed to ease her into things.

Physically and emotionally.

It took him more than a few minutes to catch his breath, but once he could see straight, Troy eased free of her and rolled from the bed, righting the covers over her naked body before going into the bathroom to dispose of the condom.

When he came back, Amelie was pulling her pajamas back on and she wouldn't meet his eyes.

She'd claimed not to regret what they did the night they met, but right now she wasn't looking like a woman with no remorse.

Troy snagged her shirt and righted it before stepping close and carefully working it over her head. "Talk to me. Tell me what's wrong."

Amelie stretched her arms into the sleeves, letting her head fall back on a little groan. "I wasn't supposed to have sex with you again."

"I don't remember anyone making that rule." He laced his fingers under the drape of her still-damp hair and pulled it free of her top.

"*I* made that rule." She lifted her brows. "I said we couldn't do it again."

"I thought that was more of a suggestion." Troy smoothed down her hair, working his fingers through the tangles he was responsible for creating. "Not a hard and fast kind of thing."

Amelie's skin flushed a deeper pink at the words hard and fast. "You said that on purpose."

Troy fought a smile. "Maybe." He reached down to pull the covers back. "Get in bed. You need to sleep."

"I need to pee." Amelie pushed at his chest a little, moving him out of her way. "The last thing I want to deal with right now is a sex-induced UTI." She disappeared into the bathroom, closing the door behind her.

Troy let the smile he was trying to hide free as he grabbed his own pajamas along with a blanket and a pillow. He was just heading out the door when Amelie came out of the bathroom.

Her brows pinched together. "Where are you going?"

"Across the hall." Troy tossed the blanket over one shoulder. "Bed's all yours."

He had to tread carefully with this woman. If he pushed too hard, she would buck, and this would all be over.

Amelie chewed her lower lip as her eyes drifted over the bed they just ruined for him in the best of ways. She grabbed the blankets, yanking them back like they'd wronged her. "You're not sleeping on the floor." Her face snapped his way, expression serious as one finger stabbed his direction. "But you better stay on your side."

ELEVEN

AMELIE

SHE DIDN'T HAVE to open her eyes to remember where she was.

Nothing could make her forget whose bed she was waking up in.

Or the fact that she was waking up next to its owner.

Amelie cracked one lid, peeking across the pillows, bracing herself for the sight of a soundly sleeping cowboy.

But Troy wasn't there.

She opened her eyes completely and sat up, staring down at the empty spot she knew he once occupied.

Knew well since she woke up at four in the morning, realizing she was accidentally wrapped around him and snuggled comfortably against his chest, leaving a little spot of drool on the fabric of his T-shirt.

She held her breath, listening for any sound that might come from the bathroom.

But the only noise to be heard was muffled and far away.

Amelie tossed back the covers and swung both feet to the floor, toes sinking into the area rug rolled across the beautiful hardwood.

Troy's house was a little unexpected. She'd seen bachelor pads before and they were usually less than comfortable and lacked the homey feel she craved.

Troy's house was nothing like that. It was small, but cozy and clean.

And warm, thank God.

Amelie crept across the bedroom, keeping her steps light just in case the floors of the old farmhouse creaked. She wasn't necessarily sneaking, this was more about having a minute to get her bearings before facing the full reality of what she'd done.

Again.

Surely the regret would come this time. Sleeping with Troy twice was a terrible idea, one she was sure wouldn't happen. But, just like last time, she was struggling to scrounge up any sort of remorse.

Which was a problem all by itself.

Amelie carefully turned the doorknob and inched it open, moving slower than slow to avoid giving herself away. Troy was somewhere in this house, and if he found her there was no telling what could happen.

Especially if his hair was still messy from sleep.

Or he said *yes, ma'am* again.

Or threatened to spank her.

If she wasn't trying to be quiet she would groan at her own bad behavior.

This was not like her. She wasn't the girl who lusted after men and threw herself at them half-naked.

That was exactly why Evelyn suggested she try it. See if stepping outside her comfort zone would snap her back into shape.

Apparently that was some sort of Pandora's box she should

have kept closed, because keeping her hands off Troy was turning out to be an exercise in futility.

Amelie finally managed to get the bedroom door open enough she could squeeze her way out, sucking in to make sure she didn't bump it as she slipped into the hallway, her bare feet silent as she tiptoed to the top of the stairs.

The tunnel of the stairwell amplified the sounds she'd heard earlier, making them perfectly clear.

"I might have to get one of those recliner chairs." Her grandmother sounded bright and cheery. "That's the best I've slept in as long as I can remember."

"That probably had more to do with the fact that you were in a warm house than it did the recliner." Troy's tone was light but carried an edge of disappointment, like a parent gently scolding their child.

Not that she was particularly familiar with any form of gentle parenting.

"I didn't want anyone making a fuss." Muriel laid out the same excuse she'd offered when Amelie confronted her about the state of her home. "I was just fine."

"Don't bring your looks into this, Miss Muriel. We're talking about your house."

Amelie didn't have to see Troy's face to know he was smiling, and it accidentally made her smile too.

Yelling at her grandmother would do absolutely no good and probably make her even more difficult. Muriel didn't like conflict. And she sure as hell didn't like being talked down to. But Troy seemed to know this, proving he was more than just the boy who shoveled her grandma's sidewalks and did a few house repairs.

"Don't you go trying to flirt with me again. I've told you I'm not interested."

"I'll wear you down eventually." Troy's voice was a tiny bit closer. "I've already got you in my house, don't I?"

Suddenly he was right there, standing at the bottom of the stairs, looking up at her with a sexy smirk and the sleep tousled hair she knew would weaken any sort of resistance she might have. "Morning."

Amelie straightened her shoulders and started down the stairs, hoping it appeared she'd just come out of the room. "Good morning."

Somehow she had to figure out how to appear like Troy hadn't fucked her within an inch of her life last night. The only way she could think of accomplishing that was to appear indifferent to his presence. Even though his presence included a T-shirt that stretched tight across his chest and biceps, and a pair of pajama pants that practically showed the complete outline of his gigantic penis.

A.k.a., Slugger.

Troy didn't budge from his spot as she reached the last step. "Hungry?"

Amelie eyed the spaces on each side of him, trying to determine which one offered more room for escape. "Sure."

Troy stretched one arm out, bracing his hand against the wall and blocking the bigger of the two paths. "I made you a plate. I'll put it in the microwave and heat it up."

Amelie frowned, forgetting that she was supposed to be trying to get around him. "What time is it?"

"After ten."

Troy's eyes skimmed down her body. "You had a long day yesterday so we decided not to wake you up."

It was after ten?

They had so much to do. If she wanted to get back into her grandmother's house, which she did, there wasn't time for her to lay in bed half the day. "You should have woken me up."

Troy's lips barely quirked and his gaze heated enough to make his thoughts clear. "I'll keep that in mind next time."

Warmth crept up her neck and inched its way across her face. "Can you move?"

Troy's gaze dipped to where her skin was flaming hot. "I can move however you want me to."

He was tormenting her. Reminding her how shamelessly she'd dragged him into bed last night. And there wasn't a thing she could do about it.

Not unless she wanted her grandmother to start doing the math and figuring shit out.

Amelie reached out to plant one hand in the center of his chest, giving it a push. "How about you just move out of my way."

The second he moved, she rushed past, doing her best to get as far from Troy, and the temptation he was, as possible.

"Well don't you look well-rested?" Her grandmother snagged a cup and filled it with coffee before carrying it her way. She passed it off with one hand and patted Amelie's cheek with the other. "Your skin even has a better color this morning."

Amelie managed a smile as she took the coffee and sucked a sip down. "Thanks."

Troy came into the kitchen, silently picking up a plate covered with a paper towel from the counter and sliding it into the microwave.

"We should get ready to go." Amelie did her best to ignore him, keeping all her attention on Muriel.

"Oh no, honey. That's all you two." Muriel went to snag her own coffee from the counter. "Troy and I talked about it and I think it's best if I just stay here out of your way."

Amelie's eyes slid to where Troy was leaned against the counter, arms across his chest, looking remarkably innocent. "You and Troy decided this?"

"Well it just makes sense." Her grandmother opened the fridge and pulled out a container of sweetened creamer, bringing it over to pour some into Amelie's coffee. "I can't really do anything to help, so if I'm there I will just be in the way."

Amelie watched as her grandmother took the creamer back to the fridge.

Muriel would never have agreed to unleash them on her house unsupervised. Something was up. And that something was either that Troy convinced her grandmother she'd be safer and happier here—

Or her grandmother was more astute than she realized.

Whatever the reason for her grandmother's sudden change of heart, the solution was still the same. Get her house habitable again and figure out where to go from there.

"I guess I'll get ready then."

Troy pulled the plate from the microwave. "You should eat first."

Sitting down at Troy's table, eating a breakfast he made—while staring at him looking sleepy and sexy—was not going to help her cause.

Her cause being to figure out how to untangle her life from his as much as possible.

It was clear she would never be able to completely get rid of Troy like she initially hoped. He and her grandmother were much closer than she realized, and it would be nice to know there was someone close by watching out for Muriel that she could count on.

Especially once she went back to her own life. Whatever that ended up looking like.

Amelie grabbed the plate from his hands. "I'll eat while I get ready." Then she turned and hurried back upstairs, leaving all the conflicting feelings this morning was bringing behind her.

She set the plate on the dresser and drank down half the

cup of coffee before grabbing her cell phone. She needed someone to talk some sense into her. Someone to help get her brain back on track.

Evelyn answered on the first ring. "Hey there, stranger."

Amelie dropped down to sit on the edge of the bed, relieved at the sound of her best friend's cheerful voice. Evelyn would know what to do. She was great at leaving men behind and moving on. Hopefully she could help Amelie figure out how to do the same.

"I've got a problem." She could waste time beating around the bush, but it was pointless. Evelyn would be way more interested in the mess than any sort of small-talk she managed to come up with. "I accidentally screwed a cowboy."

Evelyn sucked in a surprised breath. "Am, that's great news." She yelled at someone in the background, muffling the phone and making it impossible for Amelie to make out the words. "Okay, I'm back. I had to kick out the guy I slept with last night."

"And he's just leaving?"

Evelyn snorted. "Of course."

Calling her best friend was the right thing to do. "I'm going to need you to tell me how to do that, because I have to figure out how to get rid of this one." She leaned forward, resting her head in her hands. "Or at least I need to figure out how to stop sleeping with him."

She couldn't actually get rid of Troy, which was complicating the whole situation.

"You slept with him more than once?"

"Only twice." Plus a little bit of a make-out session that resulted in his hands down her pants, but she decided to leave that out. "But it can't happen again."

"Is he bad in bed?"

"No. He's not bad." Unfortunately. This would all be much

easier if Troy was terrible in the sack, like most of the other men she'd slept with. They were all pretty simple to leave behind.

And she certainly never ripped her clothes off and threw herself at them.

"Then why don't you want to do it again?"

Not wanting to wasn't the issue.

"It's just not a good idea." Amelie cringed as the sound of Troy and her grandmother joking around carried up the stairs, the muffled sounds a little louder than they were before. "It's complicated."

"I don't know, Am. I think banging a cowboy repeatedly sounds like the best idea you've ever had." Evelyn paused for just a second. "Hell, I might have to make a trip to Montana myself. Wrangle a cowboy of my own."

Amelie flopped backward to the mattress, pressing one hand to her head as she stared up at the ceiling. "You're not helping."

"Actually, I think I'm helping you a lot. You were just trying to talk yourself out of fucking a cowboy who's good at sex, which is a ridiculous thing to try to do."

It was clear Evelyn wasn't understanding the severity of the situation she'd gotten herself into, and chances were good her best friend might not ever grasp the full extent of her conundrum. Continuing to talk about Troy with her would only lead to Evelyn telling her even more of what she didn't want to hear, so it was probably time to change the subject.

"Have you heard anything about Trevor?" Talking about her ex would certainly distract her from the issues she had here in Montana. And some sick part of her wanted to hear that he was suffering horribly in her absence.

She practically ran that whole damn art gallery he owned. There was no way he could possibly be—

Evelyn groaned. "You don't even want to know."

"I probably shouldn't want to know, but I still do."

She wasn't actually that upset over not being with Trevor anymore. The fact that he cheated on her with the new-hire she'd been training to work at the art gallery stung a little, but she was under no illusions that they had a great relationship.

That hadn't been the case for a long time. If ever.

"Is he still with Olivia?" She should have seen it coming when he walked the budding artist in and announced that Amelie would be training her to work in the gallery. Olivia was essentially a younger, more starry-eyed version of what Amelie was when she first moved to New York. The kind of girl who would fall for every line he laid in front of her.

Just like she had.

"Yes." Evelyn's answer was short and clipped. Abrupt enough to make it clear there was more to that story.

"And?" Amelie huffed out a little laugh. "Are they getting married or something?" She sat up. "Wait. Is she pregnant?" Both possibilities were a little amusing. Trevor had made it almost to fifty without being tied down. It would be kind of hilarious if he jumped in with both feet with a twenty-year-old who couldn't even buy alcohol.

"He's hosting a show for her."

The smile slipped from Amelie's lips. "What?"

"See? I knew that was going to upset you. That's why I didn't want to talk about him."

"He's hosting a show for her?" She'd seen Olivia's artwork and it left a hell of a lot to be desired. "Why the hell would he—"

Amelie's stomach dropped, twisting around itself and the coffee she'd just consumed. "Oh."

She'd been in New York for over six years, spending the majority of that time working for, living with, and dating the owner of one of the best-known galleries in the city. During that time, her work had been displayed all over the city and she'd held four separate shows, all of them organized and hosted by Trevor.

He'd said it was because she was one of the most talented artists he'd ever seen.

That she evoked a level of emotion with her work few others could.

That's why Trevor claimed he first wanted to get to know her. Why he pushed her paintings and held exhibitions.

"This has nothing to do with you, Am. He's just an asshole trying to get his dick wet."

Evelyn was trying to help, but she was only making things worse.

Because what was true now might have also been true then.

Maybe Trevor never thought she was talented. Maybe he never believed she would be the next great artist. Maybe she didn't really earn any of the accolades he offered her.

Maybe it was always about getting his dick wet.

"I'm gonna go. I've got to go do some work at my grandma's house." Amelie rubbed her head, squeezing her temples as an ache started to set into her brain. "I'll call you later."

She tossed the phone to the bed and stood up, every bit of uncertainty she'd been fighting coming back to overtake her in an instant.

She thought coming to Montana was the right decision. A way to reclaim her former self. The woman who believed she could do anything.

But maybe she couldn't do anything. Maybe she should never have gone to New York in the first place.

Maybe her dream of being an artist was as stupid and naïve as her parents told her it was.

Maybe she should have listened to them and not her grandmother.

TWELVE

TROY

TROY GLANCED ACROSS the cab of his truck as Amelie sipped on the fancy coffee he practically forced her to let him stop for. "Good?"

She nodded but didn't look his way.

Something was off. He expected her to wake up just as sassy and stubborn as normal, and she did.

But something changed.

She'd gone upstairs to get ready as a woman he knew and came down as someone he was less familiar with, turning somber and silent.

He'd hoped she'd warm up a little bit on the drive back to Billings, but it didn't happen. Then he thought maybe a sweet, creamy coffee would adjust her attitude, but so far that didn't appear to be helping either.

"We will get the house fixed up. I promise."

Maybe she was worried. Concerned that Muriel would struggle being away from the home she was so attached to, though he was sure those concerns wouldn't be warranted. Muriel was as happy as a clam when she woke up this morning, bright-eyed and bushy-tailed and ready to talk his ear off.

Which was why he'd made a phone call before they left, setting up an outing for her so she wouldn't be stuck alone in his house all day.

"That's good. I'm sure it will make her happy." Amelie's words sounded optimistic, but the tone of them was flat and the most unemotional he'd ever seen her.

"Is everything okay?" He was out of guesses as to what might be upsetting her, so the only option he had left was to straight-up ask and hope she'd give him an honest answer.

"I'm fine."

So much for getting an honest answer.

The fact that Amelie didn't trust him enough to open up was disappointing, but he always did like a challenge.

"Good, because we've got a long day of work ahead of us."

Troy pulled into the driveway and parked his truck, positioning it so Amelie could step right out at the shoveled sidewalk. She slid from the cab, clutching the warm cup of coffee tight as they headed up onto the porch where she unlocked the front door and led him inside.

The house felt decently warm. Enough that he wasn't concerned about the pipes freezing, but it certainly wouldn't be comfortable to spend a winter here.

"I still can't believe she didn't tell me about what happened upstairs."

Muriel not trusting him with her problems bothered him way more than Amelie not trusting him did.

Hadn't he shown Muriel that he would take care of her? Didn't she know that he wouldn't judge or look down on her for struggling to maintain a house she couldn't physically take care of anymore?

He'd been chasing down the reasons he was single, but maybe the answers were in front of his face this whole time.

Maybe he just wasn't enough. Enough to be trusted. Enough to be appreciated. Enough to be wanted for more than a couple of nights.

Enough for either of his parents to stick around.

Amelie turned to face him, her dark eyes moving over his face. "You got quiet."

Troy shrugged, suddenly uncertain that he would ever get past whatever was holding him back. "I'm fine."

Amelie's head tipped to one side. "Whenever someone says I'm fine, it's always a lie."

Troy lifted his brows at her. "You just said it."

Amelie's full lips barely twitched. "Touché."

"How about you tell me what's wrong, and then I'll tell you what's wrong." It wasn't a deal he should make, especially when his issues would probably push her even farther away. But he still didn't like the sadness lingering in her gaze. It bothered him in a way he couldn't explain.

Amelie groaned, eyes rolling to the ceiling. "Men just suck."

That was not where he expected her to go. "Okay."

"Not you." She waved one hand around. "Just some dick I used to date in New York."

"What did he do?" That might be valuable information. Might offer a peek into why women chose the men they did.

Amelie stared down at her coffee, lips flattening into a thin line. "I'm not sure I really want to think about it right now, if that's okay."

"Of course that's okay." She'd given him something. Offered up the reason she was upset even if she didn't clarify it completely. "I'm sorry for whatever it is."

Amelie lifted one shoulder. "It's fine."

"Is that a lie?"

The flat line of her mouth barely softened as her eyes lifted to his. "Of course it is." She let out a sigh, setting her paper cup down on the table and shucking her coat. "Now tell me what's bothering you."

"I guess I'm just a little jealous that you and your grandma have each other." He kept it short and sweet. Explaining his struggles to Amelie wasn't an option. He didn't want her to feel sorry for him. Didn't want her to think he was the kind of person who only lived in the past.

Amelie tossed her coat over the back of the sofa. "If it makes you feel any better, it seems like you're stuck with her now too." She gathered her long blonde hair, pulling it up at the top of her head and wrapping it into a bun before securing it with a stretchy bunch of fabric looped around one wrist. "She sure seems to adore the hell out of you."

He hadn't really considered himself a permanent fixture in Muriel's life. More of a stand-in for the family who didn't show up. But now that Amelie was here, his relationship with Muriel wasn't quite on the same footing anymore.

She didn't need him. Not as long as Amelie planned to stay.

And the possibility of that loss pushed him to keep talking.

"She reminds me a lot of my grandma." He'd been so young when the grandmother who cared for him died, that most of his childhood memories revolved around the neglect and unhappiness that came after it.

He held the few bits and pieces of the time he spent with her close because they were the only happy moments he really spent as a child.

"She was snarky, like Muriel." Troy let himself go back, something he didn't allow often. "She was funny too. She'd play little tricks on me, like trading out my underwear for a bigger size and trying to convince me I shrank."

Amelie was quiet, but her eyes stayed on his, making it clear she was listening.

Which made him want to tell her more.

"One time, she snuck out while I was playing in the backyard and threw a water balloon at my feet." He'd been shocked as hell to look up and see his grandmother standing there with a bucketful of filled balloons, ready to go to war. "We spent the whole afternoon filling them up and throwing them at each other."

She'd enjoyed him. Cared for him. Appreciated him. Maybe that was why it had been such a shock when she died and he was thrust into a life with a woman who found absolutely no joy in his existence.

"It sounds like she loved the hell out of you."

Troy managed a nod. "She did."

"I'm sorry you didn't get more time with her." Amelie took a step his way.

He wanted to keep looking at her, but the need to hide how much pain still lingered after all these years forced his eyes to the floor. "So am I."

Some nights, when he was feeling really sorry for himself, he'd take just a minute to imagine how different his life might have been if she hadn't died. If she'd been the one to finish raising him.

If she was still around now.

Maybe he wouldn't try so hard to force everyone to see he had value.

Maybe he'd recognize the fact himself.

He stiffened in surprise when Amelie's arms looped around his neck, her soft body pressing against his in an embrace he wasn't expecting but needed more than he was willing to admit.

Troy wrapped his arms around her, spreading his palms wide over her back as he held her close. He closed his eyes as the moment stretched out, each passing second soothing the parts of him that still ached for acceptance.

Still longed to be wanted.

Amelie tucked her face into the crook of his neck, her breath warm against his skin as she continued to hold on. Her head slowly tipped back, expression soft as her eyes moved over his face. Then her lips were on his, sweet and pliant as her fingers moved into his hair. The sweet taste of her coffee still lingered on her tongue as it stroked against his in a kiss that was different from any they'd shared before.

It wasn't about desire or physical need.

It was about something else. Something he'd had far too little of in his life.

Understanding.

It was hard not to let himself believe this moment could be what he was waiting for, but thinking that he and Amelie had turned a corner would be premature. So he had to take this for what it was and nothing more. Stop himself from building expectations and instead just let it be.

Amelie's lips eased from his, but she didn't move away. Her head remained tipped back, eyes fixed on his face.

He waited for her to say something. Maybe give him a hint at what she was thinking, because at this point he didn't have a clue.

Her lips parted on a soft inhale. "I—"

His phone started to ring in his pocket, cutting her off. Troy snatched it free, silencing it without looking at the screen. "You, what?"

He needed to know what she was thinking. What suddenly changed, because something did.

Amelie's eyes dropped down to his phone. "Don't you need to get that?"

"I'm sure it's nothing."

He tried to shove it back into his pocket, but she grabbed his wrist and pulled it loose. "You didn't even look to see who it was. It could be my grandma."

"I think she would call you first."

Amelie snorted. "I'm not so sure about that." She poked him in the chest, the stab light and playful. "You're her new favorite."

Troy glanced down at the screen of his still vibrating phone, just in case it was Muriel.

Colt's name displayed on the screen so he lifted it up between them. "Not her."

"You should still probably answer it." Amelie stepped away, taking the grounding sense of closeness he'd waited for his whole life as she moved toward the stairs. "I'll go get suited up."

Troy blew out a breath of frustration and connected the call. "Hello?"

"I just kidnapped a beautiful woman from your house." Colt's grin carried through the line. "But to be fair, she practically ran to my truck."

Knowing Muriel would enjoy her day eased a little of the frustration Colt's ill-timed call brought. "She seemed real interested when I pitched the idea."

"She's already BFFs with Gertrude. They're talkin' like they've known each other forever. Already making plans for when the snow melts."

Troy chuckled. "Keep an eye on her. She doesn't know her limits."

Colt laughed. "Sounds like someone else I know. They're two peas in a damn pod."

He appreciated his friend keeping him posted, but he had terrible fucking timing. "I'm glad she's having a good time."

"She's not the only one. Gertrude hasn't stopped laughing since she walked in. Colt leaned away from the phone, directing his next words at Muriel. "Troy says he's jealous he's missing out on all the fun."

Muriel cackled in the background. "Tell him he's still my favorite."

Troy couldn't help but smile. "Tell her to behave while she's there or she'll be grounded."

"I'm guessing this one doesn't know how to behave." Colt laughed. "What time do you want me to bring her back?"

"We can come get her on our way home. I'll call you when we're headed that way." Troy finished up the call, disconnecting it as he headed up the stairs to where Amelie was already working in the second of the two bedrooms.

"Sounds like your grandmother's making new friends." He pulled on his mask and safety glasses then joined her in the room. "My buddy Colt has a neighbor that's about her age so I asked if she'd want to go for a visit today."

Amelie stopped what she was doing to stare at him. "You set up a playdate for my grandma?"

Troy moved to her side and took the garbage bag she was holding. "Something like that."

Amelie studied him a second longer before going back to cramming a pile of ruined sheetrock into the garbage bag. "That's really thoughtful of you. I don't know how long it's been since she's been able to socialize with someone her own age." Amelie continued grabbing items from the bed and stuffing them into the bag. "She never drove much and once my grandpa stopped driving she was pretty much stuck relying on taxis or neighbors." Her focus slowly came his way. "Or stray cowboys who found their way to her front door."

His next smile came a little easier. "Is that what I am? A stray?"

Amelie tossed a stained throw pillow at him. "You are kinda mangy."

Troy caught the pillow and swung it around, swatting her in the ass with it. "Careful, Miss Amelie. You might get another spankin' tonight."

Amelie sobered and he thought for sure he'd fucked up.

Gotten too comfortable.

But then her dark eyes moved down his frame. "Does that mean you plan on sharing your bed with me again tonight?"

He'd share his bed with her any night she'd let him.

But that wasn't what she was asking.

He moved closer to her, so she could see how serious he was. "You decide who's in your bed and who's not."

Amelie held his gaze, the mask covering her mouth making it hard to get a good read on her expression. She was quiet for a second, and when she spoke again her voice was so soft he could barely hear it. "I don't have a bed anymore."

It was a tiny glimpse into the secrets she still held close.

But it spoke volumes.

And pushed him to say something he shouldn't. To show more of his hand than he intended.

"My bed's your bed."

It didn't make sense and it went against everything he knew to be true. But the minute he saw Amelie stretched across his sheets, he knew that was where she was meant to be. And every second they'd spent together since only proved it more.

All he had to do was make her see it too.

Amelie's eyes lowered as she stepped in closer, reaching out to trace one gloved finger down the front of his shirt. "You're just saying that because you figured out I like being spanked."

That was the least of the reasons he wanted her in his bed. But if that was the one she was most comfortable with, then so be it. He'd play along.

For now.

Troy leaned closer, pressing up on the filter of her mask until her eyes met his. "I plan to figure out *everything* you like, Miss Amelie."

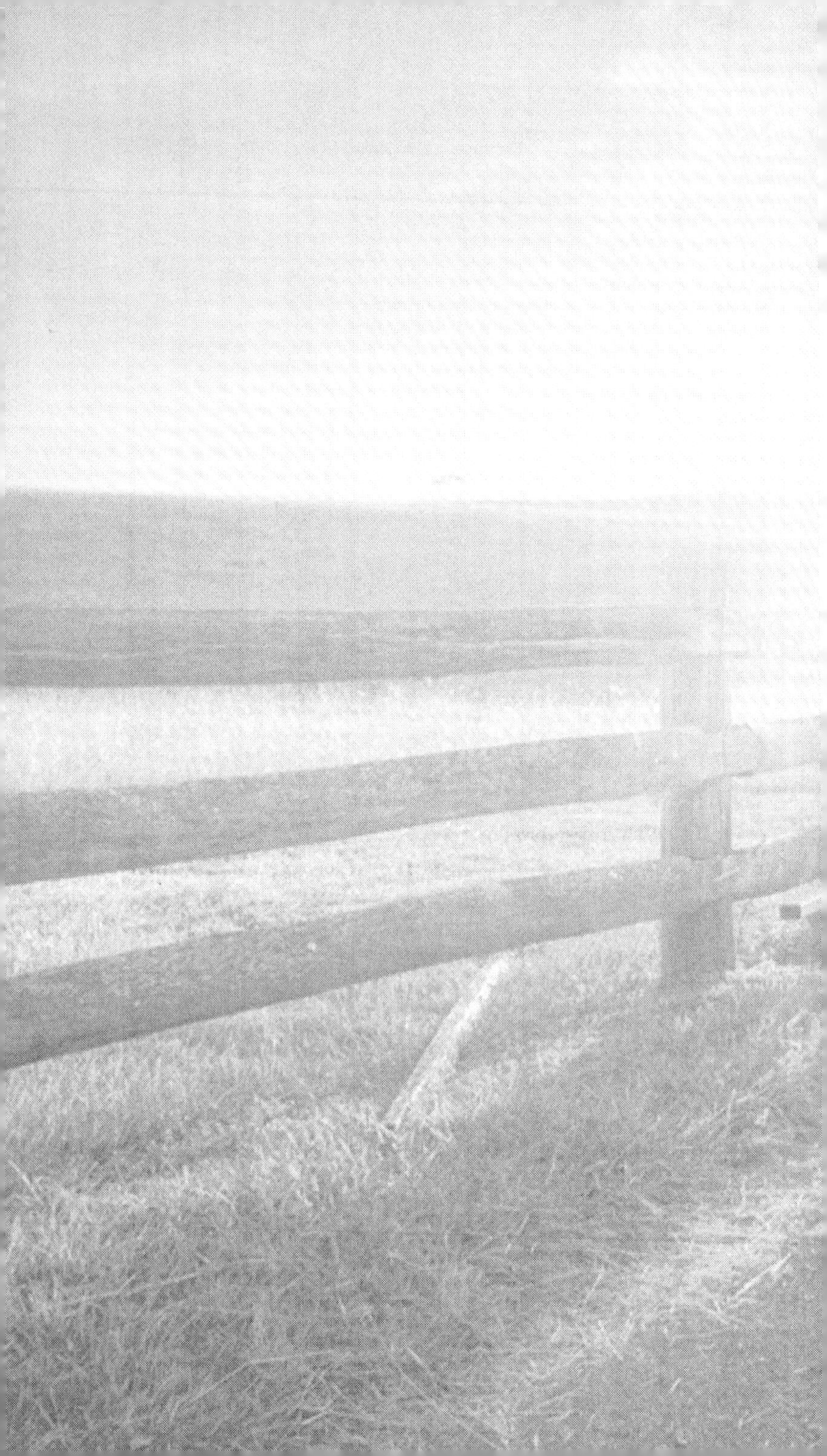

THIRTEEN
AMELIE

AMELIE WATCHED THE scenery change as Troy's truck climbed up the side of the mountain, slowly winding along the slippery roads while the sky lost the last of its color. "It's really pretty up here, but I'm not sure I would want to live on a road like this."

She'd been in New York long enough to get used to being able to walk everywhere she wanted to go, and it was still a little strange to see such long stretches of unpopulated space.

Not that she minded. It was just different.

However, the consuming darkness brought on by the towering fir trees lining the asphalt was a little unsettling.

"I feel the same way." Troy slowed down, squinting at the mailboxes sticking up out of the snow. "Colt's place is really nice and the view is amazing, but it can be hard as hell to get to in the winter."

While they worked at her grandmother's, Troy had filled her in on his friend Colt and the woman he was dating. Apparently Winter also lived around the Billings area, but her Great Aunt Gertrude was a resident of Grizzly Peak, the mountain they were currently scaling. "I guess I can understand Colt living on this mountain more than I can Gertrude." She gazed into the pitch-black darkness walled up on each side of the truck. "I don't see how it could be safe for her to live all the way out here on her own."

"I would say at this point it's not, which is why Winter is in the process of moving." Troy slowed almost to a stop before easing his truck into a narrow driveway. "From what Colt said, Winter's been spending most of her time here with Gertrude while she recovers from breaking her hip, so I don't think she's spending too much time alone these days."

"That's good." Guilt settled into Amelie's gut. Guilt that her own grandmother had struggled through a knee replacement alone while she chased her dreams in New York, painting her heart out thinking she was on the road to claiming everything she wanted.

Everything they both sacrificed so much for her to have.

"Hopefully Muriel had a good time." Troy parked next to a blue pickup, shutting off the engine as he shot her a grin. "Otherwise, we might not hear the end of it."

Amelie laughed. "I wouldn't worry about that."

The chances of her grandmother not enjoying a day out with people her own age was slim to none.

Not that the fact was making her feel any better right now.

She should be thrilled to know that Muriel wasn't still sitting around her drafty house, wearing sink-washed clothes and taking whore's baths with water warmed up in a pot, but knowing how long it had been since she had a day like this only stabbed the pain of guilt deeper.

Amelie jumped out of the truck and made her way along the cleared sidewalk, the soles of her sneakers crunching on the scattered salt.

"We might need to take you out and get you a pair of work

boots." Troy tipped his head at her dirty shoes. "Something that'll keep you safe in the snow and while we work."

She definitely hadn't come to Montana prepared for the amount of manual labor she was doing. Most of her outfits were what she wore to work in the gallery during the day, or to attend one of the many functions Trevor was involved in in the evenings. Even the clothes she wore to paint were less than ideal for scooping up drywall and insulation.

"I probably do need to make a trip to get a few things." She could use some jeans and some long-sleeved shirts and maybe a few sports bras. Nothing expensive, just stuff to get her through the work that needed to be done at her grandmother's house.

Then she could figure out how to get back to her normal life.

Whatever that was going to be.

Troy rapped on the door and it opened a second later. A pretty redheaded woman who looked to be a few years younger than her smiled out at them. "Hey, Troy."

Troy tipped his head at the woman. "Winter. Nice to see you again." His focus shifted, swinging to settle on where Amelie stood at his side. "This is Muriel's granddaughter—"

"Amelie." Winter held out one hand. "I've heard a lot about you."

"Oof." Amelie took Winter's hand in a shake. "I can only imagine what she's said."

Her grandmother was one of the few people who supported her aspirations to be a working artist, and she rarely missed the opportunity to brag on all Amelie's accomplishments.

Too bad most of them didn't really matter anymore. Not now that she knew she hadn't earned them. Not with her painting anyway.

"All of it was good." Winter stepped back, opening the door wider. "Come in out of the cold. It's freezing out there."

Amelie paused just inside the door, stomping her feet to

knock as much snow off her shoes as possible. "It does seem to get colder here than it does in town, doesn't it?"

"I said the same thing to Colt when I first came here." Winter closed the door. "I think it's because it's so much higher that the wind really cuts through and cools everything down." She smiled softly. "But I still like it here way better than I liked Billings."

"Hey there." A good-looking man who was a little shorter than Troy and just a hair leaner crossed the small, brightly-colored front room of the little house. "You get everything done you were hoping to?"

Troy tipped his head to one side. "We did okay." He reached out to rest one hand on the small of Amelie's back. "This is Amelie, Muriel's granddaughter." Troy's eyes rested on her face. "Amelie, this is my friend Colt."

Colt shoved one hand in her direction, offering up a more enthusiastic shake than his girlfriend did. "Thanks for letting me steal your grandma today. She and Gertrude did a great job of keeping my grandma company this afternoon."

Amelie peeked past Colt's shoulder and finally got eyes on her grandmother. Muriel was sitting at the kitchen table, laughing heartily along with two other ladies, both looking like they might be around her same age. "I'm sure it went both ways."

It was a little strange to see her grandmother chatting with her peers. Strange in the best possible way.

Muriel spent so many years living a life that focused on her husband and children. She'd given up any dreams of her own to take care of them, making sure they had everything she could offer.

And look where it got her. Alone. Isolated. Sitting in a rundown house waiting to die.

But maybe it didn't have to be that way. Now that she knew

what was happening she could change things. Make sure her grandmother finally lived the kind of life she deserved.

She owed it to her since Muriel had given up everything to make sure Amelie was in control of her own life and her own future.

"We're just about to eat some dinner. Why don't you guys stay?" Colt thumbed over one shoulder. "There's plenty to go around. My mom made beef stew and homemade biscuits."

"Your mom's here too?" Amelie leaned a little more, trying to get a better view of the kitchen.

Colt nodded. "She comes up here a few times a week and brings my grandma with her. They sit around with Gertrude, playing cards and gossiping like a bunch of old hens."

A beautiful woman with shiny hair and bright eyes appeared at Colt's side, wrapping one arm around his shoulders to pull him in. "I know you didn't just call me old, son."

"That doesn't sound like something I would do." Colt wiggled his brows at his mother. "But if the shoe fits."

His mother faked outrage, widening her eyes as she shoved at his shoulder. "Just for that you only get one biscuit."

"Well that's just downright evil." Colt leaned into Winter's side as his mother made her way back to the kitchen, lowering his voice as he whispered in her ear. "Grab a few extra for me."

Winter shook her head. "No way. You're on your own."

Amelie watched the whole interaction, a little fascinated by the way they all treated each other.

It was strange as hell.

No one was yelling. No one was arguing. No one was dishing out underhanded compliments and then pretending to be innocent.

And no one was acting like they were better than anyone else.

She leaned into Troy's ear as Winter and Colt followed his

mother into the kitchen. "Do you feel like you're in the Twilight Zone?"

"I feel that way a lot." He was quiet for a minute, eyes moving over her face. "The people around here are different. At first I thought it was all for show, but it's not." His gaze drifted into the kitchen, watching as Colt and his family teased and joked, their love and affection for each other blatant and undeniable. "This is how they really are all the time."

"Must be nice."

She managed a smile as Winter came back, collecting both their coats while Colt's mom ushered them into the kitchen and loaded them up with steaming bowls of beef stew and stacks of warm biscuits. Amelie ended up at the table with the rest of the women, listening to everyone chat while Troy and Colt sat together in the living room.

Occasionally, she would glance in and find him watching her while Colt talked. It was odd, but knowing Troy was there, and that he understood how weird this whole situation was, made her feel less out of her element.

Less like the outcast they didn't realize she was.

"You okay?" Winter's voice was quiet as she stole Amelie's attention from the man watching her intently.

Amelie forced on a smile. "I'm good. Just tired."

It was an easy explanation. One that was believable since she'd worked her ass off all day helping clear out the second of the bedrooms upstairs.

But the exhaustion lingering in her limbs wasn't the root of her silence.

"This can be kind of a lot for me sometimes too."

Winter's understanding of what was actually the issue surprised her.

"I'm just not used to everyone being so..." Amelie stopped there because she didn't quite know how to explain it.

Luckily, Winter did. "Nice?"

Amelie huffed out a little laugh. "Pretty much."

"I still have a hard time with it myself." Winter glanced in where Colt and Troy sat. "I don't know how much Troy told you, but my family isn't really around." Her warm gaze went to rest on Gertrude. "My aunt is all I have, and I just found her a few weeks ago."

Amelie turned to face Winter. "What?"

"It's kind of a wild story. I got stuck in the snow coming to visit her and Colt pretty much saved me from freezing to death on the side of the road. It turned out that he and my aunt were neighbors, so he helped me find her. Now I'm moving here to be closer to her." Her cheeks pinked a little bit. "And him."

"How long did you know Colt before you realized he was neighbors with your aunt?"

"Oh." Winter shook her head. "I must not have explained it well. I only met Colt a few weeks ago too." She shrugged. "Everything kind of snowballed really fast and now I'm moving and starting a new job and making new friends." She sucked in a breath and blew it back out. "It's been crazy."

Amelie understood just how crazy uprooting your life could be, and she was a little jealous that Winter got to do it for happy reasons.

"I can't believe you all just met." Amelie looked over the group lined around the table. "It seems like you've known each other forever."

Winter's expression changed in a way that made Amelie's throat tight. "Really?"

Amelie nodded. That was all she could manage. It was clear what she said made Winter emotional, and somehow that made her emotional too.

Winter sniffed, blinking fast. "They all came into my life right when I needed them most."

Amelie swallowed at a sudden tightness in her throat. "I'm glad."

She knew what it was like to feel alone, and even though she didn't really know Winter, it was evident that having these people in her life had changed it for the better. "Life can be hard when your family doesn't want to have anything to do with you."

Winter glanced at where Muriel sat next to Gertrude. She leaned closer to Amelie, lowering her voice. "They don't talk to your grandma either?"

Amelie shook her head. "We both got cut off at the same time."

And for the same reason.

Her.

That was why she had to get her life together. Put her focus back where it was supposed to be so her grandmother didn't lose it all for nothing.

Gertrude pushed away from the table, using the cane close at hand to lift herself up out of her seat. "Who wants dessert?"

Everyone chimed in with enthusiasm, and Colt's mom rose swiftly from her chair to lend a hand. "I'll grab that for you."

She picked up a pie plate sitting on the counter and brought it over to the table. "This looks amazing, Winter."

"She's been making them every couple of days." Gertrude came back with a fistful of forks and set them beside the pie. "We need something to make us happy because this weather sure isn't gonna do it." She dropped back into her seat as Colt's mother passed out dessert plates. "What I wouldn't give for just a little peek at spring."

"It's January. We've still got a few more months to wait." Winter cut into the chocolate pie, slicing it into neat wedges. "Unfortunately."

"Maybe I'll get a new picture and hang it on the wall. A nice shot of Hawaii to carry me through." Gertrude stared out into the living room where Colt and Troy still sat. "It's a shame I can't just paint my whole living room to look like Hawaii."

"Why not?" Amelie had been pleasantly surprised by the interior of Gertrude's house. It was bright and colorful and cheery. The fact that Gertrude wasn't willing to paint a giant mural on one wall was a little surprising.

"Not really in my skill set." Gertrude dug into her pie as soon as Colt's mom set it in front of her. "The best I can do is a stick figure."

"I could paint it for you." The offer was out of Amelie's mouth before she realized she was going to make it.

But the second it cleared her lips she started to hope Gertrude would take her up on it. Not just because she was itching to get back to what she loved, but because it would give her grandmother and Gertrude more time together. More time to reminisce about the decades they'd both experienced and the lives they'd led.

And maybe she'd get to see a little more of Winter.

So far the hardest part about leaving New York was being away from Evelyn, missing out on the kind of conversations only a girlfriend could provide.

Gertrude's eyes slid Amelie's way. "Your grandmother did mention you are one heck of a talented artist." A sly smile worked across Gertrude's lips and suddenly Amelie realized she might have been set up.

"I can definitely paint more than just a stick figure." She looked over the expanse of walls. "I'm sure we could come up with something nice and tropical if you really wanted to."

Gertrude pointed her fork at Amelie. "I'm going to hold you to that."

Amelie pressed her lips together, but it was impossible to hold back her smile. "You better."

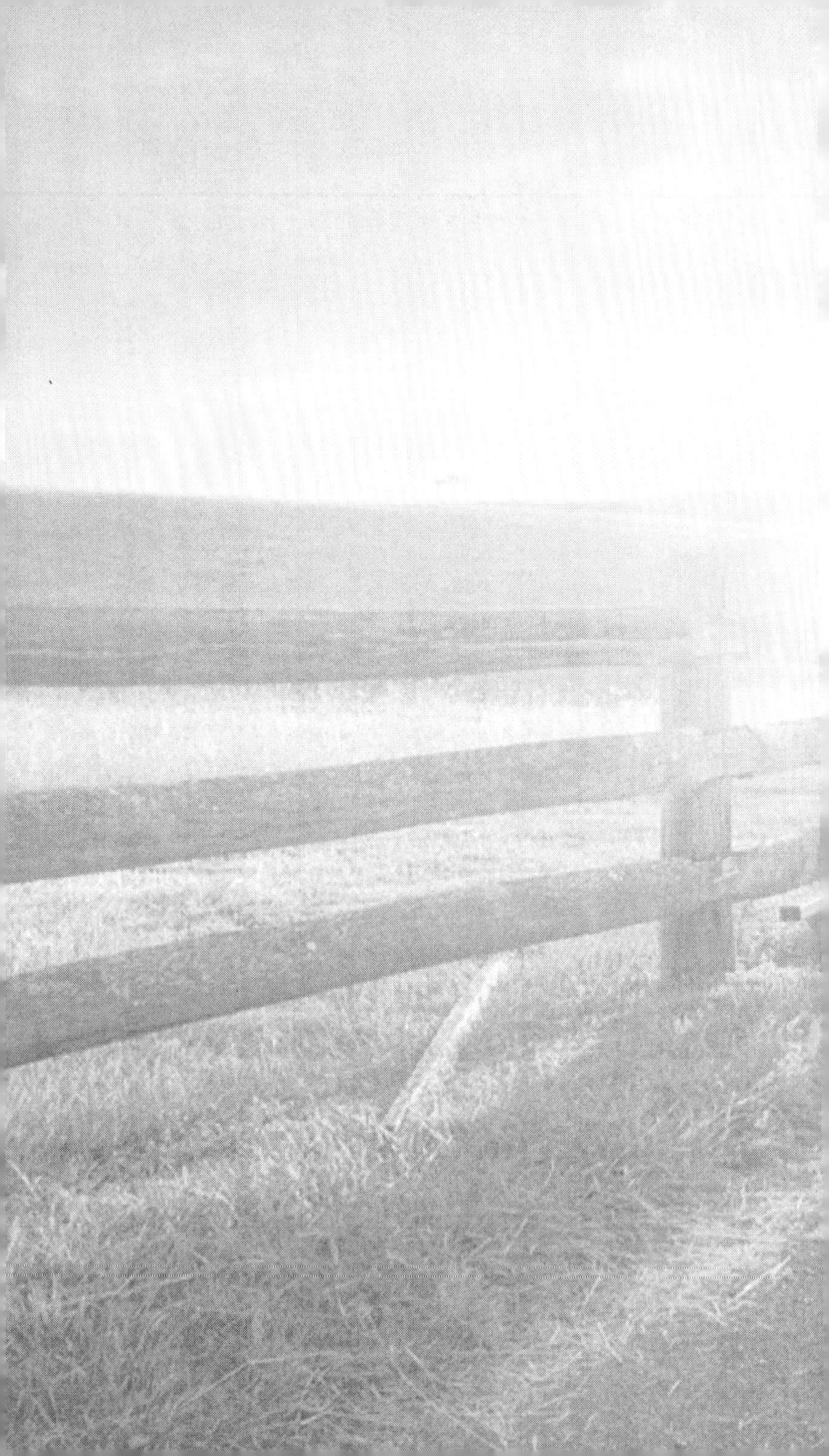

FOURTEEN

TROY

IT WAS NEARLY midnight by the time he managed to wrestle Amelie and Muriel into the truck. But even the late hour didn't seem to dim their enthusiasm over the evening.

"I'm a little excited about painting Gertrude's living room." Amelie had talked with Gertrude for almost an hour, coming up with a plan for the walls of the older woman's living room.

"I am too." Muriel sat in the front seat, carrying the stack of leftovers Colt's mother packed up for her to take home. "Maybe when you're done with hers you can paint one in my house."

Amelie's lips pressed together as if she was trying to smother out her smile. "Colt's mom asked if I could do a landscape in her dining room." Her joy over getting back to doing what she loved was palpable.

It was something he should have recognized and tried to remedy instead of dragging her to Muriel's to work for hours at a time.

It was one more way he was obviously lacking. All he'd been worried about was figuring out how to make Amelie realize they could be good together. He hadn't given a single thought to how she could be good on her own.

"You're kidding." Muriel twisted in her seat to peek into the back where Amelie was crammed into the small space behind them. "That's wonderful."

It was.

Colt's mother and grandma easily accepted Amelie into their fold, adding her to their little group the same way they'd done with Winter. Amelie started the evening off looking a little uncomfortable, but the women warmed her up immediately and brought out a side of her he hadn't seen before.

For the first time since they'd met she seemed relaxed. Her laughs were a little longer and a little louder. Her smiles were bigger and brighter.

Which was a problem.

Because at the end of the day, he didn't have a family to offer Amelie. Not like Colt did Winter.

All he had was himself.

And after seeing how much Amelie enjoyed being part of a big happy family, it was becoming clear that he probably wouldn't be enough.

Amelie and Muriel continued to talk about their new friends and the plans they'd made as he drove home. Their chatter didn't even stop as he pulled down the driveway and parked.

"I am so glad you called Colt and set today up." Muriel unbuckled her seatbelt. "Not that I wasn't going to be a happy little clam with cable TV in that recliner of yours, but it was nice to get out and spend time with people."

"I'm sure your presence will be requested again." Troy climbed out of the truck and rounded the front before opening Muriel's door and helping her down. "I expect your social calendar is about to get real full."

Muriel balanced her leftovers in one hand and gripped his arm with the other as they walked toward the house. "I guess I should get my fill in before I have to go back to Billings. I doubt they'll want to drive all the way out there to get me."

Amelie followed behind them, carrying the final slice of pie left from the evening. "I can bring you here."

Troy and Muriel stopped and turned to look at her at the same time.

"I didn't think you were going to be staying long?" Muriel asked the question he couldn't bring himself to voice.

Amelie hadn't set any parameters for her time here in Montana, and he hadn't wanted to press the issue. Mostly because he was afraid of what she might say. But Amelie looked surprisingly indifferent now.

She lifted one shoulder in a shrug. "Well, we have to finish your house. And then I have to paint Gertrude's living room and Pam's dining room, so it seems I might be here a little longer than I expected."

It was good news and bad.

Good news because the thought of Amelie leaving made his chest ache.

Bad because the thought of Amelie leaving already made his chest ache, and that pain would only get worse the longer she stuck around. Especially since he was beginning to realize maybe he might not be what was best for her.

"Well you know you are welcome to stay with me as long as you want." Muriel turned back toward the house and began shuffling along again. "Pretty soon you'll even have a bedroom of your own."

That was one more thing he really didn't want to think about.

This morning was perfect. He woke up to Amelie wrapped around him then spent his day at her side, thinking maybe this could become a more permanent situation.

But that was before he was faced with the cold hard truth of just how lacking he really was. He didn't have a family or any of the things that came with one. No mother to spoil any grandchildren he may or may not have. No brothers or sisters to be aunts and uncles. And it was probably one more reason he always ended up alone. No matter how helpful or funny or charming he was, it would never be enough to make up for the fact that all he brought to the table was himself.

"I'm going to have to get that pie recipe from Winter." Muriel leaned on him a little more heavily as they stepped up onto the deck. "That thing was fantastic."

"I'm sure she'll give it to you. She seemed really nice." Amelie held open the screen door while he unlocked the deadbolt, waiting for him and Muriel to clear the threshold before following them in. "I have her number if you want it."

"Look at you making friends." Muriel turned to give Amelie a smile. "You think Evelyn will be jealous?"

Amelie grinned. "No way. She's always telling me to put myself out there." Amelie closed the door and flipped the lock. "I think she'll really like Winter too."

Muriel's brows shot up. "When do you think they will meet?"

Amelie slipped out of her coat, hanging it in the closet before coming to collect Muriel's. "She seemed to be considering coming to visit me while I'm here." Amelie's eyes drifted his way, holding a second before going back to her grandmother's face. "She thought it sounded interesting."

"Any place can be interesting under the right circumstances." Muriel set her food in the fridge before making her way down the hall to the main floor bathroom. She yawned loudly as she flipped on the light. "I think I'm gonna brush my teeth and turn in."

Amelie turned to face him, holding one hand out. "Do you want me to hang your coat up too?"

Being with Colt's family tonight felt strange, but this moment felt odd in a different way. One that was significantly more comfortable than how the rest of the evening had been.

But everything seemed more comfortable when it was just the two of them.

Troy unzipped his coat and passed it over, the mundane task creating an unimaginable impact. "Thank you."

This was the kind of moment he'd longed for. A simple, boring interaction between two people as they came home and worked on settling in.

Coats hanging together in a closet.

Shoes lined side-by-side on the floor.

"You don't have to thank me." Amelie gave him a soft smile as she looped his heavy coat over a hanger and slid it into place next to hers. "It's the least I can do considering everything you've done." She turned back to face him. "And I understand I don't owe you anything, but you definitely deserve my appreciation."

Her recognition made him feel like he was wearing a shirt two sizes too small.

It didn't seem to fit quite right.

But confessing the full truth of his motivations didn't feel any better. "I've been trying to take care of your grandma's house for months."

Amelie's quick smile was surprising and unexpected. "I can imagine." Her dark eyes moved to the stairs. "Is it okay if I go take a shower?"

"Of course." He wanted her to feel comfortable in his house because despite the realization the evening forced on him, he still wanted to believe he could find a way to be enough. That he could figure out how to make Amelie want to stay in Montana.

Stay with him.

But after so many years of being left by so many people who should have stayed at his side, he knew the chances of that happening were slim to none.

Amelie made it halfway up the stairs before she paused, turning back to him. "Will you be up soon?"

It was an invitation he wasn't strong enough to turn down.

Troy nodded. "Let me make sure your grandma has everything she needs and then I'll be in."

Amelie smiled softly, watching him a second longer before disappearing up to the second floor.

Troy double-checked all the locks, making sure everyone was safe before getting Muriel a glass of water and helping her find a show she liked on the television. Then he made his way up to where Amelie was, the sweet scent of her body wash greeting him before he reached the landing.

It was one more thing about this time he would never be able to forget. No matter what happened, he would never look at this little house the same. Every room would somehow be marked with the memory of her.

The memory of what he thought he might finally be able to have.

Troy tapped on the door, waiting a second before cracking it open.

"You can come in." Amelie was already tucked into his bed, her long blonde hair fluffy and dry as it fell around her freshly scrubbed face and over the pale blue fabric of her pajama top. "This is your room."

"I want you to feel comfortable here. I don't want you to worry that I'll just barge in."

Amelie's brows pinched together. "I don't worry about that." She sat up a little straighter, bending her knees and wrapping both arms around them. "And I do feel comfortable here." The corners of her mouth lifted. "Definitely more comfortable than I was sleeping on my grandmother's couch and trying to race through an ice-cold shower."

Troy cringed, the reminder of what Muriel had been dealing with bothering him just as much as facing down all the things he couldn't give Amelie. "I wish she would've told me." He pulled fresh pajamas from the dresser on his way to the bathroom.

"*I* wish you weren't the only person she had to count on for so long." Amelie scooted to the edge of the bed, swinging both legs over the side as he went into the bathroom. "And I wish my family wasn't so fucked up that my poor grandmother was left on her own with nobody making sure she was okay."

Troy paused, turning to meet Amelie's eyes. "I was making sure she was okay."

Amelie twisted the blankets between her fingers. "You were doing a lot of things."

Troy recognized the shift in her expression the second it happened, saw the heat as it crept in around the edges. It meant chances were good tonight was going to go exactly like the night before.

But maybe that would be wrong. Maybe he needed to take a step back and help Amelie to do the same.

"I'm going to take a shower. I'll be out in a second." He shut the door between them, hoping the barrier would keep him from doing everything possible to find his way back into the heat of her body.

He quickly stripped down, stuffing his dirty clothes into the hamper before climbing under the heat of the water and scrubbing away the grime of the day. He rinsed off, sliding the soap from his skin with his hands as he rushed through the process. As much as he hated himself for it, he couldn't wait to get back to her—to see if she still wanted him like he wanted her—and that didn't have as much to do with sex as it probably ought to.

He barely heard the soft knock on the door over the sound of the rushing water. "Troy?"

"Yeah?"

The latch clicked open. "Can I ask you something?"

"Of course."

Amelie was quiet for a second, and when she spoke again her voice was softer. More hesitant. "How did you turn out this way?"

He shut off the faucet, squeezing the water from his hair and wiping it from his eyes. "What way?" He snagged his towel from the rack just outside before wrapping it around his waist and opening the curtain.

Amelie stood right in front of him, but her eyes stayed on his face. "Good."

She stepped in a little closer. "I was thinking about it while Winter was telling me all about Colt." Her lips softened into a little smile. "She is crazy about him, by the way." Her eyes held his as she inched in a little more. "But it made me start to think about the differences between his life and yours. I'm sure Colt's a nice guy and all, but he was sort of set up to be that way, right?" Amelie reached out to rest one palm against his chest. "But you weren't." Her eyes dipped down to where her fingers gently brushed over his still damp skin. "You should be angry at the world," her eyes slowly came back to his, "but you're not."

He didn't really understand what sort of an answer she was looking for. "Being angry won't get me what I want."

A flash of confusion moved across her features. "What do you want?"

"I want what Colt has. I want a family that likes each other and sticks around even when things are hard."

He forced his eyes from hers, knowing the anger they would carry. That it would prove she didn't know him as well as she thought. "But I can't have it, no matter how hard I try."

"Why not?" Amelie's lack of understanding made it clear that she didn't see everything he did tonight, but she would. Eventually.

And the sooner it happened, the better.

"I can't go back in time and make my mom happy I was born. I can't make my dad decide he wanted to be a part of my life." Having what Colt had was impossible, and the reality that he would never be able to create the family he desperately wanted was gut wrenching.

"Would you really want to force people to like you?" Amelie leaned closer, waiting for him to meet her gaze. "My dad doesn't really like me, and I would never wish I could make him, because honestly he doesn't deserve to like me." Amelie's voice was sharper than he'd ever heard it. "The same for my uncle. He doesn't deserve to be a part of my fantastic fucking life." She jabbed at his chest with one finger. "Just like your mom and your dick of a dad don't deserve to be a part of yours." She lifted her chin, jaw set. "They don't deserve to even know you, because you are good and kind and caring and everything they will never be."

Troy stared her down. "If I'm so good then why am I alone?"

It was a question he'd asked himself more times than he could count but never voiced to another person, and he regretted it almost immediately. But there was no escaping it now that it was between them. She'd heard his bitterness. His frustration.

Now she would see he wasn't quite as good as she thought.

Amelie's eyes searched his as her fingers spread wide, palms flattening against his chest. "Are you?"

FIFTEEN
AMELIE

THE FACT THAT Troy believed he was alone made her sad.

It also hurt her feelings a little.

But maybe she deserved that. She'd been very clear that whatever happened between them was accidental at best.

Nothing more than scratching each other's itches.

But that wasn't as true as she first thought she wanted it to be.

Amelie watched her fingers as they traced little lines across his chest. "I mean, I'm pretty sure you're stuck with my grandmother forever." She bit her lower lip as if it might help keep her from continuing.

But right now Troy needed to hear the truth more than she needed to believe a lie.

"And I'm here." She fought in a shaky breath, forcing her eyes back up to his. "With you."

Troy was silent, his expression dark as his eyes stared into hers.

Then he was on her.

Hands in her hair, warm body shoving hers back through

the open door as the towel dropped from his waist to tangle in her feet.

She started to tip, losing her footing, but Troy immediately caught her, lifting her up against him before lowering them both down to his bed.

Normally she was the aggressor, the one initiating anything physical that happened between them, but not this time. This time it was all Troy. And the frenzied way his hands stripped away her pajamas and moved against her skin was exhilarating.

It would be easy to let herself think he was caught up in a whirlwind of lust, but that's not what this was. And if she was going to face one truth, she was going to face all of them.

This moment was about need. Need that stepped outside the lines she kept trying to draw around them.

Troy's lips followed his hands, branding a path down her body before stopping between her thighs. The heat of his mouth was on her flesh before she could fully prepare, the incessant flick of his tongue sending her barreling toward a climax at epic speeds.

Amelie tried to wiggle away, but Troy's hands clamped onto her thighs, spreading them wider as he pinned her in place and continued lapping at her clit.

She shoved one hand between them, blocking his access. "I want you inside me." Her heart skipped a beat when he made a sound that was dangerously close to a growl.

She lifted her head to meet his narrowed gaze. "Now."

Troy scowled at her a second longer but finally reached for the nightstand, grabbing a condom and rolling it on before his body covered hers.

He wedged one knee between her thighs, keeping her right leg flat, just like he did their first night together, as he lifted the other one wide. But instead of letting him ease into her like she knew he would, Amelie hooked the leg Troy was lifting around his back, locked it tight, and rolled them to the right, following the weight of his body until his back was on the mattress and she was straddling his hips.

All the air rushed from her lungs as she stared down at him. "That was easier than I thought it was going to be."

Troy's frown was still in place. "What are you doing?" He tried to push up from the mattress, but she pressed both hands to his chest, putting most of her weight on her arms as she leaned forward.

"When I said I wanted you inside me," she angled her hips, sliding her seam along Troy's length before rolling them forward to notch him against her body, "I meant I wanted all of you."

She sank over him before he could argue, knowing Troy would insist on easing her into it since she'd made such a big deal about how much of him there was to manage.

And there was definitely a lot of him, but tonight the thought of leaving any part of Troy feeling unappreciated didn't sit right.

But maybe she was starting to acclimate because the majority of him fit with no problem. The last inch or so, took a little more work, and even that might have been all in her head, because once she was fully over him, the stretch of his body in hers wasn't even a little uncomfortable.

She just felt... full, but in an extremely arousing way.

"Wow." Amelie rocked forward, lifting up before sinking back down. "That—" the word strangled off as Troy slid his hands up her front, strong fingers rolling both nipples at once.

"Holy shit." She shifted her weight, bracing against his chest before sinking back down. "You feel so good."

She'd already been on the verge of an orgasm from his mouth, and it didn't take long before she was right there again. But as great as everything felt, she needed just a little more.

"Troy, I need—" She whimpered as his fingers pinched tighter, the sensation shooting straight to her core and making her clench around him. It felt fantastic, but not in a way that would make her come. "I need—"

"Do it then." Troy's voice was surprisingly demanding. "Rub your pussy while you fuck me."

All the air rushed from her lungs at his blunt demand. It was the dirtiest thing any man had ever said to her, and her first instinct was to be shy.

To pretend she didn't want to do exactly what he was suggesting.

But the allure of having her body filled, nipples pinched, and clit rubbed all at the same time was too much to ignore.

Amelie pulled one hand from his chest and slid it into place, fingertips gliding over her wet skin as she started to work them against the hardened nub begging for contact.

"That's it." Troy's voice was rough and ragged, his eyes glued to where she touched herself. "Such a good fucking girl." He bent his knees, digging his feet into the bed as he started to thrust his hips up, his body meeting hers as she continued to rock over him. "Rub faster."

When she did as he said her thighs started to shake, almost as if he knew what she needed better than she did. The combination of sensations was consuming, possessing her completely as she ground against the hard length of his cock. Her spine curled forward as she lost the ability to hold herself upright, every muscle in her body focused only on the climax shattering through her.

Amelie collapsed on top of him, weighed down by the burden of her limbs, barely managing to breathe as little aftershocks continued torturing her with bolts of pleasure.

Troy gathered her hair, collecting it from where it covered

his face and working it off to one side before wrapping both arms around her back, keeping her tight to him.

Each touch was tender and careful. Sweet and soft.

She smothered down a smile as he fought to pull the covers over them. "Do you want me to move?"

"Not particularly."

She pushed up, her eyes drifting down to where their bodies were still joined. "Did you..."

Troy chuckled. "Absolutely I did."

"I must have missed it." Amelie pressed her lips together, but finally let her smile free. "I was a little distracted."

Troy reached up to tuck her hair behind one ear. "Good."

———

"LOOK AT YOU up bright and shiny." Muriel wandered into the kitchen, blinking at the bright light reflecting in through the window above the sink. "I figured you might sleep in this morning."

"I guess I just got enough rest." Amelie pulled out the basket of the coffee pot before going in search of a filter. "Definitely more than I got sleeping on your couch." She gave her grandma a little smile as she dropped the liner into place and started scooping in grounds from the can on the counter.

"I can imagine." Muriel grabbed a couple coffee cups and carried them to the fridge. "I'm sure you got better sleep than you did in New York too." She poured a little creamer into each one. "Probably had to keep one eye open sleeping next to that snake of an ex-boyfriend."

Her grandmother had never been a big fan of Trevor. She mostly kept it to herself, but it wasn't difficult to tell when Muriel didn't like someone. She wore her heart on her sleeve in good ways and bad.

"Well he's sleeping next to someone else now." The fact didn't make her quite as bitter as her grandmother probably thought it did. She was never particularly upset that Trevor found someone new. They'd been growing apart for a while, and honestly it was just a matter of time before he moved on.

The fact that he was giving Olivia an art show though, that stung.

"Well he's her problem now, thank God." Muriel set the prepared cups on the counter in front of the coffee pot as it worked. "I'm sure she'll get too old for him too and he'll replace her with a younger model just like he did you."

Amelie propped up against the counter, crossing her arms as she considered the reality of what actually happened in New York. "I think there's probably some mutual using that goes on in the relationships he develops."

It was a tough pill to swallow, but maybe her own reasons for being with Trevor were a little...

Self-serving.

"Good. The women he's with should get something out of it." Her grandmother peered at her over the top of her glasses. "Because we both know they're not getting good sex from him."

Amelie's eyes widened so far it was almost painful. "What?"

She talked about a lot of things with her grandmother, but her sex life was not one of them.

"Oh, come on. I saw pictures of him." She went to the fridge and opened the door, pulling out the piece of chocolate pie they brought home last night. "You could tell by looking at him he was an arrogant asshole. Men like that are always shit in bed."

Amelie opened her mouth, but there were no words she really wanted to say, so she clamped it back shut again.

"You want a humble man. One who's not too good to get on his knees." Muriel sat down at the table and popped the lid off the container, digging into the pie like she hadn't just created a mental picture Amelie would never scrub out of her brain.

They needed to start a new conversation. One that didn't involve men on their knees.

"I should call Winter." Amelie turned back to the coffee pot, unable to look her grandmother in the eye. "See if she can give me the recipe for that pie."

Muriel shoved in a bite of pie before pointing her fork at Amelie. "Good idea. Ask her if Colt's good in bed when you talk to her. It'll prove my theory."

Amelie shook her head. "I'm not going to ask her that." She barely knew Winter. The last thing she would do was ask her what her new boyfriend was like between the sheets.

But Muriel didn't seem to share that opinion.

"Why not? It's an honest question." She forked off another bite. "I can find out about his daddy and granddaddy next time I go to Gertrude's."

The coffee pot beeped, providing a welcome distraction and Amelie grabbed the carafe a bit more aggressively than intended, pouring out a cupful and setting it in front of her grandmother before fixing her own.

Muriel took a long sip before peering into the cup. "That's good stuff. Troy has good taste in coffee creamer." She set the cup down on the table and went back to her pie.

Amelie let out a little sigh of relief, relaxing as she brought her own cup of coffee to her lips.

"You should ask Troy what he's like—"

Amelie's throat spasmed—reacting immediately to her grandmother's mention of Troy and what she knew was coming next—forcing the coffee down the wrong pipe and sending her into a coughing fit.

Muriel's brows pinched together. "You okay?"

Amelie nodded, working hard to clear the hot liquid from

her throat. "Fine." She set her cup down and headed for the hall. "I'll be right back."

Hopefully by the time she was finished in the bathroom her grandmother would lose interest, or at least forget where their conversation left off.

Amelie was just passing the back entrance when a shadow moved across the window of the front door. She stopped, squinting at the sheer curtains covering the glass.

It was still pretty early, but probably not too early for the ranch hands that worked on Cross Creek. She glanced up the stairs, listening to see if Troy was moving around, but the second floor was silent.

She could probably just see who it was and tell them to come back later so Troy could get a little bit more sleep.

Especially since she was the reason he was up so late.

And then again in the middle of the night.

Amelie quietly moved through the living room, past the television that was still on, set to the channel that continuously played reruns of old sitcoms.

She reached the front door and pushed the curtain to one side, peeking out to see if it was someone she might recognize.

But the man on the other side was no one she'd met before.

Amelie unlocked the deadbolt and cracked the door. "Can I help you?"

The man on Troy's front porch looked to be around her father's age, but that was where the comparisons to her father ended. Where her father was showing his age and severely overweight, this man was still in amazing shape. His broad shoulders and thick arms were obvious, even through the bulk of his coat. He was almost as tall as Troy, with a chiseled jaw and clear blue eyes.

Blue eyes that seemed vaguely familiar.

He cleared his throat, shifting on his feet. "I hope so." The man glanced behind him, looking out over the barren landscape surrounding them. "I'm not sure I'm in the right place."

"You're at Cross Creek Ranch." She didn't know the address but couldn't imagine it mattered. "Is that where you were looking for?"

His blue eyes came back to her and for a second they almost seemed identical to a set she knew.

Well.

"I'm looking for Troy Merrick."

Amelie stood a little straighter, gripping the doorknob in preparation to slam it closed in his face. "Why?"

The man was quiet for a second, his jaw clenching tight before he finally gave her the answer she already knew. "He's my son."

SIXTEEN

TROY

THE TIGHT CLIP of Amelie's tone had Troy moving down the stairs faster than he ever had before.

Something was wrong.

Muriel stood in the kitchen, eyes wide and fixed in the direction of the front door, giving him the location he needed.

Troy raced through the living room, catching Amelie around the waist the second he reached the door. He pulled her body behind his, coming face-to-face with the man she was ripping a new asshole.

At least he looked appropriately apologetic.

Troy stared the stranger down. "What in the hell is going on?"

Amelie shoved at his back, trying to push him out of her way in an effort to face the man down again. "Nothing. Don't worry about it."

Troy tightened his grip on her, keeping her in place as he looked the man on his porch up and down. "Who's this?"

He already had his suspicions, but wanted confirmation before he planted his fist in the guy's jaw.

Twice. Once for Amelie and once for Muriel.

"He's no one." Amelie managed to get one elbow into his ribs, digging it in as she continued to fight her way toward the door. "And he's leaving."

The man didn't seem concerned that a half-rabid woman was itching to get her hands on him. If anything he seemed to be completely oblivious to Amelie's existence.

His entire focus was on Troy.

"Christ." The man scrubbed one hand down his face and across the stubble covering his jaw. "It's true." The man barely shook his head, eyes moving over Troy's face. "I didn't think it could be, but it is."

Troy jerked his head Amelie's way. "What in the hell is your dad talking about?"

He'd always hoped one of Muriel's sons would show up on her doorstep, but this was good enough. He'd take any opportunity he could get to repay them for how they treated their mother.

Amelie stopped fighting him, her spine straightening the tiniest bit. "That's not my dad, Troy."

He looked the man over again, taking in his tall frame and solid stance, before turning just enough to meet Amelie's wide eyes. If this wasn't her dad then the explanation he thought he had for the situation was gone. "Then who in the hell is he?"

The man stepped closer. "I'm *your* dad."

Troy slowly turned to face the stranger staring at him.

He didn't want to believe what this guy was saying, but the longer he looked at him, the more Troy had to consider that it might be true.

The man's build was similar and the color of his eyes was almost identical. His full head of salt-and-pepper hair explained the greys Troy had already found growing on his own head. Even the way he held himself reflected what Troy saw in the mirror every day.

"Huh." Troy straightened fully, his back to Amelie as he stepped out the door. "I guess it's just one punch then."

He swung hard and fast, catching the man who claimed to be his dad right in the jaw and sending him two steps back.

Amelie quickly came around him, and for a second he thought she was trying to get between them. To stop what was happening.

Then he realized she was winding up to dish out a swing of her own.

Troy grabbed her before she could let it fly. Snagging her around the waist with one arm and catching her fist with the other, he pulled her body back against him as their early morning visitor rested one palm against his already bruising face.

"I guess I deserve that." He worked his jaw from side to side, wincing a little with the motion.

"You deserve a hell of a lot more than that." Amelie tried to rush at him again, but Troy held fast, so she resorted to kicking a clump of snow at the man with her socked foot.

Troy angled her back through the door, doing his best to get her flailing limbs into the house. "Go inside."

"Why's she gotta come back inside?" Muriel blocked his path, making it impossible to get Amelie out of the cold.

"Because her feet are wet and her toes are going to freeze off." Troy leaned back, managing to get Amelie's toes off the ground. "Can you move to one side so I can get her in?"

Muriel ignored him, looking over the guy still standing on his front porch. "Who's that?"

Amelie grabbed at the arm wrapped around her waist, still doing her best to get free. "His asshole father." She suddenly stopped wiggling and focused on Muriel. "Can you punch him for me?"

Troy quickly stretched his arm across the doorway, gripping

the frame before Muriel could move a muscle. "You two aren't punching anyone." His head was spinning, partly from the fact that a man claiming to be his dad was standing on his porch, and partly because he was scrambling to contain the wild-card women currently glaring their visitor's direction.

"You the same father who skipped out the minute you found out his mother was pregnant?" Muriel's words were icy and flat.

And laced with just enough of a threat of violence that he was grateful she didn't have her cane in her hand.

The man on the porch straightened, pushing his shoulders back. "No. I'm not."

Amelie went still, her dark eyes moving over the stranger. "You're either him or you're not."

"I'm his dad." The man's eyes moved from Muriel to Amelie to him. "But I didn't know he existed until two weeks ago."

Troy stared out at him, barely feeling the bite of the cold air as it whipped across the ranch. It wasn't until Amelie shivered against him that the chill registered. He stepped back, angling her feet onto the floor inside before turning to the man watching him with a wary gaze.

It would be easy to throw him out, send him back to wherever he came from and go on like this never happened.

But it was a hell of a lot easier to believe that his mother had been lying to him all these years.

Troy tipped his head toward the house. "Come in."

The man glanced at Muriel and Amelie, hesitating.

"We won't punch you." Muriel lifted her chin. "For now."

The man dipped his head and stepped into the house, stopping on the rug just inside the door, looking uncertain as hell.

"Take those boots off." Muriel turned toward the kitchen. "If you track snow through this house I'll have your head."

The man claiming to be his father nodded. "Yes, ma'am."

Muriel stopped and slowly turned back, her cool gaze lingering on the large man still dominating his doorway. One brow lifted before she went back to making her way to the kitchen.

Amelie stayed right at his side, arms crossed firmly over her chest as she stared the man down, still looking half interested in decking him.

Troy rested one hand on her back, reaching out with the other to slide his fingers over her cheek. "Why don't you go upstairs and put on some fresh socks."

She met his gaze, eyes defiant. "I'm fine."

She was far from fine. She was clearly pissed as hell and ready to fight on his behalf, which might be what was making this whole situation easier to face than he would have ever imagined.

"So am I." He leaned in to press his lips to her forehead, hoping to reassure her. "I promise."

He'd imagined meeting his father a million times, and every one of them started a whole lot like this one did.

With him repaying the man for walking out on him.

But what if his claim was true? What if his mother *had* lied? What if he didn't know?

That might change everything.

Amelie's eyes slid to where the man stood, narrowing a second before moving back to Troy's. "I'll be right back."

He smiled. "I'll be waiting."

She shot the man another glare before hustling toward the stairs. Troy watched her go, halfway planning to keep staring until she came back.

Something changed between them last night, but he hadn't been quite sure what it was. Not until she faced down a man fifty pounds heavier than her, spitting mad and ready to fight on his behalf.

"Looks like you found someone who cares about you a hell of a lot." The man inched off the mat, shoving both hands into the pockets of his coat. "I'm glad."

Troy didn't want to discuss Amelie with this man. He didn't want to discuss Amelie with anyone. Not yet. Not until he knew where they stood.

There was only one conversation he wanted to have right now, and it centered around the woman they both apparently knew.

"My mother didn't tell you she was pregnant?"

The man hesitated.

"We'd just broken up when she left me a message that she was pregnant and planned to have an abortion." He paused, taking a slow breath. "By the time I reached her and told her I would keep the baby, she said it was too late. That she already got rid of it."

Troy took in the slight slump of the man's shoulders. The way he still seemed to carry the burden from all those years ago.

"Were you the one who broke up with her?" He'd seen first-hand how his mother dealt with someone affecting her life, so it wasn't a stretch to think she would lie to punish a man who chose not to be with her.

The man nodded. "I didn't like how selfish she was."

Troy huffed out a bitter laugh. "I get it." He scratched at the stubble across his cheek. "You want some coffee?"

The man seemed surprised by the offer. "Sure."

Amelie raced down the stairs as they passed, sliding across the floor in her socks, bumping right into Troy's side. She peeked over his shoulder, watching the man following him through the house. "You're letting him stay?"

Troy nodded. "For now."

When they got to the kitchen Muriel had a fresh pot of coffee brewing and was unrolling a tube of cinnamon rolls. She jerked her chin toward the table. "Sit down. Coffee'll be done in a minute."

Troy pulled out a chair for Amelie before sitting beside her. The man was the last to sit, slowly lowering his big frame into the seat.

Troy had a million questions but knew exactly where he wanted to start.

"What's your name?" He held his breath, waiting to finally learn the name he might have had.

"Griffin Fraley." Griffin unzipped the front of his black leather coat, sliding it off and hanging it over the back of his seat. "I grew up a couple towns over from your mom. We met right after high school."

The timeline matched up, as did his description of the woman who might be even worse than Troy realized. "How did you find out she didn't have an abortion?"

Griffin's lips twisted into a bitter smile. "Apparently your mother decided I owed her money for taking care of a son I didn't know existed." He clasped his hands together on the table in front of him, staring down at his intertwined fingers. "I got a letter from an attorney saying she wanted to sue me for back child support."

Amelie's mouth dropped open. "Can she do that?"

"She can try." Griffin's smile turned easy. "But my attorney's a hell of a lot better than hers, so she won't get very far."

Amelie pursed her lips like she was mulling the situation over. "Is she the one who told you how to find Troy?"

"No." Griffin leaned back in his seat. "She offered to tell me where you lived for a price." He crossed his arms. "But I decided I'd pay a private investigator before I'd give her a dime."

"She must be single again." Troy sighed. "Last I heard she was with some doctor who left his wife for her."

It was his mother's M.O. She found wealthy men and used

them until they got tired of her entitled attitude and sociopathic tendencies. Then they dumped her, she keyed their cars, and everyone moved on.

Amelie's nostrils flared. "If she shows up here you better not stop me from punching her."

"You'll have to get in line." Muriel came to the table with two cups, setting one in front of Troy and one in front of Amelie before going back for the last one and giving it to Griffin. "I guessed you liked yours black."

Griffin took the cup with a smile. "You guessed right."

Muriel's cheeks almost seemed to pink up as she gave Griffin a wide smile. "I bet you work with your hands too."

Amelie's eyes widened as she slowly turned to stare at her grandmother.

Muriel leaned back, her expression full of innocence. "What?" She pointed at where Griffin held his cup. "You can tell by all the callouses."

"I actually own a few car repair shops around Seattle." Griffin took a sip of his coffee before setting it down. "I'm guessing that's why your mother decided to come after me now. She must have heard I was doing okay."

"That sounds like her." Lots of people thought they knew his mother, but most of them only saw what she wanted them to see. Her ability to manipulate everyone around her would have been impressive if it wasn't so fucked up.

But it seemed like Griffin might have figured her out. Unfortunately, it cost both of them.

Muriel slid the pan of rolls in the oven before dropping down into the remaining chair, letting out a long sigh as she turned to Griffin. "I suppose you're here because you want to have a relationship with your son."

Griffin glanced at Troy before looking back at Muriel. "I do."

"Well," Muriel leaned forward, resting her arms on the

table, "you should know that if you do anything to hurt him I will personally hunt you down and beat you to death with my walker."

Griffin chuckled, the sound dying off as Muriel continued to stare at him, completely straight-faced.

He cleared his throat, tipping his head in a nod. "I understand."

Muriel continued to stare until Griffin shifted in his seat, obviously uncomfortable but unsure what to do about it.

Troy reached out to slide his fingers across Amelie's arm, forgetting for a second that Muriel was sitting right there.

He pulled his hand away, covering his mouth with it as he faked a cough. "Where are you staying?"

Griffin turned from where Muriel was still staring at him. "There's a bed and breakfast on the other side of town called The Inn at Red Cedar Ranch. I've got a room there for the next week."

"So you're in town for a week?" Muriel's narrowed gaze moved over Griffin. "That gives us plenty of time to get to know each other then."

Griffin kept his focus on Troy. "That's what I was hoping for, but I understand if there's no room for me in your life."

The moment was surreal. Not just because of Amelie and the way she tried to protect him from a situation she thought might cause him pain, but because the man he'd spent his whole life hating might not have deserved it at all.

Troy tapped one finger against the table, resisting the urge to reach for Amelie again as he faced down what might be a pivotal moment in his life.

"I think I might be able to find some room."

SEVENTEEN

AMELIE

"I KNOW I keep saying this, but that looks fantastic." Gertrude looked over the bit of roughing-in Amelie was working on. "I can already picture what it's going to look like."

Amelie resisted the urge to smile. "Hopefully you're right, otherwise I'll have to paint over it and start from scratch."

Gertrude scoffed, looking entirely too offended. "Of course I'm right." She propped both hands on her hips. "The sketches you did were unbelievable. There's not a doubt in my mind the real thing will make me want to hire you back to paint my whole house."

"You'll have to wait your turn because I'm next." Colt's mom, Pam, snagged the coffee pot from the maker on Gertrude's counter and went around the kitchen table filling everyone's cups. "She's finishing this and then coming to my house to do my dining room."

Liza, one of the owners of Cross Creek Ranch, picked up her mug as soon as Pam finished filling it. "And I have her scheduled as soon as they have the drywall in my bedroom at the new house finished." One corner of her mouth lifted. "And I may have mentioned her to my mother who is hoping to have a mural done in my sister's bedroom."

Amelie smiled back at the group of women she was getting to know better and better. "I can't wait to meet her when they move here." She sat up a little taller on the stool she was using as she worked. "Maybe she can help me."

Liza had a younger sister with Down syndrome who would be moving to Moss Creek in the spring along with Liza's parents. They were building houses side-by-side close to the mountains at the edge of Cross Creek Ranch, forming a family compound of sorts.

Liza beamed back at her. "She would absolutely love that."

"I get priority treatment as her grandma, so as soon as those boys are finished with my house, she's going there." Muriel dealt the next round of cards, passing them out quickly before checking her own hand. "I've just got to decide what I want her to paint."

"Maybe she could do a portrait of Griffin." Colt's grandmother wiggled her drawn-on eyebrows as she stacked up her cards. "I swear if I was thirty years younger—"

"If you were thirty years younger, dad would still be alive and I am positive he would not approve of you lusting after another man." Pam replaced the carafe and went to work brewing up another pot.

"Good thing there's not much he can do about it now." Colt's grandmother leaned into Muriel's side.

Muriel cackled, head tipping back. "I know that's right."

Amelie shook her head as she focused on the area of foliage that would hopefully look like it spread out from the corner, carefully working up the basic structures of the different plants that would frame the left side of the mural.

It had been over a week and a half since Griffin showed up

on Troy's doorstep, and his appearance had turned her life upside down yet again.

But she couldn't bring herself to be upset about it this time.

Since Griffin's unexpected arrival, he'd been more than just her grandmother's favorite topic of conversation, he was also now the one working with Troy on Muriel's house. It turned out Griffin was skilled at fixing more than just cars, and having another set of capable hands was speeding up the whole process. The two men had already finished clearing the upstairs bedrooms and rehanging the new drywall. They'd also repainted the main floor and replaced the furnace, clearing most of the to-do list in just a few long days.

And that was before Ben, the other owner of Cross Creek, and Colt started pitching in. Which was so very kind of them, especially considering they refused to let her pay any of them.

But she wouldn't be upset if maybe they were a little less helpful.

Because as difficult as it was to wash away the dust and debris that seemed to cover every inch of her after a day of working at the house, she missed getting to spend that time with Troy.

She felt a little selfish even thinking it, considering Troy was now spending his days getting to know his father. And from what she could tell, Griffin was working hard to show Troy he wanted to be a part of his life, and she would never want to take that from him.

Amelie stood up from her stool, stretching out the kinks working their way into her back and legs. "If you guys could all stop objectifying Griffin that would be great." She worked her upper body from side to side, bending at the waist. "I think he can tell you're all lusting after him."

"Don't get confused," Colt's grandmother organized her

cards, "it's not just *us* lusting after him. Half the room was talking about his ass yesterday at The Wooden Spoon."

Amelie shook her head. She still hadn't fully adjusted to the small-town dynamic and everyone knowing about everyone else's business.

And their asses, apparently.

Winter lifted up a card, glancing at Liza before setting it down. "Colt said Griffin seems like a nice guy."

Winter and Liza sat next to each other, working together as one. They weren't as familiar with bridge, and the rest of the group was merciless, so they'd finally convinced everyone to let them play as a team.

The rest of the women still fought over who had to be their partner, but at least Liza and Winter were holding their own now.

Liza nodded. "Ben said the same thing."

"He's definitely nice." Muriel snagged a card from her own hand. "Nice *lookin'*."

"Can we stop talking about how hot Griffin is? Seriously." Amelie stared down the mismatched group. "You're making things weird."

"I'll get weird with him." Gertrude dropped a card to the table, elbowing Muriel in the ribs.

"And with that," Amelie grabbed her earbuds and stuffed them in, "I'm not listening anymore. Be as lewd as you want to be." She switched on her music and focused on the task in front of her, easily getting lost in a process she'd loved for as long as she could remember.

There was always something about painting that calmed and centered her in a way nothing else could. The experience of layering color and texture to create an image, and also emotion, from nothing was almost spiritual for her.

It made it easy to get lost in what she was doing as she

immersed herself in the greens and blues meant to evoke the warmth and sunshine Gertrude missed during the long winter months.

And for the first time in a long time, Amelie felt at home.

Like maybe she finally found where she belonged.

Where she was appreciated. Where she was seen.

Trevor might have only been pretending to appreciate her talent, but the women chatting and joking around the table behind her weren't.

They all believed in her skills enough that they were willing to permanently feature her art in their homes.

And to pay for it.

Making her the working artist she'd always set out to be.

Maybe it wasn't the same as the glamorous shows she'd had in New York, but right now she was set to make a decent amount of money all on her own.

And that was her real dream. To be in control of her life. To continue to pursue what she loved most instead of chasing after someone else's dream.

A soft touch on her shoulder pulled Amelie from her thoughts, sending her spinning around as she yanked her earbuds free.

Troy's smile was easy and relaxed. "You were really focused."

Amelie scanned the house, finding that most of the men had arrived. Ben was leaned into Liza's ear, voice low enough she couldn't hear what he was saying but based on the blush of Liza's cheeks she could guess.

Colt was on his knees at Winter's side, one arm around her as he teased his mom and grandma.

A week ago she felt a little awkward around the people filling Gertrude's house.

But now she was a part of it. A part of them.

And so was Troy.

But someone was missing.

Amelie gave the small house another look. "Where's Griffin?"

He usually tagged along wherever Troy went, giving Muriel and her friends plenty to talk about.

"He went back to The Inn. Said he had some phone calls to make and some work to do." Troy glanced over the work she'd done while he was gone. "How has your day been?"

Amelie set her brush down and stood, wiping both hands on the front of her smock as she glanced toward the women still whooping it up in the kitchen. "I'm sure you can guess."

She resisted the urge to move a little closer to Troy and couldn't help but resent the way Winter and Liza could openly touch and kiss the men at their sides.

It was starting to get hard to pretend there was nothing between them, but if her grandmother had a clue that Troy shared a bed with her every night, she would never hear the end of it.

But even the thought of that was becoming less and less of a deterrent.

Hell, it might be nice to hear about something besides Griffin's hot ass.

Amelie took a step back, looking over the dusty fog clinging to Troy's clothes, being careful not to let her gaze linger too long on his muscular frame. "You look tired." She tore her eyes from him and began to collect her paint. "Did you guys get a lot done today?"

Troy crouched down to help her, grabbing the line of brushes she'd been using. "We got the new water heater installed while the guys were finishing the drywall on the second floor."

Amelie smiled even though Troy's explanation made her

stomach clench. "It sounds like you're getting close to being done."

Considering the state Muriel's house was in, Troy and his dad were managing to get it together way faster than she anticipated.

Way faster than she hoped.

"There's still a lot of cleaning up to do, but I think we're coming close to having it livable again." Troy followed her to the kitchen and stood beside her as she rinsed her brushes in the sink, washing away the water-based paint she decided would be the best option for the project.

He tipped his head toward the front room. "It looks like you're making pretty good headway too."

Amelie looked over the mural as she worked any trace of paint free of the bristles. "There's a lot of space to cover, but it's coming together pretty well."

She'd been a little concerned about tackling such a large project, but after figuring out the logistics of it, the process wasn't as overwhelming as she first thought it might be.

That was how pretty much everything was shaking out lately, from her move to Montana to fixing up her grandmother's house. All of it was so much easier to handle than she expected.

Mostly because of the man standing at her side.

Once the brushes were cleaned and laid out to dry, Amelie turned to where Muriel was still knee-deep in her card game. "Are you about ready to go?"

"She's not going home with you tonight." Colt's grandma leaned forward. "She's coming home with me. We're having a girls' night."

Troy's brows lifted. "Are we taking it all the way back to teenage slumber parties now?"

"Why shouldn't we?" Muriel collected the cards and shuffled them. "What's the point of being old if you can't have any fun?"

Troy turned to Colt's mom. "Do you want me to take them?"

Colt's grandmother technically still drove, but only in town, so she relied on Colt's mom to bring her up to Gertrude's. And Gertrude still hadn't been cleared to drive after breaking her hip, so they were a whole hell of a lot like teenagers.

Reliant on other people for transportation and obsessed with hot guys.

Pam shook her head. "I've got to head that way anyway." She rinsed out the coffee pot and dropped the filter full of used grounds into the trash. "Plus, I'm not sure you'd be able to get them all out of the back of your pickup truck."

"Maybe I should have held onto my car a little longer." She'd returned the small SUV a few days into her stay at Troy's house. She wasn't really using it anymore, and she needed to save every penny she could to make sure she had enough to finish getting her grandmother's house back in order. It was the least she could do since she was the reason her grandmother didn't have the money to do it herself.

"We would have figured it out." Gertrude lifted her cane in the air, wedging the end under Muriel's butt. "We probably could've gotten in there, but you might have had to pry us out."

Amelie grinned as her grandmother laughed, cackling along with her three new friends. Somehow they'd managed to come across two women who were almost exactly like Muriel. They were fast friends and already thick as thieves.

It was freaking fantastic.

And one more thing she could blame entirely on Troy.

Without him, her grandmother would still be sitting at home alone in her house.

Without him, that house would still be cold and collapsing around her.

And without him, Amelie would be right next to her grandmother, freezing her ass off while she tried to get some sleep on the lumpy couch, worried about how in the hell she was going to fix the mess she walked into.

The mess she was indirectly responsible for.

"I'm not going to argue with you." Troy stretched, wincing a little at the movement. "I'm too tired."

"Well then go the hell home and go to bed and leave the partying for us spry folks." Muriel didn't take her eyes off her cards. "I'll get with you tomorrow."

Amelie collected her coat and purse, layering on her scarf and hat before zipping up and heading out into the cool night. Troy's truck was still warm, so the bite of the chilly air didn't linger as they made their way back down the mountain to Cross Creek.

As they drove, Troy told her about everything they accomplished on the house, and what they had left to do, keeping her up to date on the progress of the project that somehow now sat squarely on his shoulders.

"I can come help you." Amelie studied him across the cab. "I don't expect you to do this all by yourself."

"I'm not all by myself." Troy stopped, going silent.

"Is it weird to say that?"

He nodded. "A little."

"Is everything still okay with Griffin?" She was glad Troy's father was back in his life, and hopeful that Griffin really was all he appeared to be. But a tiny part of her still worried. Still wondered if all this was going to end up the way Troy deserved for it to be.

"It's been interesting hearing about his life." Troy eased into the driveway leading to his little farmhouse. "It kind of sounds like leaving my mom behind was the best thing he ever did."

There was an edge of hurt in Troy's voice, because his mom wasn't the only one Griffin left behind. Unknowingly, but still.

"I'm sure if he had it all to do over again things would be different."

"I'd like to think so, but I'll never really know." Troy pulled into his spot behind the house and parked. "And I guess it shouldn't matter."

"It does matter though."

She'd tried apologizing to her grandmother the first night she was back. Muriel made it clear there was nothing to apologize for because if she had it to do all over again, she would've done it the exact same way. Knowing her grandmother had no regrets eased a little bit of her own.

For Troy it would be the opposite. Knowing Griffin would change the past might ease a little of his own pain. It might help him to know he was always wanted by someone.

Amelie slid from the truck, her new boots gripping tight as she moved over the snow-covered gravel, the quiet feeling peaceful instead of eerie.

It was odd how quickly she'd acclimated to the differences between Montana and New York. It no longer seemed quite as barren here. The dark didn't feel quite as consuming and the cold wind didn't make her skin ache quite the way it did those first couple of days.

But she was still ready to get into the heat of the house and rushed inside as soon as Troy opened the door.

"Is it just me, or does the house seem too quiet?" Amelie hung her coat in the closet before grabbing Troy's and hanging it beside hers.

"I don't know if you've noticed this, but your grandma makes a lot of noise." Troy kicked off his boots before eyeing the stairs. "I'm gonna go take a quick shower."

Amelie looked him over, this time letting her eyes linger

wherever they wanted. "You should do that. You're looking a little chalky."

"Wait till you see the house." Troy started up towards the second floor. "You're going to be dusting it forever."

Amelie watched him go, her chest pulling tighter with each step he took.

Of course she wouldn't stay in Troy's house once Muriel's place was finished. Why would she?

It's not like they were anything.

Specifically.

Which was what she was supposed to want.

Did want.

For the most part.

As the sound of the shower kicked on, Amelie forced herself from the bottom of the stairs, moving into the kitchen that was familiar and inviting in a way few other spaces had been in her life.

She'd lived with Trevor most of her time in New York, but his apartment always felt exactly like what it was.

His.

She was always nothing more than a guest, one he barely tolerated by the end.

But Troy never made her feel that way. His home was her home. And his bed was her bed. He welcomed her into his world even though she'd done everything possible to pretend she didn't want any part of it.

But now here she was, facing down the day she would have to leave this place.

Leave him.

And it didn't seem quite as freeing as she expected.

EIGHTEEN

TROY

"WHAT'S GOING ON here?" Troy made his way into the kitchen, feeling a little more human after scrubbing off under a hot shower and shaving away the stubble making his face itch.

But that feeling was nothing compared to the one tightening his chest as he watched Amelie working at the counter in his kitchen.

"I figured you might be hungry." She turned toward him, balancing a bowl in each hand. "But my options were pretty limited."

Troy took both bowls from her, peeking in at the steaming contents. "You managed pretty well considering I haven't been to the grocery store in a week and a half."

He paused beside the table, then kept walking, skipping the hard wood chairs in favor of something more comfortable.

"This was what I lived on in art school." Amelie followed him out to the living room, carrying a set of spoons and forks. "I was broke as hell and ramen noodles are cheap, so I learned how to dress them up."

Troy set the bowls down on the coffee table. "I have eaten a fair bit of ramen myself." He tipped his head toward the couch. "Okay if we eat out here?"

Amelie smiled wide. "I love eating in front of the television." She dropped down onto the cushions, curling her legs under her as she got comfy. "I don't think I've ever sat on your couch before."

"That's because your grandmother is always here." Troy eased down beside her before passing over one of the bowls. "She's pretty much laid claim to this room."

Amelie picked up her fork, stirring around the meat and vegetables she'd added to the cheap grocery staple. "It sounds like she'll be back in her own house pretty soon, so you'll get your television back."

He shrugged, trying to make it seem like he was less bothered by the thought of them leaving than he was. "I don't watch much television anyway."

Amelie snagged the remote from the coffee table. "Good. Then you won't mind if I'm the one who picks what we watch."

"I don't mind at all." He would watch whatever horrible shows she wanted, as long as he got to sit here with her. They hadn't had an evening like this before. For the same reason Amelie hadn't yet sat on his couch.

All their time was spent upstairs.

In his bed.

Which he didn't mind, but this was different. This made what they had feel more real. Like it was more than just sex. And it was. At least for him, and he was willing to bet it was for Amelie too.

Even if she wouldn't admit it.

Troy dug into his bowl of soup, collecting a little bit of the broccoli and steak she'd incorporated, slurping it down while Amelie worked through the menu of his television.

"For a guy who doesn't watch TV you sure do have a decent

number of options." Amelie seemed to find what she was looking for and set the program to play.

"Honestly, the place came with pretty much all of it." Troy slid his bowl onto the table before going back to the kitchen to retrieve drinks. "All the televisions on the ranch share subscriptions."

He came back into the living room with two bottles of water to find Amelie staring at him, her mouth dropped open wide.

"You're a Netflix thief?"

He grinned, passing one of the bottles off to her. "Does it count if I've never watched it?"

Amelie eyed him. "I'll have to think about that."

Troy retrieved his bowl and settled back in. "You think about it. I'm going to eat."

Amelie was right when she assumed he was hungry. He was starving. They'd worked through lunch, all of them eager to get done early so they could get back to Cross Creek.

But Griffin seemed to have his own reasons for rushing through the day. Not that he'd shared them. Even after a few weeks, the man who was his father still held quite a bit close. He'd shared plenty about his business and what it entailed, but anything more personal than that Griffin kept to himself.

And it made it hard to feel like he was more than just a friend he shared DNA with.

The television started to play, stealing a little of Troy's attention and pulling it toward the screen. He watched for a minute, more and more confused by what he was seeing as the seconds ticked past. "What in the hell are we watching?"

"You said I could watch whatever I wanted." Amelie kicked her feet up on the table and sucked down a mouthful of noodles. "Now you have to live with your life choices."

"Is that what this is?" He looked over where Amelie was

stretched out across his couch, watching his TV, eating his food. "Living with my life choices?"

"Yup." She fished a hunk of broccoli from her bowl and popped it into her mouth. "So you're just gonna have to deal with it."

Her eyes went back to the television screen, watching as what appeared to be a group of vampires led their undead lives in a house on Staten Island.

Troy smiled. "I guess it could be worse."

Amelie snorted out a laugh, leaning closer until the side of her body rested against his. That was how they sat while they ate, watching a show he had no intention of following because he was too busy enjoying the moment.

Enjoying her.

Amelie tipped up her bowl as the episode ended, drinking down the last of her broth before setting it on the coffee table. "I forgot how much I love ramen." She leaned back against the cushions, tilting her head toward him. "I actually forgot a lot of stuff I think."

"Like what?"

Amelie, like his dad, hadn't opened up a whole lot about her personal life. And while he was interested to know the man he came from, he was desperate to know more about Amelie.

More about her life in New York.

More about what made her leave it behind.

"Well, I forgot how much I like Montana, for starters." She yawned, slouching a little deeper on the cushions. "I think I got used to New York because that was where I always thought I was going to live, but I never really loved it there."

"I've never been to New York."

Amelie sighed. "You're not missing much." She smiled. "But I'm probably just saying that because of everything that happened there."

He waited for her to elaborate, but Amelie went quiet.

"What happened?"

He didn't want to pry, but knowing why Amelie left New York might tell him something he desperately needed to know.

How to make her stay in Montana.

How to make her stay with him.

He might not have the big family Colt did, but it was no longer just him he was bringing to the table. Now he had Griffin, and it seemed like his dad wanted to be a part of his life. He'd extended his stay more than once and worked hard to make sure they spent time together. And he had friends. Colt and Winter. Ben and Liza. They might not be actual family, but they were starting to feel close.

Hopefully close enough to count.

Amelie chewed her lower lip for a second, leaving him wondering if she would give him what he wanted.

"I moved to New York to go to art school." She reached out to trace the lines printed on his pajama pants as she continued. "It was my dream to move there and become an artist, but my parents thought it was a stupid career choice and refused to pay for my education. They wanted me to go to school in Colorado. Major in something soul crushing like finance or business management." She followed the path of a single red line, tracing down the top of his thigh. "My grandmother was the only person who believed in me. Who thought I was making the right decision." Amelie's finger stopped. "So she paid for my school." Her eyes lifted to Troy's. "That's why she didn't have the money to fix up her house. She spent her nest egg on me."

"What about your grandpa?" When Ben and Liza first met Muriel she said her husband had only been gone for a little while, so he had to have been a part of what happened. "What did he think about all of it?"

Amelie's expression fell. "He had dementia. He was already

pretty bad when I graduated high school, but I went to a community college for a couple of years to shut my parents up." She rubbed her lips together, expression sad. "By the time I finished there he was all but gone and my grandmother made me that offer." She grabbed his arm, holding tight. "If I had known it was all they had when she gave it to me, I never would have taken it."

Amelie's lower lip quivered the tiniest bit. "So it's actually my fault that her house looks the way it does. If she hadn't helped me, she would have had the money she needed to keep it nice." Amelie blew out a shaky breath, blinking a few times. "So, I'm the one you should really be mad at. She wouldn't let anyone in because she was protecting me. She didn't want people to know that I was the reason she couldn't afford to keep the place up."

Troy didn't think, he just reacted, reaching out to pull Amelie close. She came easily, curling against him, resting across his lap as she sniffled into his shoulder.

"I'm about to tell you some things you aren't going to want to hear, but I want you to listen to them anyway." He stroked down the soft strands of her hair, doing his best to comfort her even though he wasn't entirely sure what something like that should look like.

"I haven't known your grandmother for long, but even I know that when she decides to do something, there's no talking her out of it." Muriel was about as stubborn as they came, and if she wanted to make sure Amelie had the opportunity to live her dream, then it was going to happen. "There's no way you could have talked her out of it. She wasn't going to take no for an answer."

Muriel was one of the most determined people he'd ever met, and that characteristic definitely carried down to her granddaughter. Amelie had been hell bent that she was going to take on the repairs of Muriel's house. She fully intended to repay her grandmother for the sacrifice she made. And one way or another, Amelie would have figured out how to fix every single problem there was.

Luckily, she didn't have to. That meant she could get back to doing what she enjoyed. Painting. Which she attacked with the same focus and drive.

"I know she would have done it no matter what, but I still feel guilty." Amelie curled a little closer, resting one hand against the center of his chest. "Especially since I wasn't really doing much painting anymore in New York."

Troy tucked his chin so he could peek down at her. "Why not?"

Muriel loved to brag about Amelie. Loved to tell everyone they met about all the shows she had and how her work was featured in galleries across the city. But finding out that Amelie wasn't painting made him wonder if Muriel hadn't been the only one glossing over the truth of their situation.

"Because I'm stupid." Amelie's tone was low. "I started dating the owner of this big gallery." She paused, chewing on her lower lip. "He's the reason I don't like flowers. He acted like they should fix everything, but they're the least personal gift you can give someone."

"So he was an ass."

Amelie's face twisted in consideration. "Not always. At the beginning he was really enthusiastic about my work, but as time went on he pushed me to focus more on actually running the gallery instead of filling it, so that's what happened." One of Amelie's fingers traced across the center of his chest. "I did exactly what I said I wouldn't do and let someone else dictate my life and my dreams."

"And your dream is to be an artist?"

Amelie was quiet for a minute, her finger continuing to

create a path over his skin just like it had over the plaid of his pants. "Yes."

Troy slid his hand through her hair, the quiet moment so much more than he could have ever expected it would be. This was the closeness he'd been chasing his whole life. This was what he'd been wanting for longer than he could remember. Someone who trusted him enough to tell him their dreams. Someone who looked to him to provide comfort. Someone who was there because they chose him.

Unfortunately, the last part was still up in the air.

Muriel's house was almost done. Would be finished in another week. Then he would find out if he finally had everything he wanted.

Or he would end up alone again, sitting on his couch, wishing this moment could come back.

Amelie sniffled as she lifted her eyes to his. "Was it your dream to be a cowboy?"

Troy hesitated, not wanting to drag his own history into this moment.

To muddy the waters by bringing in his own shortfalls and insecurities.

"I've always been better at working with my hands than I have working with my head." It was the easiest way to explain his struggles and the choices they left him.

Amelie smiled softly. "Me too." She huffed out a little laugh. "School was so tedious and boring to me so I had a really hard time."

"I'm sure you could have done it if you wanted to." Amelie was brilliant, and he didn't believe for a second that she struggled because of inability.

She shrugged. "Maybe, but what's worse? Failing because you tried and couldn't, or failing because you didn't even want to try?"

Her question cut straight into him, slicing down to the very core.

He wanted Amelie to stay. Wanted her in his bed even when she could go back to Billings. But asking her not to leave would be a risk. One that could end up breaking his heart.

But what would be worse? Having a broken heart because he failed? Or having a broken heart because he willingly let her go?

It might not even matter.

Because they would both hurt the same.

NINETEEN

AMELIE

"GOOD MORNING." TROY'S voice was rough with sleep, but his touch was soft as it slid up and down her spine.

"Good morning." Amelie reached up to rub at one eye, wincing a little when her finger dragged across yesterday's mascara. "Did I pass out on the couch?"

A low chuckle rumbled through Troy's chest, the sound deep and comforting. "You crashed harder than I've ever seen anyone crash without the help of a serious amount of alcohol."

A yawn started when she opened her mouth, forcing her to wait it out to explain. "I think everything is finally catching up with me."

And she did mean everything.

It wasn't just all the work she'd done at the house or the time she was spending painting Gertrude's wall. It wasn't even the weight of what happened in New York that had been wearing on her.

This went back farther than that.

"I'm sorry I dumped all my shit on you last night." She'd dropped just about every bit of mess she possessed right in

Troy's lap, confessing her deepest darkest while sniffing against his chest.

Which wasn't like her at all.

No one knew about her grandmother paying for her education besides her immediate family. She never told Evelyn, and she sure as hell never told Trevor. It wasn't their business. She didn't want them to think less of her, and she certainly didn't want them to think less of her grandmother.

But it felt like Troy would understand. Like he wouldn't judge her or hold it against her the way she continued to hold it against herself.

"Don't apologize for that." Troy pulled her a little closer. "I'm glad you told me."

Amelie snuggled her face tighter to his chest. "Okay."

Waking up next to him this morning was different. They'd shared his bed more than a few times, but never quite like this. This time it wasn't about sex or physical attraction. And it wasn't because there was nowhere else to sleep. She could have easily stayed on the couch or in the recliner.

They were in bed together because that was where they wanted to be.

Together.

"We should probably get moving." Troy didn't budge, just continued sliding his palm up and down her back. "I've got to go out and meet Colt and Ben at the barn to check on the animals, and then head out to work on Muriel's place."

Amelie rubbed her lips together as she tried to decide if the clench in her stomach was from excitement or fear.

Probably a little of both.

"I could go with you." The tightness in her belly intensified as she waited for Troy's reaction.

They were in a confusing spot. One she wasn't quite sure how they reached. They'd slept together almost every night she'd been in Montana, and when they were alone things seemed so easy.

So simple.

But this wasn't a simple situation. Far from it.

There was someone else involved. Someone she would never want to let down. Someone Troy desperately needed in his life, whether he would admit it or not.

That meant he would have to be the one to decide if what they had ever moved outside of his bedroom.

He studied her face. "Is that what you want to do?"

His tone gave nothing away. Didn't hint at how he felt about her tagging along in a way that would make it more difficult to deny that it wasn't just friendship between them.

"I'd rather go with you than be here by myself all day." She stopped short of telling him the whole truth—That as much fun as she had hanging out with Muriel and Gertrude and the women in Colt's life, she was missing the time they spent together. Missing feeling like she and Troy were a little bit of a team.

Like he was there with her and she was there with him.

"It gets real cold out there while we feed the horses." Troy's free hand came to slide along her cheek. "Are you sure that's what you want to do?"

"I'll be fine." Again, she couldn't make herself admit that she wanted to be there.

With him.

It felt too risky. For him.

For her.

Troy's lips lifted in a smile. "You better dress warm then, Miss Amelie." He swatted her on the butt before flipping the covers back. "Don't want you to freeze that sweet ass of yours off."

Amelie climbed out of bed and dug through her suitcase,

searching for the long underwear she picked up at the store the same day she bought the boots that now kept her feet toasty warm in the snow. She held the base layer up. "So I should wear these?"

His lips twisted into a pulse pounding smirk. "I'm a little disappointed I've never seen you in those before."

Amelie rolled her eyes. "Right. Because they're so sexy."

Troy slowly prowled toward her. "Sweetheart, you could look sexy in a garbage bag." He snagged her around the waist, pulling her close. "I might even pay money to see it."

She looped both arms around his neck, relaxing against him. "I'll keep that in mind when the credit card statements start coming in."

Troy's expression sobered, turning serious. "I can help you with those."

"I'm pretty sure you've already done more than enough." She hadn't worked up the nerve to ask who paid for the roof yet.

Not that she couldn't already guess.

Troy's eyes held hers. "Your grandmother is the first person to really make me feel like I was needed." He paused for just a second. "Like they wanted me around." He barely shook his head. "There will never be enough I can do to repay her for that."

The love he had for her grandmother made Amelie's stomach tight and only dug her resolution to protect that relationship at all costs deeper.

"That's not something you have to repay a person for."

Troy lifted his brows. "Isn't that what you're doing?"

Was it?

"That's not why I'm fixing her house up." Entirely. "I don't feel like I owe her for loving me."

She did owe her grandmother for other things though.

And most of them she could never repay with money or repairs.

Amelie tapped one finger in the center of Troy's chest. "And you shouldn't feel like you owe her for loving you either."

Accepting that her grandmother loved Troy was terrifying.

It meant she had to realize her feelings for him were secondary.

And so were his feelings for her.

"THEY ARE WAY bigger than I expected them to be." Amelie stared down the line of stalls as Colt and Troy worked through them. A few horses peeked out over the gates, impatiently waiting their turn.

Colt glanced her way as he carried a bale of hay across the aisle. "You've never seen a horse before?"

Of course she'd seen a horse before. "Not this close."

She'd seen plenty of horses driving around, but had never come face-to-face with one, which probably seemed pretty crazy to the men who built their lives around the animals.

Colt snapped the ties on the bale and started passing out servings. "You can get closer. All the horses in this barn are friendly."

That was an interesting way to say it. "In *this* barn?"

Colt gave her a lopsided grin. "You heard me right."

Amelie inched back, putting some more distance between herself and the giant animals that could probably kill her with a few well-placed stomps.

She nearly jumped out of her skin when something brushed up against her leg, tipping to one side as she stumbled away.

From a cat.

The little tabby cocked its head and meowed at her in a way

that sounded a whole lot like she was calling her dramatic. Amelie crouched down and tentatively reached one hand toward the feline, just to be sure she was as friendly as she seemed. The cat sniffed her fingers then immediately rubbed its head into her palm, purring steadily. "You're a sweetie, aren't you?" Amelie scratched the cat's head a few seconds before deciding to try to pick her up. The cat meowed again but didn't fight as Amelie scooped her from the floor and held her against her chest.

Troy watched from where he was helping Colt, his eyes staying on her as the cat rubbed against the underside of her chin.

"Looks like you're makin' friends." Colt dumped the last of the straw into the final stall.

Amelie cuddled the cat closer. "What's her name?"

Colt's brows came together. "She's a barn cat."

"So?" Amelie looked between the two men. "You don't name your barn cats?"

"Don't have time." Colt nodded toward the door. "And don't have enough names."

Amelie turned in the direction he tipped his head to find a line of cats loitering around the partially-open door. "Holy crap. There's a lot of them."

"We do our best to keep the population down." Troy moved close, reaching out to stroke along the cat's back. "But we can't catch all of them. Some are too mean."

"So they just keep having babies?" Amelie noticed a couple of their middles did seem a little larger than they should be. "You'll end up with a million of them."

"That's what I said." Colt bent down to snag one of the friendlier cats, tucking it under one arm as he passed and pointing a finger at Troy. "But this one won't stop feeding them so they just keep coming."

Amelie frowned out at the herd growing larger by the minute. "How many are there?"

"Too damn many." Colt opened a giant bin and scooped out a pile of dry food, carrying it around to dump it into a few wide-based bowls set in the corner. "But Troy's got a soft spot for strays, so we just keep takin' them in."

Troy was silent at her side, his big hand still softly stroking the cat in her arms.

Of course he took in all the strays.

He was one himself.

Unwanted. Unloved.

No one to depend on. No one to trust.

She looked down at the sweet and affectionate cat purring loudly as it soaked up any attention it could get. Probably because she never knew when it might come again.

"Poppy."

Troy's blue eyes lifted to hers. "What?"

"I think her name should be Poppy." Amelie pointed to a big, white, fluffy cat that was clearly one of the more skittish of the group. "And that one should be Marshmallow."

The cats all needed names. They all mattered and they all deserved to be recognized. Whether they were jaded and sour from the hand life dealt them, like Marshmallow, or still desperate for love and attachment like Poppy.

She scanned the swarm as they rushed in to eat the food Colt piled into their dishes. There had to be at least twenty cats of all different colors and sizes. "I might have to make a list for the rest."

"Careful, Troy." Colt shot him a grin. "She'll have 'em all in your house if you blink too long."

Amelie pressed her lips together as she looked around the barn. "They already have someplace to stay, right?"

Troy was quiet for a minute. "Nowhere specific."

Colt laughed, his head tipping back. "I'm callin' it now. You're gonna have five cats in that house before the month's out."

Amelie watched as Colt walked out the door, still chuckling to himself.

"I won't try to bring cats into your house." She said it just in case Troy was worried his friend was right.

Troy reached out to slide one hand over the knit hat covering her head. "I wouldn't stop you if you did." He glanced at the cats. "Unless it was Marshmallow. He's kind of an asshole." Troy lifted his brows. "But he's one hell of a mouser, so I guess I might even let him stay."

She couldn't tell if he was kidding or not. The words sounded like he might be joking, but the way he said them was so serious she almost thought he'd be okay if she lured the fluffy white cat inside.

"I won't try to bring Marshmallow into the house." Amelie glanced down at where the big cat sat in the corner, keeping his distance from everyone. "But it would probably be nice if he had somewhere warm to sleep at night." She shivered a little as the cold started to seep through the layers Troy insisted she pile on to come out to the barns. "It's probably freezing out here when it's dark."

Troy eyed her. "You know the chickens are out here in the cold too, right?"

"The chickens have a coop." She stood a little straighter. "With heat lamps."

She'd gotten a basic tour of the grounds surrounding Troy's farmhouse this morning, and while the animals were technically outside, they all had a dedicated shelter and bedding to get them through the frigid temperatures.

Including the cows.

"You want to build a house for the cats?" Again, Troy's tone left her no clue as to whether he thought the idea was brilliant or a complete waste of time and resources.

"I think they deserve a home." Amelie crouched down as another of the cats started to circle her legs. "They keep the mice out of your barns, right?"

Troy's gaze held hers a second before dropping to the cat still in her arms. He crouched down beside her to offer a pet to the one rubbing against her leg. "You know what you want it to look like?"

Amelie pursed her lips. "Not specifically."

Troy's focus stayed on her face. "I guess we'll have to make some plans then."

TWENTY

TROY

"I THINK THEY'RE already starting to get spoiled." Troy shook his head as a line of cats rushed from the wood structure he'd convinced Colt, Ben, and Griffin to help him build beside the barn.

It had only taken them a day to put the whole thing together, which was unfortunate since he was hoping to delay finishing Muriel's house as long as possible. But his friends and his father were workhorses, and they'd busted their asses, thinking Muriel was miserable being away from home.

"They're not spoiled." Amelie crouched down as Marshmallow slinked his way out the door, stretching his back legs one at a time. "They're happy." She held out her gloved hand, a small pile of treats stacked in the center of her palm, holding perfectly still as the large white cat watched her with the same wary gaze he'd given her every morning for the past week.

"I think you're wasting your time." Out of all of the cats that had shown up at Cross Creek, Marshmallow was the most feral of them all.

And the meanest.

He'd tried to trap him a handful of times, hoping to get the aging tomcat looked over by a vet, but the minute the trap's door slammed behind him, Marshmallow lost every bit of shit the good Lord gave him, scratching and biting anything that attempted to get close. He hadn't yet attacked Amelie, but Troy couldn't imagine the possibility of bodily harm would be as much of a deterrent for her as it should be.

Amelie held her position for every bit of ten minutes, staying perfectly still until her outstretched arm finally started to droop. She let out the same sigh of resignation he'd watched her produce every morning since she discovered the fuzzy gang that prowled the property.

"I was really hoping he would come to me today." She tossed the fish-shaped treats in Marshmallow's direction before standing up, watching with a frown as he immediately jumped forward to scarf them down. "I would give you more if you'd come to me, you little turd."

"Liar." Troy grinned. "You'll give him more anyway."

As soon as Marshmallow polished off the snacks he looked up at Amelie and meowed, the sound raspy enough to show his age. Amelie groaned, digging out a few more treats and tossing them his way. "You didn't have to make me a liar so quickly."

Troy shook his head as the white ball of fluff wolfed down the rest of the snacks. "I do believe we found someone more stubborn than you are."

Amelie rolled her eyes, bumping him a little as she passed. "That's because I'm not stubborn." She marched toward the barn, the crowd of cats falling in line behind her. They knew she dished out food with a heavier hand than any of the cowboys so they tended to stick to Amelie like glue.

Troy watched as Amelie fed and watered them, taking the time to offer head pets and back rubs to anyone that would tolerate it. The whole process took a hell of a lot longer than it did when he was in charge of it, but she seemed to enjoy it just as much as the cats did. If indulging her in this simple pleasure meant it took him a little longer to get started on the rest of the day's tasks, so be it.

Amelie finished up, dusting off her hands before sliding her gloves back on. She gave him a small smile. "I guess I'm ready."

At least one of them was.

They went back to his house and collected Muriel, loading her into his truck before heading to Billings. The trip seemed way shorter than he remembered it, and by the time they pulled into the driveway of Muriel's house, he was even less ready to be there than he was when they left.

Troy helped Muriel out, walking her up the sidewalk and the stairs before unlocking the door and stepping back. This was the moment he'd wanted. A reveal he'd imagined many times since he met her and realized the house she hid from him was in desperate need of help he could provide.

Then Amelie showed up, and his desire to finish Muriel's house dwindled a little more every day. But now it was done. And thanks to Colt, Ben, and Griffin, it was done much faster than he'd hoped.

Muriel stepped inside, her eyes wide as she looked around the refreshed space. "You painted."

"I figured we might as well do it while we were in here." He'd actually come up with any little projects he could to drag the whole thing out. They'd cleaned the carpet, painted the walls and ceilings, snaked out drains and scrubbed floors.

But there came a point where he had to admit there was nothing left to do.

Where he had to let Muriel go home and go back to the life he had.

The life where he came home to an empty house.

Where his television sat dark and unused.

Where he slept alone.

"I love this color." Muriel reached out to pat the pale shade of green on the walls. "It's so relaxing. Like a spa."

"Amelie picked that out." He turned back to where Amelie was following behind him, her warm gaze resting on Muriel.

She'd been thrilled when he took her through the house last night. Excited to see the home from her childhood brought back from the brink. And normally, he would have been happy to give it to her. But finishing this house meant putting distance back between them, and he was just starting to feel like they were finally finding their footing together.

He was just starting to show Amelie what a life at his side could be like.

Now that was being ripped away.

"I can't believe everything you accomplished in a few weeks." Muriel moved into the living room, heading for the stairs. "This place might look better than it did when we bought it." She reached the base of the steps and started up, moving easily to the top.

Amelie stared up at her in disbelief. "Did you just walk up those stairs?"

Muriel's eyes widened a little. "Did I?" She looked down at Amelie from the landing, expression filled with surprise. "Huh. Looks like I did." She turned to the first of the bedrooms and disappeared inside.

"That lying—"

"I'm not sure I'd say *lying*." He'd been around Muriel long enough to know that she hadn't always been able to go up and down the stairs. "I'd say conniving is a better word."

He couldn't be mad at her because they were doing the same thing.

He and Amelie worked hard to hide what was going on between them from Muriel, keeping their hands off each other when she was around and doing their best to act like they were nothing more than friends.

Amelie gaped up the stairs a second longer before her lips lifted in a small smile. She shook her head. "I should have known. She's too nosy not to know what was going on up there."

"It looks lovely." Muriel moved across the landing and into the other bedroom. "It is just beautiful."

The upstairs did look fantastic. The ceilings were new, but everything else was the same, maybe with a fresh coat of paint or polyurethane, but what was there had always been there. He'd even managed to salvage most of the wood furniture, giving it a good scrub with Murphy's Oil Soap before setting it back up. It was the easiest way to keep costs down.

And since it was Amelie's money he was spending, he did everything possible to blow through as little as possible.

Muriel came out to stand at the top of the stairs, squinting down at the hardwood beneath her feet. "I forgot there were wood floors up here."

They'd taken all the carpet out of the second floor and the stairs leading to it, choosing to clean up the existing hardwood instead of splurging on new carpet. The hardwood was prettier anyway.

At the end of the day, they hadn't spent nearly as much as he expected, so hopefully Amelie had plenty of money left to build the new life she was wanting.

"I'm glad you like it." Amelie watched as Muriel came back down to the first floor, easily scaling the steps. "I tried to pick out colors I thought you would like."

"You didn't have to do that." Muriel reached the bottom and gave Amelie's shoulder a pat. "I meant it when I told you to do whatever you wanted." She glanced Troy's way before refocusing on Amelie. "You have fantastic taste."

Amelie rolled her eyes. "I'm not sure I would say that." She gave Muriel a soft smile. "But it does seem to be getting better."

Muriel clapped her hands together, spinning toward her bedroom. "Let's talk about what you're going to paint on my wall." She made a beeline for the back corner, flipping on the newly-installed overhead lighting in her small room. She propped both hands on her hips and looked over the space. "I was thinking we could put something inspiring on that wall right across from my bed, so I see it every morning when I wake up."

Amelie lifted her brows. "Inspiring?"

"Right. Something that makes me want to be my best self." Muriel turned toward her granddaughter, the smile on her face making it obvious whatever was about to come out of her mouth was going to be shocking as hell.

She stepped closer to Amelie, resting one hand on her shoulder. "Something like Dwayne Johnson."

―――

"THIS IS A nice little place." Griffin settled into the seat across from him, looking around their booth as the waitresses of The Wooden Spoon hustled around them. "I've driven past it a few times and always thought about stopping, but never did."

"I come here a lot." Troy didn't bother picking up the menu. He didn't need it. "Everyone in Moss Creek does."

One of the younger waitresses stopped at their table, all her focus on Griffin as she took their orders. Troy got the same thing he got every time, the daily special. It didn't matter what it was, it was always good.

Griffin ended up ordering the same thing before passing over their menus and waiting until the waitress left to continue their conversation.

"You really like living here?"

"I do. It's different here than the places I lived before." Troy glanced up as their waitress stood in the corner chatting with a couple of the other girls that worked there. "The people are different."

The women all turned and stared at his table at the same time, but it took them a second to realize Troy was watching them.

Because every one of them was looking at his dad.

"I noticed that." Griffin was oblivious to the attention he was receiving. "It was really nice of your boss to come help with Muriel's house."

"Ben's how I met Muriel. He and his wife Liza are the ones who crossed paths with her first."

Ben and Liza still went to check on Muriel and take her out whenever they could, but Cross Creek was finally starting to grow and running the ranch took a hell of a lot of effort and coordination, even now that they had a good staff on hand. Which was how Troy ended up being the one making trips to Billings. He was single and had more time on his hands.

And maybe it was because he needed Muriel as much as she needed him.

"Still. I don't know many people that would go out of their way to help someone like that." Griffin paused as their waitress came back to deliver their drinks. She batted her lashes but walked away a little disappointed when he didn't pick up on her interest in flirting.

Which was probably for the best since flirting with women in a small town like this came back to bite a man real fast.

"What made you decide to move here?" Griffin leaned back. "If you don't mind me asking."

"I don't mind at all." Hopefully Griffin would return the

favor, because right now he had a hell of a lot of unanswered questions where his father was concerned.

"I've always preferred to work with my hands." Troy laced his fingers together on the table in front of him, staring down at them as he recounted a time in his life he'd rather forget. "I never did real well in school. As a kid it was all about survival. While everyone else was figuring out who they were and what they liked, I was cooking my own food and struggling with homework I didn't understand. When they were picking out careers and doing college visits, I was working whatever job could make me enough money to take care of myself since my mother made it clear I was on my own the minute I turned eighteen."

He paused, knowing none of this would be easy for Griffin to hear.

But it needed to be said.

"I was always good at getting work done. I've done just about everything you can imagine, from roofing to framing to pouring cement and running electric.

"I didn't mind any of it, but one day I came across a listing online for a job as a ranch hand. The pay wasn't much, but the opportunity to be outside, working with animals, moving around and doing something different appealed to me. So I thought I'd try it out."

Griffin's eyes dropped. "I'm probably responsible for at least some of the troubles you had in school." He picked up the wrapper from his straw and twisted it around. "I was never particularly book smart either, but I also got into a fair bit of trouble." He tied a knot in the center of the paper, adding another as he continued. "They put me into a program in high school where I went to school half the day and went to work the other half. I ended up working at a car shop for this old man who sort of took me under his wing." Griffin glanced up.

"Sometimes I think he might've saved my life. I don't know where I would've ended up without him."

"So your parents weren't around either?" It was an invasive question, but he'd spent his whole life with only half the blanks filled in. He wanted to know what the other side looked like.

"They were off doing their own thing. Not really too interested in each other or taking care of me." Griffin finished knotting off the wrapper and dropped it to the table. "I pretty much had to fend for myself."

Part of him had hoped to find out Griffin had a big loving happy family, but hearing that his dad understood the life he led offered a different measure of comfort. The same kind of comradery he'd felt with Amelie.

"Do you have any brothers or sisters?"

Griffin shook his head. "No. Just me." He tapped one finger against the table. "Never been married either."

Troy was a little surprised by that one. "Never?"

Griffin's mouth lifted in a wry smile. "Never been good at spreading my attention out." He took a sip of his drink. "I probably wasted my best years working my ass off to make sure I would never be poor again."

"That's unfortunate." Troy leaned back as their food was delivered. "I was hoping I might ask you for some advice."

The waitress slid Griffin's plate into place, lingering with a wide smile. "Can I get you anything else?"

"I think we're set." Griffin glanced at Troy. "You good?"

"I'm good." Troy tipped his head at the waitress as her smile froze. "Thank you."

"Well just let me know if I can get you anything else." She gave Griffin another glance before leaving.

Griffin forked off a chunk of his meatloaf, sopping it through the sweet glaze drizzled over the top. "I'm not sure you should be asking me for any kind of advice when it comes to women."

"I'm startin' to figure that out." Troy scooped up some mashed potatoes. "Every woman in this place has been trying to catch your eye since we walked in and you haven't noticed a single one of them."

Griffin turned, looking over the line of waitresses suddenly pretending to be wiping tables and checking salt shakers. "They're all twelve."

Troy nearly choked on his food. "They're not twelve, I can promise you that." He pointed his fork at his dad. "Each and every one of them can buy alcohol."

Griffin stared at him. "I'm not interested in girls that should be dating my son." He shoved in his bite, continuing to talk around it. "And unfortunately, the women I would love to date see me coming and realize I'm more trouble than I'm worth."

It was one more similarity he could see between himself and the man across the table.

But while Griffin didn't have advice to offer, Troy might. He leaned forward, handing over the tiny bit of wisdom he'd recently acquired.

"You've just got to find one that likes strays."

TWENTY-ONE
AMELIE

AMELIE STARED UP at the brand-new ceiling, listening to the annoying sounds of the neighborhood outside the window.

She flopped to her side, adjusting the pillow and blanket as she tried to get comfortable enough to fall back asleep.

But ten minutes later she was still awake.

Still pouting.

Still crabby that she had the whole bed to herself.

And that made her feel guilty. She should be thrilled that her grandmother's house was livable and reassembled. She should be happy they were back where they started and now had all the time she wanted to figure out where her life was headed next.

But that was not how she felt. Not even close.

Amelie kicked back the covers and slid her feet to the floor, silently walking out to the landing and down the stairs before creeping into the kitchen to start a pot of coffee.

"What are you doing up so early?"

Amelie stumbled back, hand flying to her chest as her heart did its best to spring free. "Why in the hell would you sneak up on me like that?"

Muriel came into the small kitchen, looking a little too bright-eyed considering the sun was still a couple hours from coming up. "I'm over eighty years old. I don't sneak." She took the carafe from Amelie's hand and stuck it under the faucet. "And you didn't answer my question. Why are you awake? It's barely five."

Amelie tipped back to lean against the counter. "I couldn't sleep."

Muriel poured water into the back of the maker before sliding the carafe into place. "Me either. I never realized how loud it was here." She added a filter and a pile of coffee grounds before switching the machine on. "So many damn cars going up and down the street all the time."

"Right?" Amelie raked one hand through her hair. "It's like they just drive back and forth all night long."

Muriel turned, looking her up and down. "I thought you liked the big city?"

Amelie pressed her lips together, fighting the urge to give her grandmother the truth. But Muriel deserved it. She had every right to know that her investment was a bust.

"I didn't love New York." Amelie winced a little, hating that she'd successfully proven her father right. "And I don't think I was ever really talented enough to be what I wanted to be."

Muriel stared at her for a few long, silent seconds, her eyes narrowing more and more. She was upset, and Amelie couldn't blame her. Her grandmother risked everything to help make her dream come true.

But that's all it was. A dream. One she simply could never make a reality.

"Now you listen to me, Amelie Grace Gable." Muriel came closer, practically getting right up in her face. "Just because it doesn't immediately work out the way you planned, doesn't mean you weren't cut out for it." Her eyes were sharp behind her glasses. "Your dream was to be an artist. You went to the place you thought that was most likely to happen." Muriel's chin lifted as she continued to stare her down. "But just because it didn't happen there, doesn't mean it won't happen anywhere."

"But that's why you paid for my school. So I could go to New York and have shows and sell my work in galleries."

Muriel propped both hands on her hips. "And you've done that."

"I did that because the man I was dating made it happen." Amelie grabbed the pot of coffee and poured herself a cup. "Not because I was talented enough." She slumped back against the counter. "He knew that was what I wanted and used it to get me to go out with him."

"Do you really think that man would put his reputation on the line by hosting a show for an artist who didn't have talent?" Muriel clearly thought she was onto something.

But she wasn't.

"Yes." Amelie took a big swig of her creamerless coffee, wincing at the sharpness as it moved down her throat. "He's hosting a show for his new girlfriend and she's terrible."

Muriel's brows slowly lifted. "Is she really terrible or are you just biased?"

It was a question she didn't want to dig deep enough to answer honestly.

She didn't want to be that girl. The one who shit on someone else just for making the same stupid mistake she did.

But...

"She slept with my boyfriend." Amelie took another bitter swallow of coffee. "In my bed."

"And thank the good Lord for that because he was about as worthless as tits on a boar hog." Muriel tipped her head forward, peering across the top of her glasses. "The way I look at it, that woman did you a favor. Got you to make a move you wouldn't have done otherwise."

That couldn't be true. She'd been talking about leaving Trevor for months. Even looked at a few apartments and put out a few applications.

But leaving Trevor wasn't simple. He wasn't just her boyfriend. He was the reason she had a place to live and money in the bank. Breaking off their relationship would have left her homeless and relying on the money in her savings account to live.

A lot like now.

So maybe her grandmother was right after all.

"It doesn't really matter anyway. It's not like I can move back to New York now. I don't have a job. I don't have a place to live." She gave up on drinking her coffee black and went to the fridge, adding in a healthy dose of sweet cream. "And all the contacts I had before are people who know Trevor, so I can't imagine they'll be interested in working with me now either."

Muriel crossed both arms, eyeing her. "Is that what you want? To go back to New York?"

It was *supposed* to be what she wanted.

But admitting that New York held about as much appeal as a pelvic exam felt like a betrayal. Like she didn't appreciate what her grandmother gave up for her.

Amelie turned, heading for the stairs. "I'm going back to bed."

"No you're not." Muriel worked on pouring her own cup of coffee. "You're getting dressed so you can drive me over to Gertrude's house. She's gonna tell me all about the time she slept with Kenny Rogers."

Amelie stopped and turned to face her grandma. "The '*Islands in the Stream*' guy?"

Muriel grinned. "That's the one."

Amelie pondered it for a second before finally tipping her head to one side. "Good for her I guess."

"That's what I said." Muriel carried her coffee through the living room. "I told her you would drop me off early, so we better get moving."

Amelie watched as her grandmother disappeared into her bedroom. "And why are you just now bringing this up?"

Muriel poked her head out the open door. "I figured you'd be awake early."

Amelie sucked down a few more swallows of her coffee, hoping the caffeine would give her what she needed to survive this day. "Don't get used to it. I'm not a huge fan of waking up at five in the morning."

It was another lie she was choosing to tell herself. Because when they were executed by a certain cowboy, she loved the hell out of some five AM wake-up calls.

Unfortunately, those were a thing of the past. She wasn't ditching her grandmother. Not now. Not after realizing just how lonely Muriel's life had been here in Billings.

Amelie stomped back up the steps, taking what remained of her coffee and polishing it off as she pulled on a set of long underwear and layered over a pair of jeans and a sweatshirt. Then she laced up her boots and headed back downstairs, finding her grandmother already pulling on her coat.

"Is Kenny Rogers really that exciting?" Amelie poured the rest of the coffee into a travel mug and added creamer.

"Hearing about his dick definitely is." Muriel tugged a hat onto her head. "I've never heard about a famous penis before."

"Was his penis famous?" Amelie screwed the cap onto her cup and took a sip. "Because I'm pretty sure it didn't have any recording contracts."

"I bet that thing was more well-known than you realize." Muriel wiggled her eyebrows. "If you know what I mean."

"I know what you—"

"I'm talking about sex," Muriel continued on, clearly not realizing how unappealing fornication with Kenny Rogers sounded to anyone that didn't get a senior discount at the drugstore.

"I got it." Amelie snagged her keys off the entry table before cracking open the front door and punching the button on the automatic starter of the car she picked up last night after Troy left. She slammed the door back against the cold, shivering a little as she stuffed her arms into her coat. "It might take that a minute to warm up."

She hadn't really needed a car while she was staying with Troy, but now that she was back in Billings, having a way to get around was a necessity. Especially since her grandmother seemed to be developing one hell of a social life.

"I'm going to get spoiled having someone around all the time to take me wherever I want to go." Muriel looped her handbag over one arm as she adjusted the scarf tucked around her neck. "It could be real easy to get used to."

"I wouldn't worry about it. I think I'm going to be here for the foreseeable future." Amelie grabbed her own bag, stuffing her cell phone down inside, trying to act like she wasn't giving her grandmother the answer she wanted earlier. "It'll take me forever to get all the paintings I've got booked finished."

Not that commissioned projects were the only thing keeping her in Montana. The place was really starting to grow on her. So were a few of the people in it.

"Plus, you'll always have Troy." Amelie opened the door and stepped out onto the porch. "I think you're stuck with him forever."

Muriel followed her out, looping one arm around Amelie's elbow as they made their way down the steps. "Let's hope so."

The drive to Moss Creek didn't seem nearly as long now.

She recognized everything they passed and the trip offered the perfect opportunity for her to chat with Muriel.

And Muriel had plenty to chat about.

By the time they reached the city limits, Amelie knew just about everything Muriel had found out about Gertrude and Colt's grandmother's lives. The three women definitely enjoyed spending time together, which made it even more unfortunate that they'd had to move back to Billings.

When she did finally break down and go back to New York, Muriel would be stuck forty-five minutes away from her new best friends. And relying on Troy to continue making that trip wasn't fair.

But maybe there was another option.

"Would you consider leaving Billings?" It was a touchy subject considering what happened the last time someone tried to get her grandmother to move, but it was worth a shot.

"Well I'm not moving to New York if that's what you're asking." Muriel's feathers were immediately ruffled and it made Amelie consider dropping the subject entirely.

But she decided to give it one last shot.

"I wasn't asking about New York." She came to a stop at the single light in town. "I was thinking more along the lines of Moss Creek."

Muriel gazed out the window, looking over the storefronts of Main Street. "I can't imagine there's a whole lot of housing options in a little town like this."

That wasn't a no.

"I don't know what kind of options they have either." Amelie continued through town before turning toward the road that passed Cross Creek and went up Grizzly Point. "But you probably wouldn't have any difficulties selling your house now, so you might be able to afford a new one pretty easily."

Muriel's expression turned thoughtful as they passed the

fields of Cross Creek, a herd of their cattle huddled behind one of the wind breaks. "Maybe."

Moving Muriel closer to people she knew would definitely ease a little bit of the guilt Amelie would feel when she left.

And she had to leave. She had to go back and do what she told her grandmother she would. She had to prove to everyone that they both made the right decisions.

But the dreams she'd been so set on held a lot less shine than before.

After dropping Muriel off at Gertrude's, Amelie drove back down the mountain.

And straight to Cross Creek Ranch.

Pulling into the driveway felt a little too nice. A little too comfortable. Way better than anything she ever felt in New York.

Amelie passed the little farmhouse and Troy's truck, going straight to the barns where she knew he would be helping Colt and Ben take care of the animals that relied on them for food and water.

By the time she was parked and climbing out into the cold, her heart was beating fast, racing along as she tried to pretend going back to New York was still the plan. She could fake it in Billings. She could fake it with her grandmother. But she couldn't fake it when Troy was standing in front of her, making it impossible to ignore all the reasons she wanted to stay.

One of the cats poked its head out of the house Troy built them, meowing loudly before rushing out to chase behind her across the gravel. By the time she reached the barn, most of the cats were following her.

It was a pussy parade.

Amelie snorted to herself as she stepped inside, the smell of hay and animal less of an assault to her senses than it was her first visit. She stopped, staring down the empty aisle running between the stalls and the storage area. "Troy?"

The only answer came from one of the cats milling around her ankles, meowing impatiently for its breakfast.

"Okay. Okay." Amelie pried the lid off the food bin and went to work dishing out scoops of kibble, expecting Troy to show up any second. But by the time she'd fed and watered the whole crew there was still no sign of Troy.

And he wasn't the only one missing.

Amelie crouched down to pet Poppy, stroking along the cat's spine as she scanned the furry bodies circling the dishes. "Where's Marshmallow?"

The big cat might not want her love and affection, but he never missed breakfast.

Worry for Marshmallow pulled her back outside, dragging her around the barn to peek at all the places he liked to hang out. She poked her head into the heated house. Looked under equipment and inside sheds.

But there was no sign of the little asshole.

Which dug a pit in her stomach.

She was probably a little too attached to the fluffball considering he hated her guts, but that almost made her more determined to earn his trust. Marshmallow deserved to know love before he went to the heated cat house in the sky. But she might have missed her opportunity.

The thought had her jumping back into her new crossover, tires slipping on the icy gravel as she went in search of the man she knew would help her hunt Marshmallow down.

Because Troy would help her do anything.

Amelie parked next to his truck and rushed up to the back door, banging hard with one gloved hand.

Then she knocked again.

On the third knock Troy finally appeared, hair messy as he

yanked open the door. "Amelie." He glanced over one shoulder, looking a little panicked. "You're here."

The sickness in her stomach quadrupled. "I'm here." She fought in a breath as Troy leaned against the opening. Like he was trying to keep her from seeing what was inside.

Or maybe *who* was inside.

"Um." Her brain scrambled to remember why she was there, but suddenly all it could conjure up was visions of Troy with another woman.

Touching her.

Kissing her.

Holding her.

Maybe that's why he wasn't at the barn.

Maybe that's why he was still in bed and looked a little like he had a late night.

"I just—" Amelie stumbled backward. "I should go."

Was she really this blind? This foolish after all she'd been through?

Amelie bumped into the rail circling the small deck, blinking hard as tears burned the edges of her eyes.

But then something stopped her in her tracks.

Amelie stared down at the spot just beside Troy's bare feet. "Is that Marshmallow?"

Troy ran one hand through his messy hair. "Yeah."

Amelie cocked her head as she tried to make sense of what she was seeing. "Is he wearing a cone?"

"He had a run-in with one of the horses yesterday evening and hurt his paw." Troy gently nudged the coned cat away from the open door. "I was up all night with him at the emergency vet in Billings and they said he should stay inside until—"

Amelie didn't wait to hear what else he had to say.

It didn't matter.

She rushed across the deck, tackling the man she never should have doubted.

Never should have questioned.

Troy woke up every day and showed her who he was. Proved he was someone she could rely on.

Someone she could trust.

Someone she should keep.

TWENTY-TWO

TROY

LAST NIGHT SUCKED.

Not because he spent most of it sitting on a hard chair, the skin on his arms burning like fire from the fight Marshmallow put up. But because he came home to an empty house.

An empty bed.

He knew Amelie had to move back to Billings. Understood all her reasons for it and agreed completely.

That didn't make her absence any easier to face.

But her absence was way shorter lived than he expected.

Amelie latched onto him the second their bodies collided, her lips bumping his as he stumbled back, knocked off balance by the impact.

"You took care of him." Her words were garbled and messy as she tried to talk without taking her mouth off his. "Even though he's an asshole."

Troy continued fumbling his way back, trying to regain his footing as Amelie held on for dear life, legs tangling with his to the point there was no saving them.

They were going down.

He managed to kick the door closed as they toppled over,

dropping ungracefully to the hardwood just inside the back entrance of the farmhouse. Amelie grunted out a sharp breath as they hit the floor, the impact banging her teeth against his and smashing their noses together. She jerked her head back, running the tip of her tongue across the front of her teeth before her eyes dropped to his mouth.

He grinned. "Are they all still there?"

Her expression turned serious and she slowly shook her head. "The front one's gone. You must've swallowed it."

Troy's head dropped back to the wood floor as he started to laugh, feeling like a different person now that she was here with him. He wrapped both arms around her, pinning Amelie close as he rolled across the floor until her body was under his. "Does that mean you don't want to be seen with me anymore?" He leaned down to run his nose up the side of hers. "Don't want people to think you found yourself a nice toothless boyfriend?"

Amelie's gloved hand rested against his chest. "Boyfriend?" Her brows slowly lifted. "Is that what you are?"

He didn't mean to have this conversation. Not like this. Hell, he'd been avoiding it like the plague since she showed up on Muriel's front porch, a fixture in his life even though she didn't know it yet. "I'll be whatever you want me to be, Amelie."

Amelie's eyes dropped, fixing on a spot at the center of his chest. "For a minute I thought you were in here with someone else."

The admission was shocking. Mostly because he hadn't even thought of another woman since he sat down next to her on that barstool in Billings.

Troy shook his head. "No way." He ran his hands over her hair, brushing the stray bits away from her face. "You're the only woman who's ever been in that bed, and I would be just as happy to keep it that way."

Amelie's eyes jumped to his and her mouth dropped open. "That can't be true."

"It is." He slid his thumb across the curve of her cheek. "You're the only woman I've brought here."

"Seriously?"

"Why is that so surprising?"

"Well." Amelie's eyes moved to one side before coming back to his. "I just sort of thought you were the kind of guy who brought women home regularly."

His head bobbed back in surprise.

Then she started rambling.

"Not that it's a bad thing. You're just so charming and so friendly and so flirtatious and I assumed that initially it was because you just wanted to have sex with me and so I kind of thought you were a guy who does that."

Troy frowned down at her. "You started that off with it's not a bad thing, but everything that came after that sounded pretty bad."

"I don't mean for it to sound bad. I just meant that I thought you spent time with a lot of different women." Amelie kept trying to explain what she was saying, but it wasn't getting any better.

"I don't just use women for sex, Amelie. I'm not running around trying to get laid all the time." He loved sex, but what he wanted was more than that.

He wanted the love that was supposed to go with it, but so far it had evaded him.

Amelie's head tilted, her expression thoughtful. "So what *are* you trying to do?"

"I'm trying to find the real thing."

Amelie's eyes went to where her hand rested on his chest. "How's that working out for you?"

"Up until recently, not so well." Troy snagged the tip of one of the fingers on her glove and tugged. "But I think my luck is starting to turn around." He pulled the glove free and tossed it away before repeating the process with the other one. "At least I hope it is."

Amelie's eyes came back to his as he slid the hat off her head and reached for the zipper of her coat. "I felt like I was going to throw up when I thought there was someone else in here with you."

"Good." Troy slid down the zipper and pushed the sides open. "Because the thought of you with someone else makes me want to throw punches."

He'd been holding back for so long, and one night away from her was all it took for him to be ready to confess all of his sins. "Maybe dig a few holes."

Amelie huffed out a little laugh. "You can't just go around digging holes."

"Oh, I can." He worked the heavy bulk of her coat from under her body before snagging the bottom of her sweatshirt. "And I will."

Amelie lifted her arms over her head, arching her back as he peeled away both of the layers still covering her top half.

"Well, now I'm embarrassed that all I was going to do was throw up." She ran her hands down the center of his chest, sliding one into the waistband of his pants.

Troy groaned as the warmth of her palm wrapped around his cock. "There's a backhoe in the barn. I'll get you a set of keys."

"Thanks." Amelie worked her fist up and down his length. "Because I'm pretty sure I'm not much of a digger."

Troy braced his knees on either side of her hips, thrusting into her hand as his head dropped to the floor above her shoulder. "You just haven't had the right motivation." He struggled to get the words out. "Because I know damn well you're stubborn enough to do anything you want to do."

Her hand stilled, offering him back a little of the focus she stole. "You really think that?"

Troy lifted his head to meet her eyes. "I know it."

Amelie looped her free arm around his neck and pulled his mouth back to hers in a chaste kiss.

One that snowballed almost immediately.

They'd always had chemistry. A sexual connection that bound them together from that first night. But now it was more than that. And the intensity of being with her was almost more than he could handle.

Troy yanked at her pants, growling when he stripped them free to find another pair layered beneath them.

"Don't growl at me." Amelie kicked her jeans away. "You're the one who told me I had to wear these when I came to the ranch."

Troy's eyes slowly found hers. "So you were planning to come here when you got dressed this morning?"

Amelie's mouth opened before clamping shut again. She blew out a sharp breath. "I like it here."

All the frustration he'd been fighting since driving her back to Billings faded away. "Good." He gripped the waistband of her thermal pants and slid them down. "I like having you here."

Amelie lifted her hips off the floor as he dragged away the last of the fabric between them. "Only because I feed the cats and you don't have to."

When he glanced up her eyes were on his face and her lower lip was pinched between her teeth.

Like she was waiting for his response.

"You know that's not the only reason I like having you here, Amelie." Troy tossed her pants to the pile of clothes stacked on the wood floor. "And if you don't, then I've done a shitty job of showing you how I'm feelin'." He eased over her, slowly lowering his body against hers. "But I'm happy to lay it all out for you if you want to hear it."

Amelie pressed her lips together. "I think that might be a good idea."

He'd been working so hard not to pressure her with any expectations or assumptions. But that left a hell of a lot of room for interpretation. The fact that Amelie thought he'd ever have another woman in his bed meant he wasn't doing a great job of showing her the truth of what he felt.

It was one more way he was lacking and one more reason he'd slept alone for so long.

"I like having you here because you're funny." Troy resisted the urge to stop there. "Because you're smart." He leaned in to slide his lips down the side of her neck. "Because you smell good." He hesitated, the need to keep all this close enough to protect him from the very real possibility of rejection making it hard to breathe. "Because you stood up for me when Griffin showed up."

His voice cracked a little, exposing the vulnerability he would always carry. He'd been abandoned by the people who were supposed to love and protect him. Left to fend for himself in just about every way. It forced him to learn how to make sure everyone liked him. Enjoyed his company.

But it also forced him to keep them all at arm's length, holding them just close enough they couldn't hurt him when they left.

Because they always did.

Amelie's lips pressed into a thin line. "I'm still not sure I trust Griffin."

Troy smiled even though he was struggling to get enough air. "That's another reason I like havin' you here. You worry about me." He swallowed down the fear trying to keep him quiet. "No one's ever done that before."

Amelie's hand came to press against the side of his face, her eyes soft as they held his. "Maybe you're right. Maybe I haven't ever had the right motivation." Her fingers curved, stroking across his skin. "Because if Griffin hurts you, I will absolutely dig a him-sized hole and roll his ass into it."

Nothing she could have said would have affected him more.

It made him blind to anything except her and the need to be what she wanted.

What she deserved.

Troy ran his hands over her skin, slicking his tongue against every part of her. Memorizing the feel of her under his palms and his mouth as the soft sounds of her gasps made his body burn with a kind of need he'd never felt.

When he reached her belly, Amelie locked her knees under his arms as she hooked her legs around his back, using the hold to haul him upward until they were almost face-to-face. "I want you." She looped one arm around his neck. "And don't give me any of that *ladies first* shit."

"But—"

Her limbs suddenly tightened, holding on as she rolled, switching their positions. "I knew you were going to say that."

Troy gazed up at her. "Stubborn."

Amelie's hair was wild and her skin was flushed. A smirk slowly twisted her lips as she leaned forward, lining her body with his. "Maybe I am."

The wet heat of her against his skin was consuming, stealing his ability to do anything but stare at her as she rocked over him, taking every inch of him with ease and owning them all.

Claiming him for herself.

He couldn't look away from her. From the way her eyes were

locked onto his as she took what she wanted and gave more than he could stand.

She was everything.

Everything he'd been waiting for.

Everything he never thought would be his.

Amelie's movements started to become irregular as her fingers dug into the skin of his chest. "Troy—"

He blinked away the daze blanketing him like a veil, reaching between them to give her what he knew she needed. "I've got you."

Amelie whimpered as he worked her clit in steady strokes, her head falling forward, the soft strands of her hair tickling his face. "You are so good at that."

He gripped her hip, holding tight as he helped her keep moving, pressing both feet to the floor so he could thrust up into her. "I had to make you like me somehow."

"Smart." Her lids lifted, jaw slack as her gaze leveled on his, the tight clench of her pussy as she came dragging him along with her.

She slumped against him, breathing heavy, blonde hair everywhere as she fought to catch her breath.

Suddenly she went still, pressing both hands to his chest as she pushed up, her eyes dropping to where their bodies were still joined. "Oh shit."

His stomach clenched. "What's wrong?"

Did she already regret everything she said?

Or maybe it was what *he* said that had the remorseful look on her face.

"I'm so sorry." Amelie tried to move off him. "I wasn't thinking straight and—"

Troy grabbed her before she could get away. "Talk to me. Tell me what happened."

Amelie's eyes were wide and a little panicked when they

finally came to his. "I got caught up in the moment. I didn't mean to—"

His whole body went cold. "Didn't mean to, what?"

He was going to make her say it. Make her remind him why he kept the way he felt close.

But Amelie just kept rambling. "I've been checked out and I'm on the pill." Her focus dropped back between them. "I didn't mean to put you in this position."

Confusion stalled out the fear making his stomach roll.

What in the hell was she talking about?

Troy followed her gaze to where a line of wetness ran down the inside of her thigh, the evidence of what they'd just done unobstructed and uncontained.

He stared at it, unable to take his eyes off what had Amelie so upset.

"I've never—" He forced himself to look at her as he tried to ease her fears. "I always wear a condom." He brought one palm to the side of her face. "Always."

He'd never accidentally forgotten, knowing firsthand the burden a man can put on a woman.

And a child.

Amelie pressed her hand to the back of his, holding it tight to her skin. "I'm so sorry. I wasn't thinking."

"Don't be sorry." Troy reached for her, pulling her close. "It was an accident." He tucked her face against his shoulder, working his fingers across her scalp.

She relaxed just a little. "You're not upset?"

"Not even a little." He closed his eyes, letting himself consider for just a second what might have happened if Amelie wasn't on the pill.

If this accident led to another, more permanent one.

It was a fleeting thought, one he had to bank.

Because the only way he would ever bring a child into this world was on purpose.

"That's good." Amelie sniffled, straightening to turn toward the kitchen. "Because right now Marshmallow is looking judgmental as hell."

TWENTY-THREE

AMELIE

"I HAD NO idea this place existed." Muriel peeked out the front window of Amelie's new SUV, looking impressed by the sight in front of them. "It's beautiful."

Troy leaned between them, one hand gripping the side of her seat, his fingers barely brushing her left shoulder. "It looks even nicer in the summer." He pointed toward the backside of The Inn at Red Cedar Ranch. "There's a swimming pool and patio where they host events and parties when the weather's nice."

Amelie tried to focus on what he was describing, but all her attention was on the spot where Troy touched her, the point of contact just out of Muriel's sight.

A few days ago he'd told her he would be whatever she wanted, but so far Troy hadn't put any action to that statement, making her wonder how much longer he wanted to keep what was between them a secret.

At some point they would have to tell her grandmother, right?

Unless maybe he wasn't as in this as she thought. Maybe it was fun when he knew there would be an end, but now that there wasn't, Troy was trying to figure out how to get out of it without losing Muriel.

But that didn't seem like him.

She was just overreacting. Letting her past color her future.

And her past sucked.

Amelie pulled into one of the available parking spaces before shutting off the engine. "I guess I can see why Griffin keeps extending his stay." She glanced at where Troy's face was inches from hers, pulling her eyes off him after only a second. "I mean, besides the fact that his son lives here."

Troy's dad had been in Moss Creek for almost a month, and she was starting to worry. The longer Griffin stayed, the harder it would be for Troy when he left. And Griffin had to leave. Unlike her, he had a life to get back to.

"I wouldn't want to leave either if I was staying in a place like this." Muriel pulled the loose hood of her coat over her tightly curled hair, carefully setting it into place.

She'd spent most of the day primping for this party, going through at least five outfit changes by the time it was all said and done.

Amelie wasn't far behind her. She didn't know a whole lot about the family they were meeting tonight, but from what she'd picked up during her days with Gertrude and the rest of the girls, this family was almost like royalty in Moss Creek.

And you didn't show up to meet royalty in jeans and a hoodie.

"You don't want to leave Montana as it is." Amelie gave her grandmother a little grin, eyes meeting Troy's in the rearview mirror. "Not that I blame you. This place does sort of grow on you."

Troy's eyes stayed on hers, but only for a second before dropping away. "We should get inside before they wonder where we are."

They unloaded from the car and headed to the porch, Muriel walking between them so they could make sure she stayed steady on her feet as they crossed the slippery lot.

They'd barely reached the door when it flew open and they were greeted by a woman who looked to be about her mother's age. "It's about time you got here." The woman's smile was wide and warm, her eyes falling on Amelie's grandmother first. "You must be Muriel."

Muriel immediately flipped back her hood, ready to show off the hairdo she'd spent so much time on. "I would worry that my reputation precedes me." Her smile turned sly. "But I sort of hope it did."

The woman's head tipped back on a loud laugh as she reached for Muriel. "I knew I was going to love you. Get your asses in here before you freeze to death."

Troy leaned close while Muriel was distracted, his voice low in her ear. "That's Maryann Pace."

Amelie nodded. "I figured."

It wasn't hard to narrow her identity down, but the line of men and women filling the open space in front of them might be a little trickier to identify.

According to Gertrude, Maryann and Bill Pace had four sons and all of them were tall and good-looking.

She was pretty spot on.

Muriel stayed beside Maryann as they made their way into The Inn, the two women chatting and laughing together as they passed down the main hall and into the open common area, leaving Amelie and Troy to follow behind them.

The Inn was one of the nicest places she'd ever seen. It had soaring ceilings and a huge kitchen with a center island that was almost as big as most of the apartments in New York. A giant table sat off to the side of the kitchen, ladder-back chairs lined down each side. The sitting area had a leather sectional that could easily seat ten people.

And it was being put to very good use.

Most of Maryann's family filled the cushions, watching a football game. An older man Amelie assumed was her husband Bill sat with what looked to be three of his four sons, beers in hand. Two teenage boys sat with them, looking happy and comfortable as the grown men included them in the conversation. A set of women, probably three of Maryann's daughters-in-law, leaned back on the sofa, feet propped on the ottoman. Two had babies on their chests and one either had a volleyball shoved under her shirt or was well on her way to having a baby of her own.

Griffin sat in the middle of the group, laughing and chatting along with them like he'd known them his whole life. He jumped up the second he noticed Troy, stepping over legs and feet as he worked free of the cozy looking space. "You're here."

Griffin came straight to his son, pulling him in for a quick embrace before motioning toward the kitchen. "You want a beer?"

"Sure." Troy followed his dad to the fridge, looking over the meal the chef was putting together. "Smells good in here."

The young woman cooking gave him a quick smile. "Thanks."

"Have you all met Mariah?" Maryann rested one hand on the chef's shoulder. "I swear I would be lost without her. She's a godsend."

Amelie sat down at the island and leaned across the counter to get a better look at what was cooking. "I can see why." She smiled at Mariah. "I'm Amelie."

"Amelie the artist." Mariah grinned. "I might have heard a thing or two about you around town." She stirred what appeared to be a pot of grits. "I'd say you should get some business cards made, but Gertrude seems to be enjoying the hell out of gatekeeping your information."

Amelie laughed, shaking her head. "That sounds like her."

Muriel slid into the seat next to Amelie, expression serious as she focused on Mariah. "Did you know she slept with Kenny Rogers?"

"Everyone knows she slept with Kenny Rogers." Mariah snorted out a laugh. "She told me all about it five minutes after we met." She paused to empty a bowl of shrimp into a skillet. "Not that I blame her. I'd probably tell everyone I met if I'd slept with someone famous too."

"I'm sure you could make that happen." Muriel looked Mariah up and down with an appraising gaze. "You're a gorgeous girl."

Mariah's cheeks pinked up the tiniest bit. "I think you need to be invited over more often." She grinned at Muriel. "You're great for my ego."

The women continued to chat, but Amelie kept her eyes on where Griffin stood with Troy a few feet away.

Something was off with both of them tonight.

Griffin popped the lid off a beer and passed it Troy's way. "How's it going?"

"Good." Troy took a sip of the Pilsner, swallowing it down. "Thanks for inviting us."

"It wasn't actually me." Griffin glanced at where Maryann was standing beside Muriel, chatting happily about anything her grandmother wanted to bring up. "Maryann said we all needed to have dinner together before I headed back."

Amelie sat a little straighter in her seat, watching Troy's expression.

She knew this moment was coming. Griffin couldn't stay forever. He had a whole life waiting for him somewhere else.

Businesses to run. A house to maintain. Staying in Moss Creek wasn't an option for him.

"When are you leaving?" Troy took another swig of his beer, his voice a little tight.

Amelie bounced one leg under the cover of the island, forcing herself to stay seated, doing her best to resist the urge to butt into the conversation.

"In the morning." Griffin scrubbed one hand over the back of his neck. "I put it off as long as I could, but there's some things that only I can handle."

"I get it." Troy's eyes moved around the room, slowly scanning the space until they finally found hers.

What she saw in them made her heart stop and her chest ache. He was trying so hard to hide it, but it was still there. The loss. The fear.

He pulled his gaze from hers almost immediately, but the damage was already done. She couldn't ignore what she saw, and she sure as hell couldn't let it go.

"I'm gonna go get a beer." Amelie slid from her seat and rounded the island, going straight for where Griffin and Troy still stood beside the fridge.

"Hey." She bumped into Troy's side, all her focus on Griffin. "What's going on?"

Griffin eased back the tiniest bit. "I was just telling Troy that I have to head back to Washington tomorrow."

Amelie lifted her brows. "Tomorrow? That's sudden."

"I know." Griffin's head dropped forward. "I've been dragging my feet and I think I waited longer than I should have. It sounds like I've got a shitshow waiting for me."

"When are you coming back?" Amelie fired the question off, knowing Griffin's answer would determine his fate.

Griffin met her gaze. "Soon."

"Soon, when?" Amelie crossed her arms, really regretting

that she didn't make Troy give her the keys to the backhoe. "Next week? Next month? When?" She stepped a little closer to Griffin. "Specifically."

Griffin's face fell. "I wish I knew." He raked one hand through his salt and pepper hair. "I really wish I knew."

"Hmph." Amelie tipped her head to one side and narrowed her eyes. "It seems to me like you're the boss. You should be able to—"

"It's okay." Troy leaned in until she finally pulled her eyes off Griffin and brought them to his. "Really."

Amelie held his gaze for a few long seconds, teeth clenched tight. "But he shouldn't just leave you like this."

"Oh," Griffin moved closer, holding his hands up, "that's not what's happening here." He reached out to rest one hand on Troy's shoulder. "You're stuck with me. I've got a lot of years to make up for." His blue gaze moved to where Amelie was still glaring. "I'll be back in a month. I'll book my stay before I leave."

Amelie's chin barely lifted. "Good. I look forward to it."

"Me too." Troy rested one hand on her back, gently sliding it up and down.

He was acting like he was genuinely okay with the fact that Griffin was just leaving. That he was fine with his father packing up and shipping out on short notice.

"You better come back." Amelie inched closer to Griffin, staring him down. "Because if you don't, I'll—"

"Dinner is ready." Maryann clapped her hands and Troy yanked his hand from her back. "Come on. Get your asses to the table."

Griffin seemed to look a little relieved at the interruption.

He should be.

Troy was finally starting to see what it was like to have

people around that planned to stay, and no way was she letting anyone take that from him.

Griffin turned to where Maryann was, expertly taking himself out of the conversation. "Where do you want me to sit?"

Maryann led Griffin to the table, putting him at one side before directing Troy to the seat beside him. She put Muriel across from Griffin and Amelie across from Troy. Everyone else filled in the rest of the chairs and started passing around dishes, serving up the shrimp and grits Mariah made family-style.

"Well, we know when Griffin is leaving." Maryann dropped a few shrimp onto the pile of grits already at the center of her plate. "How long do you plan on staying in Montana, Amelie?"

It was a question she knew was coming, she just didn't expect it to be Maryann who asked it.

But maybe that was because Maryann wasn't afraid of what her answer might be.

What if Troy was still holding back because he was worried she would leave him just like everyone else had?

Amelie took the bowl of shrimp and added a few to her own plate, taking a steadying breath before spilling the truth she hoped would push Troy forward. "Indefinitely." She passed the bowl to her grandmother before meeting Troy's eyes across the table. "Now that I'm adjusting, I really like it here."

Troy continued to stare at her until Griffin barely bumped him, passing over the bowl of grits circling the table.

"Well of course you like it here." Maryann added a serving of greens to her plate before passing the bowl to Amelie. "I don't know if you heard, but I moved here from a bigger city." Her eyes found Bill on the other side of the table. "And I can tell you from experience that Montana has so much more to offer."

"Unless you're trying to find high-end upholstery fabric." The woman with the pregnant belly gave her a wry smile. "Then you're screwed."

Amelie smiled back. "Luckily I don't buy much upholstery fabric, so I should be okay." She stabbed one of the shrimp and lifted it. "I do buy a lot of paint though, and I need to get a few things, so I'm going to have to find a good art supply shop."

Maryann lifted her brows. "I heard about your waitlist." She leaned a little closer. "That's impressive."

Amelie smiled wider. "I'm excited." She glanced at Muriel. "My grandma and Gertrude have been one hell of a marketing team."

"Oh, they have." Maryann took a sip of her water. "But word is starting to spread fast, and I might have heard the city is looking for someone to add a mural to the side of one of the buildings downtown."

Amelie stared at Maryann, ignoring the tug of excitement in her belly. "A mural on the side of a building?" She shook her head. "I think that's a little above my skill set."

Maryann lifted a shoulder. "Maybe now, but by the summer I'm sure you'll have a whole lot more under your belt."

The conversation turned to the woman who was definitely pregnant, Nora, and the plans they were making for her baby shower, giving Amelie time to process all the possibilities that might be in front of her.

Her dream was to be a working artist. To get paid for doing what she loved and providing people with the set of emotions only art could supply.

Her grandmother was right. She'd gone to New York because that seemed like the most logical place to accomplish that. It was filled with galleries and wealthy people looking to line their walls. But did they really appreciate art more than an old woman who sat and stared at a painting every morning while she drank her coffee and tried to feel a little less bad about the piles of snow outside her window?

No. They probably didn't.

And maybe that made what she could do here better.

More important.

They all lingered after dinner was finished, continuing to talk about the goings-on of Moss Creek and when spring might start and what the week's specials were at their favorite restaurant in town.

She'd walked in expecting to be a little uncomfortable to have dinner with people she didn't really know, but by the end of the night Amelie was hoping she'd be invited back again. Not just because of how happy her grandmother was or how the whole Pace family seemed ready and more than willing to treat Muriel like one of their own, but because she felt like they treated her the same way.

Maryann's daughters-in-law, Nora, Camille, and Clara were some of the nicest women she'd ever met. They were funny and easy to talk to. Warm in a way few people were in New York.

Evelyn would love them.

Unfortunately, with so much attention on them, she and Troy had to keep their distance, and it was tough watching all Maryann's sons holding their wives close when she couldn't even put her eyes on Troy without risking one of them noticing.

"Well that was fun." Muriel held tight to Amelie's arm as they walked out to the car.

"I agree." Amelie unlocked the doors and started the engine using her fob. "I really like them."

"Well that's good." Muriel dropped down into the passenger's seat. "Because Maryann mentioned to me that she would love to have us over once a month."

"Really?" Amelie couldn't help but smile.

"Of course, really. We're fantastic." Muriel settled into her seat and pulled the door closed.

"I think her fan club gets bigger every time we take her somewhere new." Troy walked Amelie around to the driver's side. "But to be fair, I knew she and Maryann would get along. They are a lot alike."

"I can see that." Amelie snagged his arm, lowering her voice. "Are you really okay with your dad leaving?"

Troy held her gaze. "I'm really okay." He brushed his fingers over hers. "I promise. I've got Griffin's number and he's got mine. He's not leaving my life, just Montana."

Amelie inched a little closer. "Which is stupid because Montana is pretty nice."

She thought maybe he would say something about her decision to stay, but Troy tipped his head toward the car. "We should get in before your grandma starts trying to figure out what's taking so long."

The fact that Troy still didn't seem even a little ready to break the news of their connection to Muriel, even now that he knew she was staying, stung. "Yeah." Amelie pulled her hand from his. "You're right."

Muriel and Troy didn't stop talking the entire trip to his house, discussing everything from The Inn to Maryann Pace and how many grandchildren she was up to now.

Amelie stayed quiet, doing her best to smile and nod at appropriate times.

But it wasn't easy.

She'd expected Troy to be happy that she planned to stay in Montana, but his reaction was leaving a lot to be desired.

And maybe that was only because Muriel was with them.

But that was an issue all its own because at a certain point shouldn't he value their relationship just as much as the one he had with her grandmother?

Even after Troy was dropped off at his farmhouse and they were on the road to Billings, Muriel continued to talk about everyone they met, dishing out all the information she'd managed to get about each person there.

"That Mariah is a peach." Muriel bumped down the temperature of her seat warmer. "She's the sweetest thing and one hell of a cook." Her eyes slid Amelie's way. "I wonder how much it would be to have her come cater one of our Bridge Club luncheons."

"Is that what you're calling it now?" Amelie smiled, happy to have a distraction from the admittedly convoluted thoughts milling around her brain. "Bridge Club?"

"It sounds a whole lot better than Old Women Playing Cards and Talking Shit Club."

Amelie tipped her head to one side. "I don't know. I think I like the second one better." She turned into the neighborhood she now called home. "It would look great on a t-shirt."

Muriel didn't laugh like she expected her to.

Amelie glanced at her grandmother and found all Muriel's focus on a spot ahead of them. She was frowning as she peered through the windshield. "Who in the hell is that?"

Amelie turned and nearly ran the car off the road.

"Holy shit." She whipped her little SUV into the driveway, resisting the urge to plow into the man standing there.

"Want me to hit him with my door?" Muriel grabbed the handle. "Cause I'll do it."

"No." Slamming the gear shift into park, Amelie jumped out of the car, fixing her glare on where Trevor stood, looking completely out of place in his expensive clothes and wool coat. "What in the hell are you doing here?"

He jumped back when Muriel shoved open her door, barely missing him as she swung it as wide as it would go.

"Shoot." Muriel hefted herself out. "So close." She glared at Trevor as she walked past, shuffling over the cleared cement on her way to the porch. "Can't win them all, I guess."

Trevor watched her go before turning back to Amelie. "She seems great."

Amelie crossed her arms. "Why are you here?"

She was already edging on a bad mood and Trevor's appearance shoved her right into pissed off territory. She'd literally just decided New York was in her past, but here it was, acting like she didn't get to call the shots.

Her ex seemed a little shocked by her open hostility, which made her regret missing him with the bumper. "I came to see you."

She'd known Trevor for over five years. Long enough to realize he only did shit that benefited him, which meant his reasons for being here were self-serving. "Why?"

"I wanted to see when you were coming back to New York." He slowly moved around the front end of her new car, coming closer than he probably would if he knew she'd considered vehicular assault less than two minutes ago. "People have been asking about you."

Amelie snorted. "Right."

"It's true." Trevor continued coming toward her. "I've had multiple calls from people asking when you're having another show or where they can find your work."

Amelie opened her mouth to argue, but nothing came out.

People wanted her work?

"Come back to New York." Trevor came a little too close. "I'll pay for your flight back. There's an apartment over the gallery available. They're holding it for you."

The shock of Trevor's arrival began to wear off and everything he was saying started to sink in.

"So you want me to come back." Amelie stood a little taller. "And you're going to pay for my flight and get me an apartment and host my show."

"I'll handle everything." Trevor reached out to grab her hands. "New York misses you." His expression heated. "*I* miss you."

Gross.

How did she ever look at this man and think he was what she wanted?

Honestly, she didn't.

It was everything he promised that made her decide Trevor was the right fit. Not the man himself. She'd fallen into the same trap so many women did, easily letting Trevor take the reins of her life and direct it where he wanted it to go. Because it was where she'd always imagined and dreamed of winding up, it felt different than what her mother and grandmother did.

But it wasn't.

And here he was, thinking she would do it all over again.

Maybe she would have if things had gone differently in Montana. If she hadn't finally found a group of people who genuinely liked her and appreciated her talent. If she hadn't found a place that finally felt like home.

Amelie pulled her hands from his grip, the contact already making her skin crawl. "No thanks."

TWENTY-FOUR

TROY

TROY TURNED AS Amelie came into the barn. "You're up awfully early." He quickly added hay to the stall he was working in before closing the gate and coming out to meet her. "Did Muriel want to get a head start on her social schedule?"

He loved watching Muriel blossom as she found her footing within her steadily growing group of friends. The difference in her was night and day and he couldn't wait to see how she continued to change as she felt all the love coming her way.

"She was actually still in bed when I left." Amelie went to the food bin and popped off the lid. "I think last night at The Inn wore her out." She scooped out a pile and carried it to the first of the dishes. "I think she's finding out the hard way that being a social butterfly can get exhausting."

The group of cats Amelie continued to care for every morning circled around her legs, making it difficult for her to move around, but she didn't seem to mind. She offered up sweet words and gentle pats to any cat that tolerated her affection as she gave them breakfast and fresh water.

"What about you?" Troy watched as she worked. "You were just as popular as she was last night."

Last night had gone a whole lot different than he expected. Between Griffin's announcement that he was leaving and Amelie's announcement that she was staying, he'd been hit from both sides. And honestly, he wasn't sure which punch was easier to handle.

He knew how to chase Amelie. Knew how to flirt and how to charm her. But it was starting to be clear they'd moved past that, and that scared the hell out of him. Because while he knew how to get Amelie, he didn't know how to keep her.

He didn't know how to keep anyone.

"I really liked them." Amelie scooped Poppy up as the cat circled her feet, cuddling her close. "Especially Nora."

"I can see that. You two have a lot in common. You're both from the city and both creative." Nora and her husband Brooks ran a remodeling company. They bought run-down properties in Moss Creek and the surrounding areas and renovated them, with Nora putting her years as an interior decorator to full use. "She's the one who decorated The Inn."

Amelie smiled as Poppy rubbed against her chin. "That's what Maryann said." She gently put the little cat back on the ground. "Actually, Nora asked if I would ever be interested in working with her on their houses." Amelie dropped the food scoop back into the bin and pushed the lid into place. "Apparently she thinks murals are going to get really popular and would love to incorporate a few to see if that helps their resale value."

It was something he would expect Amelie to be thrilled about, but she seemed a little less enthusiastic than he anticipated. "That's great."

She gave him a little smile. "It is."

Something was different this morning, but he couldn't quite put his finger on it. She seemed almost sad.

But maybe he knew how to fix that. "You should come check on Marshmallow. See how much better he's doing."

Amelie's face brightened. "Is he?" She clasped her gloved hands together. "I was starting to get really worried when his limp got worse."

"Me too, but I think I figured out the issue." Troy followed Amelie to her car, sitting in the passenger's seat as she drove them up to the farmhouse. He turned to look through the compact, but still decently spacious interior. "You still liking this?"

"I love it." Amelie shut off the engine. "I didn't realize how much I missed driving."

It was one more thing that he should be thrilled to hear.

Amelie liked life in Montana. It was what he wanted, what he'd been working so hard to make happen.

But now what? How did he go from pursuit to whatever it was that came next?

It was a question he obviously didn't have an answer to. So at this point, he just had to throw shit at the wall and hope something stuck.

Which is what he was about to do.

Troy quietly opened the back door, holding one finger against his lips as he silently stepped into the house, moving slowly toward the front room. He motioned for Amelie to follow him, keeping one hand against her lower back to make sure she didn't miss what he wanted her to see.

Or notice what he wasn't quite ready for her to find.

Marshmallow sat in the sling he'd installed on the front window, tail swishing back and forth as he stared out into the snow. The big cat slowly stood, stretching before jumping down and sashaying across the living room at a leisurely, and completely limp-free pace.

He froze the second his eyes found them, going completely

still before meowing and continuing on his path, holding up one of his back legs as he hobbled closer.

Amelie's mouth dropped open. "That little faker." She pointed at Marshmallow. "That's not even the leg he hurt."

"Nope." He'd been so distracted by everything else going on that he hadn't immediately realized Marshmallow's limp kept changing sides. "I think he's decided he likes being an indoor cat and figures I won't put him back outside if he's still hurt."

Amelie laughed, shaking her head. "Of all the cats out there, he's the last one I would have expected to like living in a house."

"Not *a* house." Troy chuckled. "*My* house."

Amelie's smile held. "On the plus side, I hear he's a great mouser." She turned and wandered toward the back door, glancing up the stairs before her focus moved to the kitchen.

She stopped in her tracks. "What's that?"

Troy moved in behind her, apprehension and excitement warring for control of his insides. "That's for you."

Amelie stared at the items on the kitchen table a second longer before stepping toward them, reaching out to run her fingers along the collection of paintbrushes he'd worked into a mock bouquet. "These are my favorite brushes."

"I noticed they were what you used when I helped you rinse them out at Gertrude's house, so I ordered another pack just in case those started to wear out." He didn't actually know how it worked, or if brushes could even wear out, but figured it was worth a shot. "It sounds like you've got a lot of jobs lined up and I didn't want you to be low on supplies."

Her hands dropped down to the stack of threadbare flannels he'd fished out of the back of his closet. "And those are just a few of my old shirts that I thought might come in handy to use over your clothes so you don't mess them up."

He'd never had to buy a Valentine's Day gift before, but he knew Amelie wouldn't be happy with something impersonal, which was fine. He'd worked hard to get to know her and wanted her to see that. Especially since chances were real good he was gonna make a hell of a lot of mistakes.

Amelie turned to face him, her brows pinched together. "Why did you do this?"

"Because it's Valentine's Day." He tucked both hands into the pockets of his jeans. "There's a card too."

Amelie reached for the card, sliding it from the hot pink envelope it was in before reading the front, her expression thoughtful. She opened it, scanning the signature before setting it back on the table. "Does this mean I'm your valentine?"

There was something a little off in her tone.

"Of course you're my valentine." She was his favorite person to be around. The one he wanted to spend every bit of his free time with.

Amelie squared her shoulders, facing him fully. "So we can tell my grandmother then."

Troy hesitated.

"Don't you think it's a little soon?" He moved closer. "I want you to be sure before—"

"I am sure." Amelie's eyes moved to the gifts on the table. "And it seems like you're sure too."

"I am. I just want us to be positive this is going to go the way we think it is before we tell her."

Once they told Muriel there would be no going back. No recovering if Amelie decided he wasn't what she wanted after all. He would lose both of them. End up just as alone as he was before.

But now it would be worse, because now he knew what it was like to have people in your life who really gave a shit about you.

"So you just want to keep sneaking around behind her

back?" Amelie shook her head. "Because I don't. I'm tired of wondering if you're hiding this for a different reason."

Troy took a step back, the suggestion that he would have any other reason for waiting, hitting him like a punch to the chest. "What are you trying to say?"

"I'm saying there's only so many reasons a man doesn't want to hold your hand in front of all the people he knows." Amelie crossed her arms. "And none of them are good."

He did want to hold her hand in front of everyone he knew. Hell, he wanted to parade her around town to make sure everyone in Moss Creek understood Amelie was his.

But he would never put that kind of pressure on her. She came to Montana hell-bent on living the life she chose, and come hell or high water, he was going to make sure she was the one who chose this.

Especially since it wasn't the life she planned.

Moss Creek, Montana was a far cry from New York City. Painting murals on walls would never be the same as displaying her creations in a gallery.

And he wasn't a rich art dealer with connections and clout. "I just want you to be sure this is where you want to be."

"You keep putting this back on me like I'm the only one who matters." Amelie's voice got a little louder. "Like I have to decide what we're going to do because you don't care either way."

"That's not true. I do care." He cared a hell of a lot. Enough to hold back until Amelie made her decision.

"Well it sure doesn't seem like it." Her shoulders slumped a little. "It seems like you're just looking for someone who won't leave you instead of someone you really love."

"That's definitely not true." His own anger started to bubble up. "I'm looking for something real."

"Are you?" Amelie threw her arms out. "Because it seems

like you're just waiting for someone to decide they want to be with you and that's who you'll end up with."

"No." He shook his head. "I'm not."

"I know you've got abandonment issues, Troy, but I want to be with someone who knows I'm what they want." She shook her head. "Not someone who waits until I decide I'm not gonna leave them."

"That's not what I'm doing."

"Yes it is. You're putting all this on me because you're too scared to carry any of the burden." Her lips pressed into a frown. "And it's confusing as hell, because you were all in until suddenly you weren't. And then I was left trying to figure out what in the hell happened."

He pointed at the table of gifts. "That's confusing you?"

Amelie snatched the card, holding it up between them. "The card's from Marshmallow." She slapped it back down. "It says I'm 'his favorite human'." Her head bobbed in an exaggerated nod. "Yeah. It's confusing."

"Well, if that's not a double standard then I don't know what is." Troy stared her down. "Because you're the one who didn't want this to be anything." He moved closer. "Lied and told me you were going back to New York."

Amelie scoffed. "That was the first freaking night we met." She raked both hands through her hair, fisting them tight to her scalp. "I told you I wasn't leaving last night."

Troy shook his head. "No, you didn't. You told Maryann." He lifted his shoulders. "Last I heard you were still planning to leave."

"So you want full transparency from me even though you don't want to give it back?" Amelie squared up to him, just like she had a hundred times before. "Fine." Her chin lifted and her nostrils flared. "Trevor showed up at Muriel's last night. Said he wants to host a show for me. That people have been asking for my work."

"Good." Troy held her gaze. "You should do it then."

Amelie's head bobbed back like he'd slapped her. "What?"

"You should go back to New York." It had been hard enough to say it the first time and he nearly choked on it the second. "Back to the life you want."

Amelie's mouth dropped open, brows pinched tight as she stared up at him, the ache in his chest burning hotter with each passing second.

No one had ever stayed in his life long enough for him to fall in love. Part of him didn't think he'd even know it if it happened. Wouldn't be able to recognize the emotion if he was ever lucky enough to cross its path.

But he did.

And it fucking sucked.

Because it meant he would do whatever it took to make sure Amelie was happy.

That she had the life she wanted.

The life she deserved.

No matter what it cost him.

"Do you really mean that?" Amelie's expression shifted from shock to disbelief.

And all he wanted was to pull her close. Tell her he loved her and beg her to never leave him.

"I do."

Amelie sucked in a deep breath through her nose as disbelief morphed to anger. "Fine." She stepped around him, pausing with one hand on the back door. "I guess I'm glad you finally decided to have an opinion on things."

Then she walked out, quietly closing the door as she left him behind.

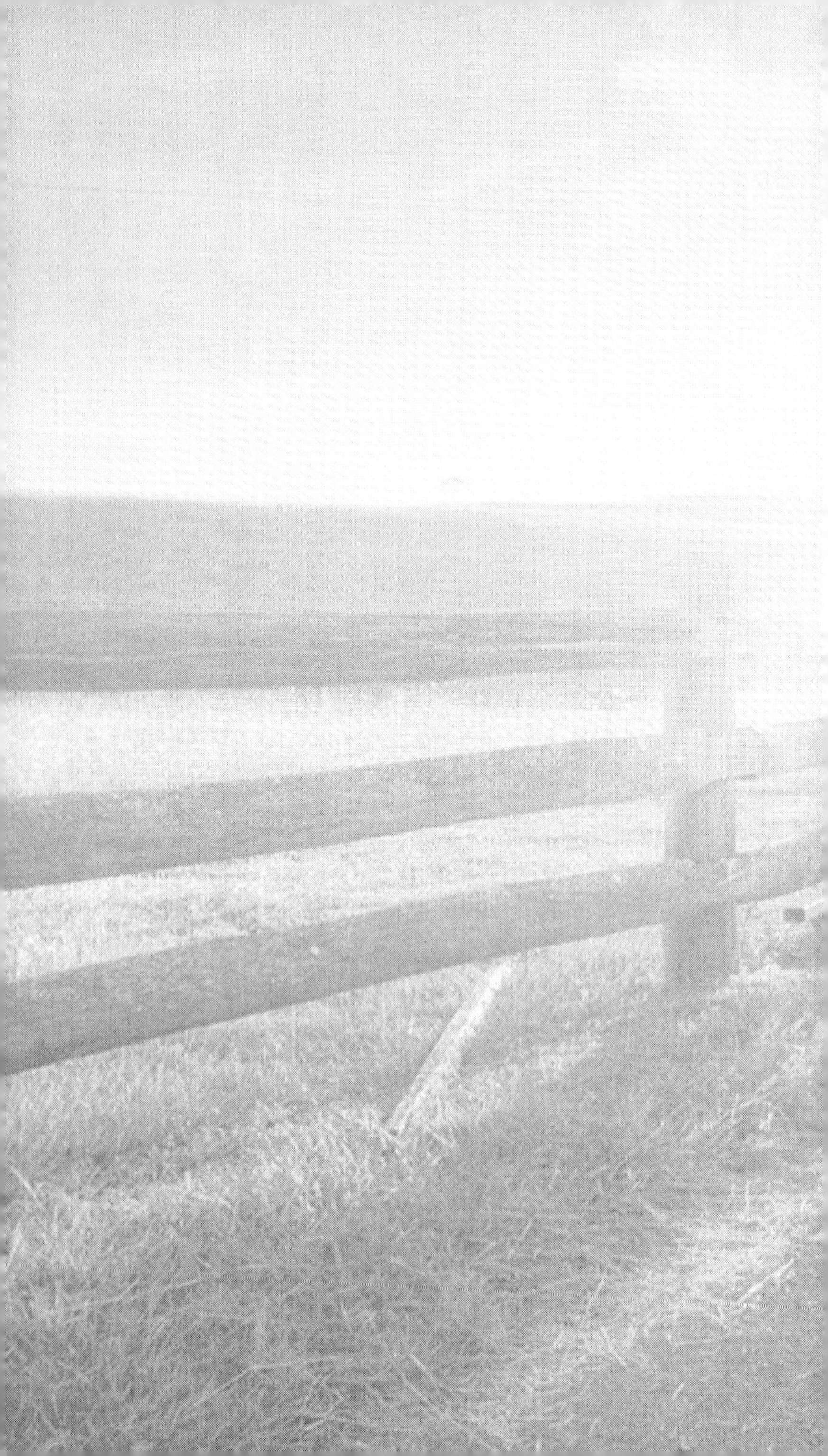

TWENTY-FIVE

AMELIE

"HOW ARE YOU feeling?" Muriel sat in the living room, eying Amelie as she came down the stairs. "Any better?"

"No." Amelie forced out a cough as she went to the kitchen in search of something that might ease the emptiness inside her.

"Maybe you should go to the doctor." Muriel scooted to the edge of her new recliner, leaning forward as Amelie dug through the refrigerator. "See if they can give you an antibiotic or something."

Amelie grabbed a bottle of water and a pack of string cheese. "I'm sure I'll be fine." She started to shut the fridge but went back in for a second stick of cheese, tucking it in the crook of her arm as she bumped the door closed with her hip. "It's probably just something that's going around." She grabbed an unopened bag of Cheetos and a king-sized sleeve of Reese's Cups from where they were stacked on the counter with the rest of the non-perishables from their last delivery, adding them to her load before going back to the stairs and forcing her feet to move up them. She was almost at the top when the doorbell rang.

Amelie stopped, blowing out a frustrated sigh before crouching down to peek into the living room. "Did you order another delivery from the grocery store?"

"No." Muriel leaned back in her chair, making it clear she wasn't interested in being the one to see who was on the porch. "I think we have everything we need."

That wasn't true.

They were out of the tequila she'd decided didn't taste as bad as she once thought, but she was just going to have to suffer through with chocolate and cheese because leaving the house right now to hit a liquor store wasn't going to happen.

Amelie turned to stomp her way back down the stairs. "It's probably just someone trying to sell you something." She didn't bother looking through the peephole before flinging the door open.

When she saw who was on the other side, Amelie nearly lost her grip on the snacks she was planning to snarf down while wallowing in self-pity. "Evelyn?"

Her best friend stood on the porch, eyes wide as they scanned her from head to toe. "You look like hot garbage."

"Thanks." Amelie turned, walking away from the door. "I haven't been feeling well." She headed for the base of the stairs. "You should probably get a hotel room so you don't catch what I have."

Evelyn trailed behind her, rolling her leopard print suitcase at her side. "I'm not worried about it." She gave Muriel a little wave as she passed. "I've got a great immune system."

Amelie sighed, reaching one hand out toward Muriel. "Evelyn, this is my grandma. Grandma," she motioned to her best friend, "this is Evelyn."

Evelyn beamed at Muriel. "It's about time I got to meet you. I've heard a lot about you."

"Likewise." Muriel wiggled her eyebrows. "I heard you can

put your feet behind your head." She smiled slyly. "Maybe you can teach me to do that."

Evelyn peeled off her gloves and shoved them in the pockets of her coat, grinning. "Get me a letter from your physical therapist and a signed waiver and I'm sure we can work something out." She wiggled out of her thigh-length coat and draped it over the back of the new sofa. "Your house is beautiful."

Muriel smiled. "Thank you. I had a lot of help with it."

Amelie started to groan, barely managing to cover the sound with a fake coughing fit. "I'm going to go lay down. I'm sure you two can entertain each other."

She was being rude and didn't care in the slightest.

Everything sucked and the world was trash.

She was miserable. And misery did not love company, despite what everyone said.

Amelie stomped her way back up to the second floor where she'd been holed away for almost a week, playing sick to cover up what she was really struggling with. She flopped onto the mattress, pulling the covers over her head before prying open the bag of Cheetos and shoving a fistful into her mouth.

The blanket she'd been using to block out the world suddenly flipped back, flinging her dirty hair across her face and stealing the isolation she craved.

"Whatcha doin'?" Evelyn dropped to sit on the edge of the mattress, stretching her legs out as she kicked off her boots.

"I told you. I'm sick." Amelie swallowed the mouthful of snacks. "I have the plague."

"Right." Evelyn grabbed away the Cheetos. "You might be able to convince your grandmother of that, but you can't convince me." She fished out a few of the crunchy sticks and popped them into her mouth. "Is this why you haven't been returning my phone calls?"

Amelie stole back the bright orange bag. "Don't act like I ignored you. I texted."

Evelyn's dark eyebrows lifted. "You sent me a series of incoherent GIFs."

"They were coherent." Amelie dug out another fistful of Cheetos, adding a new layer of orange stain to her skin. "And they were all from the same show."

Evelyn started collecting the empty food wrappers scattered around the mattress, piling them up at the foot of the bed. "They were all of David from Schitt's Creek being dramatic." Her brown eyes moved around the room. "And now that I'm here, maybe they were more coherent than I realized."

"I'm not being dramatic." She was acting exactly like anyone else would in her situation.

Evelyn reached out to trace the edges of a stain on Amelie's shirt. "That's what I'm afraid of." She took the bag of Cheetos for a second time, setting it on the nightstand before grabbing Amelie's hands with hers. "Come on. You're taking a shower."

Amelie went limp as Evelyn dragged her across the sheets. "I don't want to take a shower. I want to lay in bed and eat my Cheetos in peace."

"Then you should have answered my phone calls and pretended like you weren't having a complete meltdown." She managed to get Amelie on her feet and continued pulling her toward the door.

"I'm not having a meltdown." She blinked a few times, trying to restrain the emotion she'd been fighting all week. "I'm sad."

Evelyn wrapped one arm around her shoulders, keeping her close as they walked across the hall to the bathroom. "I know." She flipped on the light and started the water. "But you can be sad and smell good at the same time." She backed toward the door, motioning to the sweatpants and oversized T-shirt Amelie had worn for more days than she was interested in keeping track of. "Take those off and throw them out the door. I don't want to risk you putting them back on."

Amelie whipped the shirt over her head, throwing it right at Evelyn's face. "I won't put them back on. I'm sad, not a monster."

Evelyn peeled the shirt away, cringing as she pinched it out between two fingers. "What all did you spill down the front of this?"

Amelie shrugged as she kicked away the rest of her clothes and stepped into the shower. "I don't know. Probably a little orange chicken. Maybe some cheesecake." She eased under the hot spray, letting the water run over her head and down her body. "I think the big stain is enchilada sauce."

"At least you're eating." Evelyn pulled back the shower curtain and peeked inside. "I'm going to go grab you something fresh to wear. I'll be right back."

Amelie gave her friend a little smile. "Thanks."

Tears bit at her eyelids yet again, but this time she let them go. There was no sense trying to pretend everything was fine. Evelyn clearly knew the truth. And the fact that she flew across the country because of it was the first thing to make Amelie feel a little human since she walked out of Troy's house on Valentine's Day, heartbroken and confused.

Evelyn came back into the bathroom, her strong stride making the shower curtain sway. "Okay. I've got new pants, a new shirt, new underwear, and a new bra."

Amelie poked her head out of the curtain. "I'm not wearing a bra."

"Yes you are, because we are going out in public." Evelyn pointed at her unwashed hair. "Put some shampoo on that mess before it all mats together."

"Ugh." Amelie let the curtain fall back into place. "I don't want to go out in public." She tipped the shampoo bottle up and squeezed a pile directly onto the top of her head. "Going out in public sucks."

"And laying in your bed surrounded by empty candy wrappers and dirty socks is better?" Evelyn barely paused. "Don't answer that."

Amelie scrubbed at her scalp, digging her fingers in as she worked the soap through her strands. "You don't understand."

"Of course I don't understand." Evelyn pulled the shower curtain back again. "I've never been lucky enough to fall in love with a gorgeous cowboy."

Amelie shot her friend a glare. "You're calling what's in front of you right now, lucky?"

"I'm calling what's in front of me right now a woman who should have called her fucking best friend to discuss this before everything went tits up." Evelyn tossed a washcloth at her face. "Now hurry up. We've got shit to do."

Amelie scowled as she rinsed out her hair and slicked conditioner down the ends. Anger and frustration had her skin rubbed pink by the time she was finished washing it.

But at least she finally felt something besides sad.

Evelyn was waiting with a towel when she stepped out. Her friend wrapped the bath sheet around her shoulders before trying to work another one around her head. "Tell me what happened."

"He dumped me." Amelie slowly dropped down to sit on the closed lid of the toilet. "Told me I should move back to New York."

Evelyn frowned down at her, dark brows pinched together. "That doesn't sound right."

"That's what I thought, but what the hell can I do about it? If he doesn't want to be with me, then that's it."

"Is that what he said? That he didn't want to be with you?"

Evelyn gave up on trying to wrap the towel around her head and started using it to squeeze the water from her hair.

"I told him about Trevor coming here and asking me to move back and Troy told me I should go." Amelie slumped down, shoulders sagging. "Can I go back to bed now?"

"No, you can't go back to bed." Evelyn grabbed the wide-tooth comb from the sink and started working it through her hair. "When did all this happen?"

"Valentine's Day." Amelie winced a little as the comb hit a tangle. "He gave me a set of my favorite brushes and some of his old shirts to use as smocks while I work and then he told me to go back to New York."

"Of course he told you that." Muriel stepped into the small space, taking up the last bit of free room. "That boy loves the hell out of you." She wiggled one finger up and down in front of Amelie. "And based on the looks of it, you love the hell out of him too."

She should pretend they were talking about someone else.

Try to salvage the connection her grandmother and Troy shared.

"Oh, don't look at me like that." Muriel crossed her arms. "I'm old. Not dumb." She leaned against the tiny bit of available wall. "I knew you two were boning from the get-go."

Amelie closed her eyes against a sudden and piercing headache. "I'm going to need you to not say boning ever again."

"Fine." Muriel leaned forward. "Fucking."

"Okay." Amelie took a slow breath. "That's worse."

"You know what I mean." Muriel lifted one hand. "Doing the horizontal tango. Bumping uglies. Hiding the salami. Pounding the pu—"

"Nope." Amelie shook her throbbing head. "That's enough."

She'd been through too much this week. Hearing her grandmother say the word punani would send her over the edge.

Muriel tucked her loose hand back against her chest. "All I'm saying is that anyone with eyes can see you two have something going on."

"Had." Amelie croaked it out. "We *had* something going on."

"Pshht." Muriel made a face. "That kind of thing doesn't just stop." She lifted her brows. "Let me guess. You got close and he pushed you away."

Amelie glanced up at Evelyn. Her friend shrugged and went back to combing her hair.

"When I told him about Trevor showing up he said I should move back to New York." Amelie fiddled with the worn end of the towel wrapped around her body. "He made it seem like he wanted me to leave."

Muriel stared at her for a few long seconds. "Does that seem like the kind of thing Troy would want?"

Amelie rolled her lips inward, pressing them together in the hopes that it would help keep her chin from quivering. "No. That's why I was so confused."

"Listen." Muriel dropped her arms and came closer, slowly easing down to sit on the edge of the pale pink tub. "That boy wants to be loved more than he wants almost anything else in the world."

Amelie scrunched her face up. "Almost?"

"That's right." Muriel reached out to take Amelie's hands in hers. "He wants the people he loves to be happy more."

"But I told him I was staying. I told him—"

Muriel shook her head. "He's not listening. He's just reacting." She squeezed Amelie's hands. "And you've got to remember, he has no idea how to be loved, Amelie."

The lump that set up shop in her throat a week ago got a little tighter. "But he deserves to be loved."

Troy was unlike anyone she'd ever met before. He was kind and caring and selfless.

He was sweet and funny and thoughtful.

That's why all of this was so freaking hard to deal with. Especially the part about him not knowing how to be loved.

"He is loved." Muriel sniffed and sat a little straighter. "By a hell of a lot of people."

Amelie swallowed hard, fighting against the feelings she'd been trying to smother with chocolate, Cheetos and tequila. "So what do I do?" She wiped at the corner of one eye with her towel. "He told me to leave."

"Well, not leaving is a good start." Muriel tipped her head toward Evelyn. "I've got a feeling that one's not gonna leave either." Her lips pulled into a sly grin. "Especially once she sees all Moss Creek has to offer."

Amelie sat up a little straighter. "Moss Creek?"

Muriel lifted her chin. "You gonna tell me you don't think that would be a nicer place to live than here?"

"But this is your home." Amelie leaned closer to her grandmother. "You've been here almost your whole life."

Muriel slowly smiled. "Then I'd say it might be time for me to try something new."

TWENTY-SIX

TROY

"WHAT IN THE hell are you doing now?" Liza crossed the stretch of stomped-down snow that ran between the mess hall and the barn.

"I'm building another house for all these damn cats." Troy lined up the two-by-four in his hand before using the nailer to secure it into place. "The other one was a little more cramped than I realized." He grabbed another of the precut two-by-fours stacked at his feet and put it in place, nailing it tight to the one he just secured.

Liza looked over the first of the houses, the one he built with Ben, Colt, and Griffin. "These houses are almost as nice as the one I'm building." She leaned down to peek through the plastic flap covering the entrance. "Is that a heat lamp in there?"

"The chickens have one. I figured I'd give the cats one too." The reasoning wasn't his own, but it still held up. "Do you need something?"

"Nothing specific." Liza leaned against the side of the barn, watching as he worked. "I just thought I should come check and see how you were doing."

Troy added another two-by-four, focusing all his attention on the project. "I'm fine."

Liza snorted. "That sounds familiar."

Troy glanced over the roofline of the small structure to where his boss stood. "What's that supposed to mean?"

The question sounded defensive. And maybe it was. Right now all he could do was be defensive, because there was no offensive. There was nothing he could fix. Nothing he could change. Nothing he could do to rid himself of the burning ache of loss making it hard to function.

"It means I've said it myself more times than I can count." Liza crossed her arms, looking a little smug. "It was a lie when I said it too."

He wanted to argue with her. Tell her it wasn't a lie. But he was so far from fine he couldn't even work up the motivation to fight about it.

"Is that what you came out here to tell me?" Troy finished attaching the last of the nailers and hooked the gun to his belt.

As he tried to reach for one of the sheets of wood paneling that would serve as siding, Poppy ran under his feet, forcing him to sidestep to avoid tripping over her lanky body. He scooped the small cat up from the ground, holding her out so he could look her right in her green eyes. "You're really getting in my way this morning, you know that?"

He'd recently taken to talking to the cats. For some reason it seemed like they understood him and could commiserate over the loss they shared. They were sad because he didn't feed them quite as liberally as Amelie did, and he was sad because—

"Does that cat have a collar on?" Liza pushed away from the side of the barn and came toward him, her eyes zeroed in on Poppy's neck. "Does she belong to somebody?"

Troy tucked Poppy into the crook of his arm, the defensiveness he couldn't seem to shake amping up. "Of course she belongs to somebody. She belongs to us."

Liza stared at him for a minute before turning to the cats scattered around the space. Her gaze slowly moved from one to the next before finally coming back to Troy. "They all have collars."

"Not all of them." Technically, there was a collar for each of the cats, he just hadn't figured out how to get some of them on yet. A few of the animals were still skittish as hell. And after wrestling Marshmallow into a carrier when he broke his leg, he wasn't in a hurry to repeat the process of arguing with a feral feline.

Liza stood there for a minute, looking around at the cats and the houses. Finally she refocused on him. "I'm going to go ahead and assume this has to do with a certain woman I haven't seen lately."

Troy set Poppy down and went back to work. "I don't want to talk about that."

He couldn't deny that he was upset, and he didn't want to argue about the reasons.

He actually didn't want to talk about Amelie at all.

He couldn't. It was too much.

"Oh, I know." Liza shook her head, letting out a low chuckle. "Trust me, I know." She stepped in as Troy wrestled with the sheet of paneling, grabbing one side and helping him get it into place. She worked silently alongside him, keeping her mouth shut for long enough that he hoped the conversation was over.

But it wasn't.

"You know, it doesn't make sense to do all of this for her if she's not gonna see it."

"I'm not doing this for her." Specifically.

This wasn't technically about Amelie. Sure, she loved the cats and would be thrilled to find out they had plenty of warm space to hunker down for the rest of the winter. But he wasn't doing this to make her happy. Like Liza said, she would never know.

He was doing this because he understood what it felt like to be out in the cold. To be alone with no one to belong to. He'd been there before and he was there again.

But while he couldn't fix his own situation, he could fix it for these cats. He could give them a home. A place to belong.

Liza helped him fix the next sheet of siding into place. "I take it that means you haven't heard from her?"

"Nope."

It shouldn't upset him as much as it did. He was the one who told Amelie to leave. Pretended like he was fine if she went. Hopefully she listened. Hopefully she was back in New York living the life she wanted.

Even though the thought of it made him sick to his stomach.

"So that's it? You're just going to be miserable?" Liza almost sounded mad.

"What else am I supposed to do?" Troy ran the nailer along one side, putting down the line of shots. "Go tell her she should give up everything for me?" He shook his head. "That's not gonna happen."

Liza sighed, the sound long and loud as she stepped closer, eyes boring into the side of his head. "Listen, Bacon Boy. I know you think you're doing the right thing, but I feel like you might just be being a dumbass."

Troy shook his head, frustrated she wouldn't just leave this alone. "You don't understand."

"Are you sure?" Liza slung one arm over the roof of the little house. "Because I feel like I was the queen of the dumbasses for a long damn time."

Troy peeked Liza's way, looking her over out of the corner of his eye. "This is nothing like your situation with Ben was."

"Okay, but that doesn't mean you can't still be a dumbass." Liza leaned in, waiting until he turned her way before continuing. "You really liked that girl and she really liked you. We all saw it. I don't know what happened, but I can't imagine you would be as miserable as you are if you didn't still like her."

"I do still like her." The admission didn't feel right. It was too much like a lie, and he didn't want to lie about how he felt where Amelie was concerned. "No. I don't like her. I love her."

Liza's brows lifted, like he'd surprised her. "And you're just going to let her leave?"

"I didn't *let* her leave." Troy's jaw clenched. "I told her to go." He forced his teeth apart as he turned back to the building. "She deserves to be happy."

"Oh. I didn't realize you were the happy police." Liza nodded like everything suddenly made complete sense. "It's good that you decided what would make her happy and dealt with it accordingly. I'm sure she really appreciated you handling that for her."

"That is not what happened."

Liza scrunched her face up, wrinkling her nose. "Are you sure?" She gave him a sympathetic smile. "Because you said you told her to move back to New York. And that sounds an awful lot like you deciding that's what she should do."

"I said it because that's what she wants. It's what she's always wanted." He shouldn't have to defend what he did, especially when it came at such a high cost.

He gave up everything so she could be happy.

"Well I always wanted to be a princess, but you don't see me flying over to Europe trying to snag myself a prince." Liza zipped the front of her work coat higher as a blast of frigid air cut between the buildings. "Dreams don't always stay the same, Troy. What we want can change as we discover more options."

She pressed her lips together, pursing them as she eyed him thoughtfully. "Did you know I lived in New York too?"

The revelation was shocking. He knew Liza wasn't from here, but he'd assumed she'd lived a similar life before moving to Moss Creek. "You lived in New York?"

She tipped her head in a nod. "Yup. Moved there the second I graduated so I could be a model."

He was a little dumbfounded—Not that Liza used to be a model, that he could completely see—It was something else that had him confused.

"How in the hell did you end up in Moss Creek, Montana?"

"I came here for a man." Her expression soured. "That was a terrible idea, but it did get me where I was supposed to be. So I can't really claim it was a mistake." Her eyes came back to his, serious and focused. "I could have moved away, and honestly it might have been easier." One side of her mouth lifted in a half smile. "But this is where I belong. Cross Creek started out as a nightmare for me, but somewhere along the line it became my new dream." One gloved hand came up to rest in the center of her chest. "A dream that *I* decided was what *I* wanted." Her expression softened. "And I'm here to tell you that if anyone told me to go back to New York, I would be pissed as hell that they wanted to send me back to a place where I no longer belonged."

"I get what you're saying, but Amelie does belong in New York." It was a bitter pill to swallow but a reality he had to face. "People love her there. They want to buy her paintings and host shows for her."

"So?" Liza scoffed. "People love her paintings here too. They want them inside their homes and on the walls of buildings downtown." Liza re-crossed her arms. "So by your argument, she belongs here."

"But Montana and New York aren't the same thing."

"Definitely not." Liza's head tipped to one side as she huffed out a laugh. "Thank God. New York is fucking insane." Her eyes dropped as a group of collared cats milled around between them. "Not that this place is too far behind."

"I don't want her to stay in Montana just for me." He'd spent his whole life wishing people would stay, but he couldn't make himself do that to Amelie.

"Why not?" Liza straightened away from the house. "Would you move to New York for her?"

The possibility hadn't really occurred to him. For one specific reason.

She hadn't asked.

"That's different."

Liza's head craned to one side. "Is it?" She clicked her tongue. "Because I don't think it's different at all." She stretched her arms out, motioning around them. "You love it here, I know that." One gloved finger came to point at him. "But you would leave it all behind to go with her if she asked you to." She smiled. "And you would be happy to do it because it meant you would get to be with her."

"But working at Cross Creek isn't my dream." He held one hand up. "No offense."

"We talked about dreams, Bacon Boy." Liza reached out to rest one hand on his shoulder. "Dreams change. And you don't get to tell someone else what theirs should be." She gave his shoulder a little slap before turning to the second of the cat houses. "You want me to send Ben out here to help with this?"

Troy shook his head. He couldn't handle anymore deep conversations and there wasn't a doubt in his mind Liza's plan was for Ben to have a stab at talking some sense into him. "Nope. I got it."

Liza paused, turning back toward him. "I know you do." She gave him a wink. "I have faith in you."

TWENTY-SEVEN
TROY

TROY DRAGGED HIS eyes from the television as someone knocked on his door.

He jumped up from the sofa, heart racing as he rushed around the coffee table, banging his leg against the corner, the pain from the impact making him hobble like Marshmallow as he hurried to unlock the deadbolt and fling the door open.

Griffin smiled. "Surprise."

Troy blinked, taking a second before forcing on a smile of his own. "Hey." His eyes fell to the set of luggage at his dad's feet. "You're back early."

"Maryann said the same thing when I showed up at The Inn." Griffin reached up to scrub down the back of his neck with one hand. "And unfortunately, The Inn is currently full because they're hosting a wedding this weekend." He paused, expression tightening a little. "So I was wondering if I could crash on your couch for a couple days."

Troy blinked again, still struggling to recover from the rush of adrenaline coursing through his veins. "You want to sleep on my couch?"

"If you don't have any room that's okay." Griffin thumbed

over one shoulder. "I can go into Billings and get a hotel. I just thought it might be easier if I could stay in town until The Inn opened up again."

"No, yeah." Troy stepped back as he tried to get his brain back on track. Griffin was not who he was hoping to find standing on his porch, and it was starting to show. "You can totally stay here." He raked one hand through his hair. "There's no reason for you to go all the way to Billings."

Unfortunately, it was true for him too.

Muriel was probably pissed as hell at him. She hadn't called him once since Amelie walked out of his house two weeks ago. And he was too scared to call her first. Too afraid she would tell him she didn't need him anymore now that her house was fixed.

Griffin grabbed his bags and rolled them in. "Thanks. I really wasn't looking forward to driving all the way back to Billings." He lined the bags up against the wall and looked around, taking in the quiet space. "Where's your bulldog?"

Troy didn't have any clue what in the world Griffin was talking about. "I don't have a dog." He pointed to where Marshmallow was stretched out across the sling in the front window. "I do have a cat now though."

"I was talking about your girlfriend." Griffin unzipped his heavy black leather coat and shrugged it off. "The one who likes to attack me."

"She wasn't attacking you." Troy closed the door and went to flop back down onto the couch. "She's just—"

He stopped short, shutting down the explanation before it cleared his lips.

He almost told Griffin that Amelie was just protective of the people she cared about, but thinking about the fact that Amelie cared for him was too raw right now.

"She's just, what?" Griffin stacked his coat on top of his bags before coming to sit on the couch beside Troy.

"Gone." He reached out to grab his most recent beer from the table and tipped it back, swallowing down the rest before sliding it back onto the wood surface.

"Gone?" Griffin's blue eyes moved across the cluttered table, taking in the empty beer bottles and discarded plates surrounding the small stuffed bear he hadn't been able to bring himself to mail back to its owner. "Gone, where?"

"Probably New York." He shrugged. "That's where she really wanted to be."

Griffin's grey brows lifted. "She told you she'd rather live in New York than Montana?"

Why did everyone want to get into semantics on this? "She's an artist. New York was always where she wanted to live, so when an opportunity came to move back I told her she should take it."

Griffin nodded. "Oh."

The room was quiet except for the sound of the Staten Island vampires filtering out from the television.

"I wasn't trying to tell her what to do, if that's what you're thinking." He'd been wrestling with what Liza accused him of for almost a week. And every time he came to the same conclusion: He couldn't have been making that decision for Amelie if it was what she wanted in the first place.

Griffin lifted up both hands. "I'm not thinking anything." His hands dropped to his lap. "I'm the last person who should judge anyone when it comes to relationships."

"It wasn't a relationship."

Griffin's eyes rolled his way. "But she was staying here with you."

"Because she couldn't stay at her grandma's house."

Griffin's expression turned thoughtful. "And you helped her fix her grandma's house."

"Because her grandma is my friend." Troy's head dropped. "Was my friend."

Griffin pointed at Marshmallow. "Where did you say that cat came from?"

"He's one of the barn cats. One of the horses accidentally stepped on him and hurt his back leg so I took him to the vet and he had to have surgery."

"You paid for surgery on a barn cat?" Griffin looked from Marshmallow to Troy and then back to Marshmallow.

"Amelie—" He caught himself again.

That was one of the hardest parts of all this to deal with. Everything in his life seemed to circle back to Amelie. She was everywhere he turned. And it was hell.

He couldn't get into his truck without imagining her there beside him, dirty and exhausted from tackling a project she wasn't equipped to handle.

He couldn't go to the barn without expecting her to walk in with a line of cats waiting for her attention.

He couldn't sleep in his bed.

He couldn't use his shower.

He couldn't sit at his kitchen table.

Even the fucking floor beside his back door was ruined.

There wasn't a place in his life that was safe.

"Listen." Griffin leaned closer, his deep voice softening a little. "I may not know much about how relationships work, but I can tell you that it was clear that girl cared about you." He half-smiled. "Most men won't square up with me, but she was in my face every chance she got." He pointed at Troy. "And she did it for you." He shook his head. "People willing to fight for you don't come along every day, and that woman was ready and willing to fight for you."

Troy tried not to let what his dad was saying sink in.

But he hadn't stopped thinking about Amelie and what happened between them for two weeks, and this minute wasn't going to be any different.

"Liza said I was trying to decide Amelie's future for her." He glanced toward his dad. "That I was telling her what to do."

"Were you?"

"No. Amelie said it was her dream to be an artist in New York. I was just telling her what she wanted to hear." He held firm on his stance.

"So you lied to her."

Troy's head swung Griffin's way. "No. I would never lie to her."

"But you told her she should go to New York even though you think she should stay here." Griffin laid it out like it was simple.

"I'm not going to hold her back." Troy shook his head. "She would resent me forever. There'd be no coming back from that."

It might not happen right away, but eventually Amelie would hate him for it. Would realize all she gave up and hold it against him.

"You're telling me an awful lot about how you think she feels and what you think she wants." Griffin stood up from the couch. "And I don't know much, but I do know that women hate being told how they feel." He went into the kitchen and came back with a couple of beers, passing one to Troy as he sat back down. "Like, will throw your shit out in the street, hate it."

Troy smiled for the first time in weeks. "That sounds like it might be a personal experience."

Griffin drank down a few sips of beer. "I wish I could say it only happened once." He tipped his head Troy's way. "I should also tell you I have a history of choosing women with a little too much of a wild streak."

Troy thought of Amelie's determination and the stubbornness she refused to admit she possessed. "There's nothing wrong with a little bit of a wild streak."

"As long as you're man enough to handle it." Griffin sighed. "And history has shown that I am not."

Troy chuckled. "At least you know it now."

"I'm not sure how much it matters. I think I've decided I'm just meant to be single." Griffin focused on Troy. "You don't have to make the same mistakes I have, though."

"You think telling her to go to New York was a mistake?"

Griffin tilted his head to the side. "I'm not saying it was a mistake." His mouth flattened, tipping down at the edges. "I'm just saying I'm surprised your clothes didn't all end up thrown out a window."

"I just want her to be happy."

"They don't like when you tell them how to do that either." Griffin pointed the mouth of his beer at Troy. "Really chaps their asses."

"So what, I should have made her tell me she wanted to leave me?" The frustration he'd been fighting crept into his voice. "Because I'm not sure I could have handled that."

"So this was actually about you." Griffin met his gaze. "Not her."

Troy opened his mouth to argue.

Then clamped it shut again.

"But..." He ran out of steam immediately, sealing his lips together for the second time.

He leaned forward, catching his head in his hands. "Fuck."

Griffin sat beside him, drinking what was left of his beer as Troy rubbed both hands down his face, beating himself up for an all new reason.

He was an ass.

A selfish ass.

One that was too wrapped up in his own insecurities to see when everything he wanted was right in front of him.

Begging to be let in.

He'd pretended to be all in. Did everything he could think of to show Amelie he was worth having.

And she'd believed him.

The problem was, he didn't believe it.

He didn't think he was worth staying in Montana for.

Worth changing her dreams.

"You want me to go with you?"

Troy turned his face toward his dad. "Where?"

"To find her." Griffin set his empty bottle on the table and leaned against the cushions, stretching his long arms across the back of the sofa. "That's what you're planning to do, right?"

"She's probably in New York by now." Troy dug the tips of his fingers into his burning eyes. "I'm so fucking stupid."

"We all are. But the first step to recovery is accepting you have a problem." Griffin stood up, reaching out one hand. "Come on. Let's get you sobered up a little so we can come up with a plan to get this all straightened out."

―――

"I DON'T SEE how this is going to help." Troy stood in line at The Baking Rack, waiting behind a bunch of middle-aged women who were doing their best not to blatantly stare at his dad.

"Then you've never had the coffee here." Griffin studied the display cases filled with what remained of the day's baked goods.

He'd heard plenty about Moss Creek's newest bakery, but hadn't checked it out for himself yet. He enjoyed the food at The Wooden Spoon and wasn't particularly interested in trading one of their loaded omelets for a scone and fancy coffee.

"We could have made coffee at my house." Troy shoved his hands into the pockets of his coat, trying to temper the impatience making his skin itch.

Griffin seemed to think they could fix this. Figure out a way to repair the damage he'd done. And standing in line for an overpriced cup of bean water felt like a waste of time he didn't have.

It might already be too late.

They finally made it to the front of the line and the pretty woman on the other side flashed them a quick smile. "What can I get you?"

"We are in desperate need of some coffee." Griffin leaned against the counter. "I told my son here you made the best in town."

The woman's eyes came to Troy before moving back to his dad. "Well, I hate to call you a liar, but Blue Moon at the end of the block roasts their own beans." She held one hand up to the side of her full lips, like she was telling them a secret. "And we buy beans from them, so technically *they* have the best coffee in town."

"But I bet they don't have the same exceptional service." Griffin's smile was different than normal. "And good service goes a long way."

The woman, Dianne, according to the plastic tag pinned to the front of her apron, tapped one finger on the counter. "But I can tell you that they also have exceptional service." She straightened. "But, they do not have fresh-baked cookies, so you'll just have to decide what's more important to you."

Griffin didn't hesitate. "Definitely cookies." He pulled out his wallet. "Give us a dozen of those too."

Dianne smiled wide. "A man after my own heart." She

flipped up the side flaps on a flat box printed with the same logo as the one stamped on the front awning. "What kind?"

"Dealer's choice." Griffin pinched his credit card between two fingers, tapping it against the counter. "If you like it, I'm sure I'll love it."

Troy slowly turned to look at his dad.

Was Griffin flirting with the bakery owner?

He hadn't noticed it at first, caught up in his own misery, but it was starting to seem like Griffin's motives for coming to The Baking Rack weren't completely innocent.

He didn't fault his dad for trying to catch Dianne's attention. She was an attractive woman. And if seeing firsthand the misery that loving a woman could unleash didn't deter him, nothing would.

Troy slapped his dad on the back. "You have fun in here. I'm gonna go wait outside."

He pushed through the door and out into the cold, the scents coming from The Wooden Spoon tempting him to head that direction. But it sounded like he was about to have a giant coffee and a box of cookies to get through so he turned and walked the opposite way.

He didn't come to this part of downtown very often. Most of his trips to Main Street revolved around food or alcohol, and this particular section was devoted primarily to shopping. He passed an antique store. A shop that looked like it sold fancy soaps and lotions. A salon. A clothing store.

Troy turned to look back at The Baking Rack, checking to see if there was any sign of Griffin. His dad was nowhere in sight, so he decided to walk off a little more of the beer still pumping through his veins.

The next few shops were more of the same, but the scent of coffee beans roasting meant he was coming close to the place Dianne mentioned. A sign for Blue Moon Coffee Brewery hung on the last building of the block, dangling from a fixed arm over the door. The place was clearly popular. A number of people filled the sofas and chairs inside, working on computers or chatting over their lattes.

The sight was so distracting he almost missed the small storefront right next door to it. It was a narrow building with limewashed brick and windows that spanned nearly the entire front, making it easy to see the art lining the walls inside.

He stepped closer, drawn in by the familiarity of the graceful strokes and color choices.

He hadn't realized how personal art was until this moment.

How identifiable it could be.

Troy pulled on the door, expecting it to be locked, but the heavy slab of wood and glass swung open, making the tiny bell dangling from the inside handle chime softly.

He stepped into the building, immediately going to one of the portraits.

And stood staring at his own face.

He didn't have to hear Amelie to know she was there. Even after two weeks without her, it was so easy to feel her presence.

Troy turned, coming face to face with the owner of the shop. He looked at the painting before bringing his eyes back to hers. "It's me."

Amelie lifted one shoulder, her smile hesitant. "Of course it's you."

TWENTY-EIGHT

AMELIE

"YOU DIDN'T GO back to New York." The words rushed out of Troy's mouth, either in surprise or relief.

She couldn't tell which.

"No." Amelie shook her head. "It turns out you were right." She smiled, the expression feeling real on her face for the first time in weeks. "I might be a little stubborn."

Troy continued to stare at her like he couldn't believe what he was seeing. "So that's why you're here? Stubbornness?"

Her heart ached a little at how tightly he still clung to the fears he held close. "No." Amelie walked toward him. "I'm here because this is my home."

She could tell Troy he was the reason she stayed. It was partially true.

But that confession would have to wait until he could digest it enough to understand that it wasn't a bad thing. That being a reason someone found a home might actually be one of the best things in the world.

"This is where I belong." Amelie glanced at the line of paintings that had poured out of her in the days since she'd rented the space. "It's where I feel inspired." She smiled at one, a colorful interpretation of the sun setting over the fields of Cross Creek. "It's where I feel happy." Her focus shifted, going to the first piece she'd created after moving into the space just over a week ago, resting on the clear blue eyes she easily painted from memory. "It's where I feel safe."

"I—" Troy inhaled sharply. "I don't know how to do this, Amelie." He shook his head. "I don't know how to be what you deserve."

"Yes, you do." She'd seen it. Caught glimpses of the man who was dying to be hers. "I'm the one who has the problem."

Troy's brows pinched together, creasing a tight line between them. "You?" He shook his head. "You could never be the problem."

Her next smile came a little easier as the weight that had been sitting on her chest started to lighten. "I'm frequently the problem." She tipped her head toward the back of the building. "Do you want to see the rest?"

Troy nodded immediately. "Yes."

Amelie led him past the partial collection currently hanging on the walls and into the second, larger portion of the space.

Troy stopped just inside the door, his eyes drifting around her studio before falling to the project still sitting on her easel. His lips barely lifted. "It's Marshmallow."

Amelie peeked Troy's way. "I had to paint him since I'm his favorite human."

Troy's head fell forward. "About that."

Amelie resisted the urge to blow the Valentine's Day card off, but that wouldn't help either of them.

Troy wanted to know how to be part of something real and she wanted him to be able to tell her how he felt, so this conversation needed to happen.

No matter how awkward or uncomfortable it might be.

Troy's eyes lifted to meet hers. "I love you."

Amelie gasped, sucking in a surprised breath at the lack of caution in his declaration.

She expected Troy to explain that he cared about her. That he got a card from the cat because he was scared to admit it.

She did not expect him to immediately confess his love for her.

But now that it was out there, she wasn't going to leave him alone.

She never wanted to do that again.

"I love you." Amelie lifted her chin, staring him down. "But you better not tell me to leave you ever again or I might lose my fucking mind."

Troy tipped his head in a single nod. "Fair enough." His eyes moved over her face. "I missed you."

Amelie managed a full breath for the first time in what felt like forever. "I missed you too."

Then she ran straight at him, jumping into his arms the way she had so many times before. But this time wasn't about attraction or desire. It wasn't because of the way he said '*yes ma'am*' or his messy morning hair or the amount of skill his fingers carried.

It was because of how he saved feral cats.

It was the way he cared for her grandmother.

It was the fact that he knew which paintbrushes were her favorite and saved his old flannels for her.

It was because of shoveled snow and salvaged stuffed animals.

Troy caught her the second she was within arm's reach, holding her tighter than she'd ever been held as he buried his face against her neck, breathing deep slow breaths that she tried to match.

"I'm sorry I told you what to do." His apology was as startling as his confession of love.

"For a guy who says he doesn't know how to do this, you are doing a pretty spectacular job." Amelie pressed her hands to the sides of his face, leaning back until their eyes met. "I'm sorry that I didn't see what was really happening."

Troy shook his head. "That's not your job."

"Good point." She curled her fingers, dragging them over the surprising amount of hair peeking out across his cheeks and jawline. "Then I'm sorry I didn't tell you I was staying whether you liked it or not."

Troy's expression turned serious. "You're sure this is what you want?"

Amelie's jaw dropped open a little bit. "I love you. If that's not—"

"I'm not talking about this. About us." Troy jerked his chin toward the street outside. "I'm talking about Montana." He reached up to slide one hand into her hair. "If you want to be in New York then that's where we'll be."

Was he offering to leave Montana for her?

It shouldn't be shocking. She would leave Montana for him.

"I like Montana." Amelie couldn't help but smile. "I like Moss Creek." Her smile widened a little. "And I'm not the only one. You should probably know my grandmother is looking for a new place to live so she can hang out with her friends all the time."

Troy's surprise was immediate. "Muriel wants to move?"

Amelie shrugged. "I was surprised too, but she's already talked to Gertrude and Colt's grandmother and they are all asking around to see if anyone knows of a place that might be available soon."

"What about you? Are you looking for a place in Moss Creek too?" Troy's question was hesitant.

It made her want to be hesitant too, but holding back with

him had created a giant mess. And she said she wanted to be the one to control her fate, so it was time to prove it.

"There is a little farmhouse I'm partial to." Amelie tilted her head. "Unfortunately, someone else already lives there, so I guess it would depend on how they might feel about having permanent company."

Troy's lips pulled into a slow smile. "One of the occupants of that farmhouse is completely open to the idea." His blue eyes sparkled. "The other occupant is sort of an asshole, but he doesn't pay the bills so he doesn't get a vote."

Amelie pushed out her lower lip. "Don't pick on Marshmallow. He's had a rough month."

Troy laughed. "Right. Sleeping on the couch with me has been the hardest thing he's ever been through."

Amelie's smile slipped. "On the couch?"

Troy sobered, his eyes falling between them. "I couldn't make myself sleep in the bed without you."

Amelie stared at him for a second.

And then all the feelings she'd been trying to juggle for the past two weeks had her latching on, fingers in his hair as her mouth hit his.

Their chemistry had always been undeniable.

Unavoidable.

But it was more than simple chemistry that had her pressing against him as his tongue stroked hers, their bodies tangling together in a moment of uncontrollable need.

Uncontrollable lust.

Uncontrollable love.

"Well it looks like they made up."

Troy went still, his eyes flying open to focus on the doorway, even as his lips stayed on hers.

Amelie pulled back and turned to find her grandmother, best friend, and Griffin smiling at them.

Muriel thumbed over one shoulder at Troy's dad. "We found this one out wandering the streets and decided to take him in." She leaned to one side, craning her neck to look Griffin over. "Doesn't seem like he belongs to anyone. Maybe we should keep him."

"I'm not sure you have a choice at this point." Griffin shot Amelie a wink. "Seems like we might all be stuck with each other."

Evelyn grinned, wrestling one of the cups free of the cardboard holder she was carrying before passing the rest off to Muriel. "There are worse people to be stuck with." Her grin dimmed a little. "Trust me."

TWENTY-NINE

TROY

"WHAT DO YOU think?" Troy stood in the living room of the small house Ben and Liza would be moving out of as soon as their new home was finished.

Muriel peeked into the back bedroom, looking over the space before coming back down the hall. "You're sure they wouldn't mind me living here?"

"I'm positive." When he'd explained to the owners of Cross Creek that Muriel was wanting to move closer to her friends, Ben offered up the small cottage almost immediately. "They like the idea of having you close too."

"Of course they do." Muriel poked around the kitchen, checking out cabinets and drawers. "I'm hilarious."

"Among other things." Amelie leaned into his side, wrapping her arms around his waist and resting her head on his shoulder.

"Hard of hearing is not one of those things." Muriel shot her a scowl that immediately turned to a grin. "And you better be careful because most of what I am is probably genetic."

Amelie laughed as Muriel finished checking the place out with Poppy, her new best friend, close on her heels.

When she was done, Muriel let out a breath. "I think this is perfect." She gave Troy a serious look. "As long as you're sure they don't mind—"

"I'm sure." Troy fished the house keys from his pocket. "And I'm willing to bet Ben and Liza will tell you that themselves as soon as they get back from their trip."

He'd been in charge of the ranch for the past week while Ben and Liza flew across the country to help her parents and sister start the process of moving to Montana. Their house, along with the one Liza and Ben were building right next door to it, would be ready in less than two months. And everyone was chomping at the bit to get things going.

Not that he could blame them. He was feeling the exact same way about his own life, which sounded like it was now partially dependent on theirs.

"This will be so damn nice." Muriel gave the place one last look. "No neighbors. No traffic noise."

"No stairs to pretend you can't climb." Amelie grinned when Muriel shot her another glare.

Muriel's sour face didn't hold and she was back to smiling as they walked out the door onto the small porch. "Think of all the money you'll save on gas."

Amelie and Muriel were still technically living in Billings, spending about half their nights in the newly redone house since leaving it alone was risky. All it took was a power outage or a furnace failure and the pipes would burst and the whole damn thing would have to be redone. Again. So they rotated, spending a day or two in Billings and then coming to spend a day or two in Moss Creek. It was a pain in the ass to keep coming back and forth, but it was worth it to have the two women most important to him close at hand.

"Think of all the extra time you'll have to get into trouble when you aren't in a car two hours a day." Troy offered Muriel an arm as they went down the few stairs leading to Amelie's suv.

"We might end up using all that gas money for bail." Amelie hooked her hand through Muriel's other arm. "We should probably give Grady a heads-up so he knows what's coming."

Muriel tightened her hold on each of them. "Don't you warn him. The surprise is half the fun."

"I'm willing to bet Grady won't feel the same way." Amelie opened the passenger's door and waited while Muriel worked herself inside. "And I think if he has to arrest all three of you at once he'll have a breakdown."

"Grady is about as laid back as they come." Muriel got situated before buckling in. "I don't think anything could make him have a breakdown."

"Well let's not be the reason we find out there is." Amelie closed the door, rolling her eyes at Troy. "She's going to make me have a breakdown."

Troy wrapped one arm around her shoulders, pulling her close to press a kiss to her temple as they walked around the car. "She's definitely coming into her own."

"She's definitely something." Amelie stopped beside her door, tipping her head back to look up at him. "I really do think we should warn Grady."

Amelie was starting to find her footing in the small town they would both soon call home. Her little spot of Main Street was already known to just about everyone in Moss Creek, and her schedule was booked up for the next six months with everything from private portraits to painting the side of the building next door to The Baking Rack.

She was as famous as an artist could get in Moss Creek.

"We'll talk to him the next time we see him at The Wooden Spoon." Troy leaned in to catch her lips with his. "And Grady is a big boy. He can handle anything that comes his way."

Amelie's brows pinched together on a frown. "I wouldn't count on it."

Troy reached out to open her door. "I won't tell him you doubt him."

Amelie dropped into the driver's seat and Troy slid into the back, working one leg behind each seat in an effort to get as comfortable as possible for the trip to Gertrude's.

The Bridge Bitches, as they called themselves, were meeting on the mountain today and planned to play late into the night, so Muriel would be gone until morning.

That meant he and Amelie would have an evening alone, which didn't currently happen much given their situation.

But he wasn't complaining.

Gertrude, Colt's grandmother Betty, and a new friend they'd recently acquired, Agnes, were already wound up and loud when they walked in.

Gertrude pushed up from the table as soon as they walked through the door, moving even better than she did the last time he saw her.

"You're getting around pretty well." Troy pointed to her empty hands. "No cane?"

"No cane." Gertrude smiled, standing a little straighter. "They said I'm doing better than most fifty-year-olds." She peeked back toward her friends in the kitchen before stepping closer. "Speaking of fifty-year-olds," she lowered her voice, "is that dad of yours into older women?"

Troy chuckled, thinking she was teasing him.

But Gertrude's expression was serious.

"Uhh." He looked to Amelie for help.

"Are you trying to cut in line?" Betty was up out of her seat in an instant, moving quickly to Gertrude's side. "We played for it you hussy. I won fair and square." She elbowed Gertrude, using her slim body to bump Gertrude back. "When is your dad moving? I want to be sure I drop off a welcome to town gift at his house."

"Uhh." Troy was still struggling for words.

Amelie looped her arm through his, smiling as she saved him from the expectant looks all coming his way. "Griffin doesn't actually have a house yet. He's having a hard time finding a place so he's going to stay with us at Troy's until he finds something."

"He's gonna sleep on the couch." Muriel sat at the kitchen table, looking like the cat that ate the canary. "Right next to my recliner."

Gertrude and Betty spun around, their expressions a combination of shock and outrage. Muriel smirked at them, and for a second Troy was worried they might be too late to warn Grady.

But then the whole house erupted in laughter.

He turned to Amelie and she shrugged at him.

Troy leaned into her ear. "I feel like we should leave before we get caught in the crossfire."

Amelie nodded. "Agreed."

They backed toward the door, ducking out with a quick wave, leaving the Bridge Bitches to whatever fate they created.

When they got back to the farmhouse, Poppy was waiting at the back door, meowing to be let in.

He'd been a little worried that once word got out there was a real house with a sucker of an owner, every cat on the property would be trying to break in. But so far, Marshmallow and Poppy were the only two that showed any interest in being inside. And part of him was pretty sure Poppy only liked to come in so she could annoy the shit out of Marshmallow.

He opened the door and the little cat raced in, going straight for the sling that Marshmallow spent most of his day stretched across.

"She's going to make him want to live outside again." Troy

held the door while Amelie went in, pausing to take off her shoes and line them next to his.

"No way." Amelie wiggled out of her coat, hanging it up before taking Troy's and adding it to the rack. "He likes sleeping in the bed at night too much."

Marshmallow still didn't love outright affection, but every morning he was curled at their feet when they woke up, purring like a madman. At least until one of them opened their eyes. Then he would hiss and jump down, hiding until Amelie shook the container of snacks he didn't have the willpower to resist.

Troy locked the door and went to the kitchen, digging through the fridge for the leftovers from the meatloaf Amelie made the night before.

When she found out about his love of the meal at The Wooden Spoon, she'd called Maryann Pace. Her daughter-in-law Mae was the owner, and somehow Amelie managed to sweet-talk Maryann out of a few of the recipes.

Including the glazed meatloaf he loved.

He scooped out the meat, potatoes and green beans onto two plates, warming each in the microwave while Amelie fed the cats and checked her emails. She was just closing her laptop when the second plate came out of the oven. He passed one over before grabbing forks.

"Couch?"

Amelie smiled. "Absolutely."

When Muriel was there, they had dinner at the table. But when she was gone, they piled on the couch and watched whatever show Amelie chose.

Troy dropped into his normal spot, waiting until Amelie had the television started and was situated at his side before he started to eat. He took a bite of the meatloaf, closing his eyes at the familiar, comforting taste. "This is just as good as it was last night."

Amelie beamed at him. "Thanks." She scooped up a bite of her own. "I'm going to have to see if I can bribe Maryann into giving me more recipes." She pursed her lips. "I wonder if I could bargain with paintings."

"Careful, you might end up doing a family portrait." Troy kicked his feet up on the coffee table next to the stuffed bear that seemed to be a permanent fixture there. "And I'm not sure you can fit them all on one canvas."

"They do have a pretty big family." Amelie went quiet for a minute. "Once Nora has her baby they'll be up to eight grandkids." She pressed her lips together, poking at her food. "Have you ever thought about having kids?"

It was a topic they hadn't covered. Probably because they both had such complicated feelings around what it meant to be a parent. And what could happen when you weren't cut out for it.

"I've thought a lot about making sure I don't have kids." Troy answered honestly. He learned the hard way what happened when he held back, and didn't want to make that mistake again if he could help it. "But I've never really been in a place where I could even consider what it might be like to have kids."

"Oh." Amelie went quiet again.

"What about you?" He turned the question back on her, hoping she would offer him the same honesty.

"I think I would want to have kids someday." She slowly lifted her eyes to his. "It would be nice to have a second chance to have a happy family."

Troy smiled, easily imagining something that he wouldn't have before.

Not until her.

"It would be better than nice."

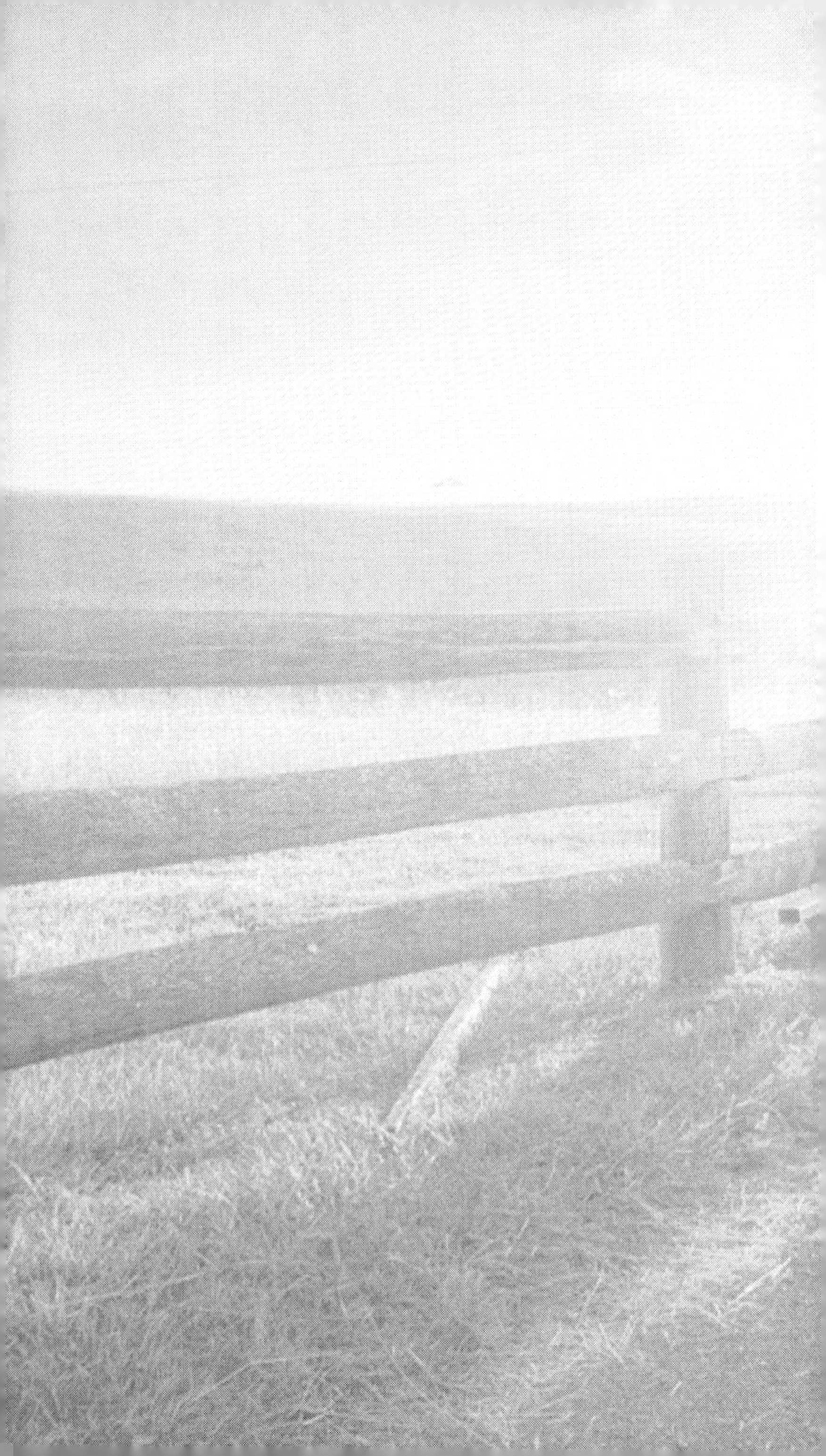

EPILOGUE

AMELIE

Three months later

"YOU LOOK UNCOMFORTABLE." Amelie let her eyes drag down Troy's long frame where he was pressed beside her in the cramped backseat of the cab. "Sexy, but uncomfortable."

Troy smiled, the sight only slightly reassuring. "I'm fine." He reached up to adjust the lapels of his jacket. "I've worn a suit before, remember?"

Amelie fanned one hand in front of her face, desperately trying to cool the heat prickling her skin. "Yes, but that was different. That was our wedding day and it was just the two of us." She grabbed the flowing skirt of her dress and started to shake it, trying to move the air against her skin in an effort to cool down.

She didn't want to walk into this place all sweaty, looking like the nervous wreck she was.

Because chances were good someone would get the wrong idea.

Troy grabbed her hand, lacing his fingers with hers. "Relax. Everything is going to be amazing."

Amelie let her head drop back against the seat, staring up as she forced in a few deep breaths. "I can't believe I let you talk me into this."

She was happy in Montana. More fulfilled than she had ever been in her whole life.

She would have been just as happy to never set foot into New York again.

"Why does he get all the credit for talking you into this?" Muriel leaned forward from where she sat on Troy's other side, the three of them crammed into the back seat of the taxi taking them from their hotel to Trevor's gallery. "I helped too."

"Fine. Then I'm mad at both of you right now."

She'd never been nervous like this before a show, but so much was different this time. This time she was invested in her paintings in a way she never was before. And this time her grandmother and husband were there and would have a front row seat if she failed.

"You'll be mad at us for about two seconds. Right up until that prick lays eyes on you and the man beside you. And the rock on your finger." Muriel slowly grinned. "I can't wait until that happens."

"I don't give a shit about Trevor." She couldn't care less if her ex was there or not. And she definitely couldn't care less what he thought about her or Troy, or even what he thought about the paintings she'd shipped across the country for him to display.

Tonight was about validation. She shouldn't need it, but deep down she wanted it.

She wanted it for her and she wanted it for her grandmother.

The car pulled to a stop and her stomach rolled, the queasiness she'd been fighting all day gaining steam. "I changed my mind. I don't want to do this anymore."

"Yes you do." Troy reached across her to open the door.

"Now get your sweet ass out of the car so we can get this show on the road."

Amelie blew out a breath, flapping her skirt one more time just for good measure before giving their driver a smile and stepping out onto the sidewalk. Her brain started spinning while she waited for Troy to help her grandmother out. She'd convinced herself this trip would be fun. That it would be nice to dress up and eat at fancy restaurants and show her grandmother around the city she once thought would be her home.

And Muriel was having fun. She loved the lights and the glamor and everything else that made New York what it was. But it was all a lot to manage at once. They could still do all the fun things without the stress of potentially facing her ex.

Muriel held tight to Troy's arm, her other hand gripping her cane as they rounded the back of the car and stepped up onto the sidewalk. Amelie frowned down at the smooth piece of wood Muriel didn't usually need. "Have we been walking too much?"

Muriel shook her head. "No." Her expression froze, eyes dropping down to the cane in her hand. She suddenly leaned against it a little more heavily. "I think I'm just a little tired is all."

Amelie reached up to dig the tips of her fingers into her temples as she realized what was happening. "You cannot assault Trevor, okay?"

Muriel's mouth dropped open. "Is that something you think I would do?"

Troy and Amelie answered at the same time. "Yes."

Amelie pointed at the cane. "Do I need to take that?"

Muriel picked it up and held it close to her chest, pressing it to the layers of sequins covering her brand-new gown. "You would steal an old woman's cane?"

"Now you're an old woman?" Amelie propped one fist on

her hip. "Because last week you were trying to convince Griffin you were flexible enough to stick your feet behind your head."

Muriel's spine straightened. "Evelyn's been helping me. It'll be true eventually."

"Good Lord let's hope not." Amelie snagged away the cane before bending down to look Muriel right in the eye. "Don't forget you promised to be on your best behavior."

"I'm always on my best behavior."

Amelie took another deep breath, hoping to ease the nausea still irritating her belly. "That's what I'm afraid of."

Muriel held her hand out. "Give me back my cane. I promise I won't cram it up his poop chute."

Amelie gave her grandmother a stern look. "It troubles me that you weren't just thinking about swinging it at him." She passed the cane back over. "And I appreciate the restraint you're showing."

Muriel's chin lifted a little. "Thank you."

They had barely made it two steps when a group of older women blocked their path. One of them stepped forward, eyes raking over Muriel's sparkling gown. "I love your dress."

Muriel immediately struck a pose, shifting her shoulders around dramatically as she did a three-point turn. "Thank you. I got it on sale."

The other women all seemed appropriately impressed as Muriel explained the deal she'd managed to work out after browbeating the sales associate for fifteen minutes and finding every imperfection on the clearance-rack garment.

One of the women turned to glance at the building behind them. "Is this where you're going all dressed up?"

Muriel nodded. "It's my granddaughter's art show this evening." She reached to press one hand on Amelie's back, shoving her forward. "She just got married." Her other hand shoved Troy forward. "To a cowboy."

Once again, the women acted impressed, which only encouraged Muriel more.

"You all remember Kenny Rogers?"

"Nope." Amelie stepped forward. "No stories about Kenny Rogers."

Muriel shot her a frown. "Fine." She refocused on the group. "Where are you girls from?"

The woman who complimented Muriel's dress pulled a flask from her fanny pack. "Florida. We all live together in a retirement community." She tipped back a drink before offering it to Muriel.

"I've never been to Florida." Muriel immediately took the flask and swallowed down a mouthful, her eyes widening. "Oh. That's good."

The woman took her flask and recapped it. "It's flavor infused moonshine. I order it from a little place in West Virginia."

Muriel nodded in approval. "Nice."

She looked from the gallery to the group of women. "Do you guys want to go to the show with us?"

Amelie glanced at Troy, unsure how this situation got out of hand so quickly. "Grandma, it's an invite only event."

"Well I'm inviting them." Muriel linked arms with the woman with the flask, turning her toward the entrance. "All of these paintings are of where we live in Montana. They're just beautiful." She paused, turning to the group. "And the owner of the gallery is Amelie's ex-boyfriend, but we're not allowed to put our hands on him." She shot Amelie another frown. "Unfortunately."

Amelie stood staring as her grandmother filed into the building with her new group of friends. "She just drank alcohol from a random person on the street."

Troy nodded, coming in close at her side. "I saw that."

She looked up at him. "Who does that?"

Troy barely smiled. "The same kind of woman who will bet the farm on something she believes in."

Amelie let her head drop back as she groaned. "Fine." She rolled her head toward Troy, letting it fall against his shoulder. "But I'm still not letting her hit Trevor with her cane."

"I think that's fair." Troy slid his hand into hers, lacing their fingers together. "You ready?"

"No." She pressed her lips together as her nerves morphed into full-blown fear. "What if no one buys anything?"

"Then we'll take them back to Montana and sell them to all the people who wanted them there." He leaned in, resting his forehead against hers. "Is that the worst thing you can imagine happening?"

"Did you not hear the poop chute comment?"

Troy chuckled. "I don't think she has the leverage to make that happen." He glanced in through the windows. "And I'm pretty sure Trevor's smart enough to steer clear of her."

"I hope you're right." Amelie straightened her shoulders. "About all of it."

She would never have done this without Troy. He was the one who convinced her to give New York another chance, explaining that she could do it on her own terms. And when she'd offered a collection to Trevor, he'd jumped at the chance. So hopefully that was a good sign.

"Let's do this." Amelie held Troy's hand tight as they walked through the doors, facing down the packed gallery.

Muriel pushed her way through the crowd, elbowing people out of her way as she rushed toward them. "People are pissed."

Amelie's stomach dropped, threatening to empty out right on the tops of her shoes. "Why?"

Muriel slowly smiled. "Everything's already sold."

NO COMING BACK